S0-EIG-928

Small Crimes

Other books by Michael Bracken

Fiction

All White Girls
Bad Girls
Canvas Bleeding
Deadly Campaign
Even Roses Bleed
In the Town of Dreams Unborn and Memories Dying
Just in Time for Love
Psi Cops
Tequila Sunrise

Anthologies

Fedora: Private Eyes and Tough Guys
Fedora II: More Private Eyes and Tough Guys
Hardbroiled

Small Crimes

edited by
Michael Bracken

BETANCOURT
& COMPANY
Doylestown, Pennsylvania

Small Crimes
A publication of
Betancourt & Company, Publishers
P.O. Box 301
Holicong, PA 18928-0301
www.wildsidepress.com

FIRST EDITION

For Sharon.
Always.

Table of Contents

Introduction

Michael Bracken

It's the little things we do that send our lives careening in directions we never anticipate – turning left one block too soon and finding ourselves lost in a dangerous neighborhood, being kind to a stranger before learning she's the company's new CEO, placing an erotic phone call to a wrong number – and yet every minute of every day is filled with little things.

How can we anticipate that stomping on a roach will break a bone in our foot that will send us to the hospital the day a fire destroys our employer's business and kills many of our co-workers? How can we anticipate that speeding to the airport will lead to a traffic ticket that makes us miss our flight and traps us in the terminal where we spend six hours deep in conversation with the woman who will become the mother of our children? How can we anticipate that picking up a dropped penny will delay our progress a fraction of a second, keeping us from stepping off the curb in front of a pickup truck that slams into a light pole where it would have crushed us?

Don't sweat the small stuff? Get real. It's the small stuff that changes our lives forever.

The stories which follow explore what happens to people when small crimes change the course of their lives. Stealing apples, failing to leave contact information after a minor traffic accident, accepting a small bribe to overlook faulty wiring – all have consequences beyond the imagination of the characters involved.

Small crimes. Big consequences.
Enjoy.

Michael Bracken
Waco, Texas
February, 2003

Chainmail

Neil Schofield

I've been thinking recently that even if you *are* lucky enough to live in a lovely English village like Handlebury, life isn't always as idyllic as uninformed opinion might have it. As James says, at the very least you need to have no nerves to speak of because there are things seething under the surface that simply don't bear thinking about. He's right as usual and I should know. Take this present situation which goes back to the Friday before last, when Tricia, my very dearest friend, said to me, rather rudely I thought, "So what did you pinch this time?"

"What do you mean, 'this time'?" I said.

"Come on, Emma, you know you can never resist. You've always been a closet klepto. Sticky-Fingers, we used to call you at school."

I had to blush. It is true, ever since I was a child, I have found it impossible, when in a shop, to fight off that little urge to pocket something, something small, just a little thing. I don't know why, it's just a habit I have. Well, we all have our little ways, don't we? I know people who do far worse things.

"So what was it?" Tricia was insisting.

"A small bag of chick-peas."

"A bag of chick-peas? You don't even eat chick-peas. And I doubt if James even knows what they are. A bag of chick-peas. Worth what?"

"One pound twenty-five," I said miserably.

She rolled back on the sofa and cawed with mocking laughter.

We were sitting in what Tricia calls her studio. In fact, it's just a front room in her cottage. There is a large, old-fashioned desk in front of the window, cluttered with all the materials she uses for her graphics work. I know she's an artist, but why these people have to live amid such disorder, I don't know. You should see that room. It's a complete tip. For one thing, it's packed with far too much furniture, including a hideous sofa, and then there are things thrown here and there all higgledy-piggledy, clothes, rolls of colored paper, masses of materials, tea-chests full of art books, all sorts of junk, even her golf clubs lying just anyhow in a corner.

But then what did I care? It was a lovely morning and Handlebury was looking the very picture of a little Suffolk village, with its age-old, rough-built cottages and its age-old, rough-built cottagers going about their little tasks and duties. The sun was streaming gloriously in through the windows: streaming, unfortunately, onto that disastrous carpet of hers. For someone who has, apparently, highly developed artistic sensibilities (her words not mine), her taste verges, sometimes, on the abysmal.

I was musing absently on Tricia's lack of color sense and thinking that she should never sit on *that* sofa wearing *that* lilac and green jump-suit, especially given her high color and the shade she dyes her hair, and most especially not with *that* carpet in the room. It was like being in the middle of an explosion in Harrod's Soft Furnishings.

Tricia was saying: "You must be barking mad. Shoplifting in Camilla's shop, of all places. Camilla Battersby, the most dangerous woman in Handlebury. Which is quite an achievement for someone who only arrived five bloody minutes ago, damn her eyes."

Actually, let's be fair, Camilla arrived in Handlebury ten months, not five minutes ago. But it *is* true that she's been nothing but trouble ever since. She has put it about that she's taking a sabbatical from her job with "a major advertising agency." To write a book, she says. Tricia, who used to work for a graphics outfit in London, and who is still in The Loop, whatever *that* might be, told me that was a load of old toffee.

Camilla had actually been sacked and blacked. I asked what for, and Tricia said "Gross moral turpitude." *I* said that I would have thought that gross moral turpitude would be rather an asset in a major advertising agency, but Tricia said that Camilla's turpitude had been *exceptionally* gross, even for advertising.

And she's completely taken over. She's everywhere.

"And then she has the nerve to open a damn shop," Tricia said. "What a bloody cheek. As if we needed a health food shop. I mean we're in middle of the bloody country for God's sake. If we need wheatgerm we can go out and dig it up. Or shoot it or whatever you do with it." She was pouring coffee really quite viciously. I did notice, incidentally, as she leaned into the sunlight, that her upper lip was rather due for a waxing. Tricia does sometimes neglect these little personal attentions. James says rather unkindly that once, admittedly in a bad light, he had mistaken her for Saddam Hussein. I told him, *please* try to keep a grip on reality. I admit that Tricia does have that slight moustache problem *and* rather a stocky build, but why would Saddam Hussein be staring into the "Knicker Box" window in Bury at eight o'clock in the evening? Even if there *was* a Sale on.

"And the latest is," Tricia was moaning now, "she's joined the Fitness Club." I could see that this would be a body-blow for her. Welcome to Cellulite City, I thought. If Camilla had decided to join the Fitness Club, it could only be with a take-over in mind. Tricia wouldn't be able to stand that, and she'd leave and start to *balloon* again. She lives on an absolute knife edge, poor thing.

"She's really got to be stopped." Tricia said, "All this flirting. You should see her up at the Golf Club."

James had mentioned that. He, for one, is terrified of her. She belongs to a class of woman he calls – for reasons that are beyond me – Ladies Who Lunge.

I wondered, not for the first time, how Tricia could manage to afford to play golf on the money she earns with her freelance graphics work and the occasional book illustration, and what she calls her calligraphy, though that's just a posh name for joined-up writing if you ask me. James plays golf but only as a sort of extension of his business life and even he says that the cost of playing these days is horrendous. So how did Tricia manage it? That bag of clubs chucked carelessly in the corner of the studio must have cost a bit and then there's the membership and the green fees. But perhaps the graphics game is better-paid than one imagines, I thought.

"She's been seen hacking round nine holes at seven in the morning," Tricia said, "pretending to be all serious about it. But we all know she only joined to get next to a lot of men."

This was getting us nowhere with my problem and I said so.

"All right," said Tricia, "so, for reasons that are buried in the primeval slime of your appalling psyche, you knicked a bag of chick-peas in the shop run by The Thing That Ate Handlebury. Then what?"

"Well," I said, "I was sure I'd got away with it. But lo and behold, she came round to see me last night. James was taking the late train back from London, thank God. Anyway, she jumped right into it. Said I was a shoplifter and she had proof."

"What sort of proof?"

"She's got a closed-circuit thingy in the shop. She said she's got a very nice recording of me taking a bag of chick-peas and stuffing it in my pocket."

Tricia rolled her eyes.

"Emma, you really are a silly cow. So she's threatening you with the police."

"Not in so many words. She was very – oblique – about it."

"I'll bet."

"All she said was, wouldn't it be a pity if a respected person like me, pillar of the community and all, got a reputation. That's all she said. But it was enough."

"So what does she want? I assume she wants something."

I sighed. "You won't believe this. She wants an invitation to the Fur and Feathers."

Tricia shouted with delight.

"You what? She hasn't got a hope. Even I don't get invited to that. And you only get invited because your father was in with them."

I should explain that the Fur and Feathers is what we

irreverently call The Game Ball, which is one of *the* events in the county. It's held at the beginning of September at Monkby Hall, which is the home of Sir Richard Ffiennes, who is the Lord-Lieutenant of the County, our local aristo and a total nitwit. The Ball is officially to mark the opening of the season, but it's really just an excuse for all the blokes who like killing things to get together and compare notes on their latest massacres.

It was easy to see how the Fur and Feathers would attract Camilla like a honeypot attracts wasps. She must have heard that the guests usually include the great, the good, and, more importantly, the rich of the county and anyone can understand why a gathering of this sort would fire her interest.

"Tricia, stop guffawing like that, it's very common, and help me," I said. "What am I going to do?"

"My advice is don't do anything. Let her do her worst."

"But if she *does* do her worst – and she's capable of it – my name would be mud. I might even be prosecuted for theft. It's been known. They might want to make an example of me. I'd be hounded out of the Women's Institute for a start. James would have to leave the Golf Club. He'd be absolutely – well, he'd leave me. I can't risk it, Trish, I really can't."

"All right, then." Go and ask what's his name at the Hall, that secretary, Gervase Fincham, to send her an invitation. You know him well enough. More than well enough at one time, I seem to remember."

That was quite enough of that.

"Tricia, she's got a shop, so she's Trade. They don't invite Trade. Even James only just scrapes in and he's a merchant banker."

She sighed.

"Right then. If that's out, let's think sideways. Who's in well with the Hall?"

"Well, lots of people. The Vicar, the Major, Bernard Heptonstall . . . I don't know, Tricia."

I stopped. Her face had taken on a look I know well.

"Bernard Heptonstall," she said. "Of course, That's your way in."

"But Bernard's only a doctor."

"Yes but he knows everyone. And he knows what everyone's

up to."

"So?"

"And *we* know what *he's* up to with Marjorie Lamb."

I was shocked more than I could say.

"Tricia, you don't mean that we blackmail the doctor?"

I couldn't believe we were actually talking like this. Things were assuming the proportions of a nightmare.

"No, of course not. All you have to do is go round and have a word with Marjorie, she's one of your dearest friends, isn't she? Well then, tell her what's what and leave it to her to do the dirty work."

I thought about this. I had to admit, it wasn't such a bad idea. Married Doctor Having Affair With Patient is a disciplinary affair.

"But what if she goes to the police?"

"Don't be silly. She'd never risk it," said Tricia scornfully.

Tricia was right. The one thing that Marjorie would *not* do in the circs was inform the law. I mean, let's face it, she would hardly risk her *louche* fumblings with Doctor Heptonstall being plastered all over Page One of the *British Medical Journal* (which James, incidentally, always refers to as *The Bleeders' Digest,* I am at a loss to understand why).

Tricia pleaded to be allowed to come with me, but I was adamant. This was something I had to do by myself. She said she'd wait in the car, but I refused absolutely. I knew she'd only end up eating the seat covers.

So I went round alone to see Marjorie, who is indeed one of my dearest friends and who wasn't expecting me, but then, I hadn't been expecting to see *her.*

Our interview started off as most of our conversations do, and then changed direction, and ended up being very nasty, in fact.

After we'd caught up with local matters, the Bring and Buy and the local Red Cross of which she is the mainstay, I asked delicately about Marjorie's health.

"Because we couldn't help noticing, Marjorie, that Doctor Heptonstall seems to be making rather more visits than usual. I couldn't help noticing, dear, you see, since he parks his car in your little drive."

That did it. She went bright red. It was like having traffic lights in the room. But I ploughed on.

"A word to the wise, dear. Because if I've noticed, then perhaps so have other people. You know what they're like round here. The gossip! All it takes is for somebody to say something and there you are. And the General Medical Council are so – well, you remember what happened to Doctor Brimble over in Uppish."

She made all the usual denial noises, as I knew she would. Then I changed the subject to give her a breather and launched onto the social scene. And I made sure that it was Marjorie who mentioned the Game Ball – very easy to do, since it's the only affair of any consequence at this time of year.

"Oh, yes, I'll be there. But," I said, "I'm really very upset about it because Camilla Battersby, who is a very dear and close friend of mine, hasn't received her invitation."

"Oh, dear," she said, clearly not caring in the slightest. "Why is that do you think?"

"I'm sure I have no idea. She's very cut up about it, as you can imagine. And so am I, rather. I'm sure they're not trying to make a point. I'm quite certain that it's just an oversight."

"Have you spoken to the Hall?" she asked. Stupid woman. Of course I hadn't.

"No, Marjorie, to be honest, I couldn't do that. But of course, all it needs is for someone influential to say something, and I'm sure they'd put matters right." Then, ever so gently, I said, "Doctor Heptonstall is well in with that sort of people isn't he?" Well, so he is. Very friendly with all the country nobs.

Of course, she balked at that straightaway. Couldn't possibly, interfering in things that don't concern him, putting his oar in, really not on, all that sort of thing.

Marjorie really is a very stupid woman. I had given her all the information she needed and yet she couldn't make the connection. I practically had to paint it in foot-high letters on the sitting room wall before she realized that there was a real and potentially causal connection between Camilla receiving an invitation to the Game Ball and her – whatever it was – with Doctor Heptonstall staying under wraps.

When she did get it, however, things went very quiet. She

sat with her hands in her lap, and stared at me.

And then she began to say things, terrible things that I'm sure she regretted later but which, while she was saying them, she seemed to be relishing. Well, I left. There was nothing more to be gained by staying there to listen to all that. And after all, I had what I had come for.

So I went home. James was down at the Sheep and Two Magnets, so I had the house to myself. I took a long hot bath and then climbed gratefully into bed. I went over the conversation. Dreadful though it had been, I realized with a slight shock that I had really rather enjoyed it.

And I could hear, just as clearly as if I was there, the conversation that would take place, perhaps *was* taking place even now, between Marjorie and Bernard. He wouldn't believe her, not at first.

"What do you mean, she threatened you? How?"

"Well, she didn't so much threaten me, as say things."

"Things? What *things? Marjorie, pull yourself together, for God's sake. What things?"*

"Well first she asked after you. She said she had noticed that you seemed to call here rather a lot and that I should be careful because it only needed someone to say something."

"Well, we know that. So?"

"Well, then, we somehow got talking about the Fur and Feathers and how that bloody Camilla Battersby of hers hadn't been invited, and how it only needed someone to say something to somebody and she was sure it could all be sorted out."

"Is that all?"

"It wasn't what she said. It was the horrible way she said 'it only needs someone to say something' – as though there was a connection. As though if someone didn't say something about the Invitation, someone would say something about us. *And your career would be ruined . . ."*

And so it would go. I could imagine it all.

In the end though, she would convince him, I knew. She may be rather stupid, but Bernard Heptonstall is far from daft.

I slept very well that night. I didn't even wake up when James came back from the pub, and rolled in beside me.

I reported back to Tricia the next morning.

"Right," she said, "all you have to do is wait. All things will come to pass." She still sounded rather sulky about not having been there, but I ignored that.

So I waited. And the waiting was dreadful. I didn't dare leave the house, because, silly as it was, I was still expecting to be arrested. I jumped a foot every time the phone rang. And it meant that I was trapped in the house with James who was like a caged wild beast. Now, I know he's having a rough time of it – well, everyone is, aren't they? – but he must realize that there are things in life other than load-restructuring and DotCom Meltdown. Whatever *they* might be. I asked him quite civilly on the Sunday if he saw any prospect of us having the new kitchen shelves up before the Third Millennium, and he simply slammed out to the pub.

So I waited. And eventually it came to pass.

In a little village like Handlebury, there's always some activity: people going hither and thither about their daily business. But if you have eyes to see, there are always patterns.

There's Mrs. Cakebread going to see her great friend Mrs. Hinchcliffe for another session of character-assassination. There's Mr. Boddy on his tardy way to solve someone's plumbing problems which he had probably helped to create in the first place. Mr. Boddy lives in a parallel universe which is identical to ours in every detail except that it's three weeks behind.

Then there will be Miss Fish on her way to collect her pension from the Post Office, a large portion of which she will spend on Gordon's Gin. When you live in a village High Street, you see all this movement, which to the unpracticed eye would seem aimless and random, but it has its patterns. And when something breaks the pattern, it stands out like a sore thumb. If you have eyes to see, that is. Tricia and I have eyes to see . . .

The Monday after I had been to Marjorie, there was quite a lot of unusual activity, if you knew what you were looking at. In Handlebury terms, it was the equivalent of the San Francisco earthquake.

The first thing that happened was that Tricia rang me in a state of some excitement.

"Guess what? Doctor Heptonstall called on Major Batty,

this morning."

That was interesting. Major Batty, whose house is directly opposite Tricia's cottage, is a detestable little man, and has never been known to have a medical visit in his life. Not publicly, that is. He puts it down to a life lived in hot places. The names "Eal Alamein" and "Rangoon" often crop up. Believe that if you will, he is a very fit little swine for his age.

"This is interesting," I said. "Why would Bernard Heptonstall be calling on the Major?"

Tricia said, "The only reason I can think of is that the Doctor is under pressure from Marjorie and went to pass some of the pressure on to the Major."

That made sense. The Major was well in with all our local notables.

"Perhaps Heptonstall's got something on the Major," I said.

"Yes, and I bet it's something to do with those little trips he keeps making to Southeast Asia," said Tricia, "to visit his so-called 'old pals.'"

There *were* some appalling rumors.

Anyway, according to Tricia, Doctor Heptonstall had emerged from the Major's cottage half an hour later. And it hadn't been a comfortable consultation. She said he was sweating like a pig, and he looked in a dreadful temper. Something, Tricia said, was up.

And up it was, because late in the morning, who should I see, as I did my shopping, but the Major walking briskly down the hill towards the center of the village. I hovered outside the village shop, trying to be inconspicuous. It looked as though he were heading for – yes, he was going into the Vicarage. He seemed to hesitate a little before actually opening the gate, and square his shoulders, like a man facing some unpleasant task.

I went in to do my shopping, thinking furiously. So, the Major was going to see the Vicar. Possibly it was entirely unrelated. Geoffrey Bolton was such a nice man. But, could he possibly have been up to something? Of course, I thought, the Major was on the Parish Council, so perhaps it was something to do with that – and hadn't someone mentioned to me once that the Vicar occasionally enjoyed a trip to the races? Perhaps his trips had become a little more than occasional? And perhaps, who knows, oh how terrible – irregularities in the Parish Fund? Or – worse? The mind boggled.

I was beginning to enjoy this, despite myself. And later, when I saw the Major coming back up the hill, looking a little grayer and stooped than usual, I knew that the fuse I had lit was burning merrily. Especially when I saw the Vicar speed past in his car, white-faced, not even bothering to hoot at the Major, as he usually did. The Vicar was heading out of the village in the direction of the Hall. And when you think that Geoffrey Bolton is the Spiritual Counselor and Guide for the Ffiennes, who get up to God knows what – well, it was all clearly going swimmingly.

All that went on on the Monday.

On the Tuesday morning, someone rang the doorbell, and when I opened the door, who should be standing there but Marjorie. She pushed her way in and glared at me. Her makeup was a mess; evidently she'd put her face on in the dark. All in all, she looked as though she had been colored-in by a three-year-old, who had then panicked and tried to rub her out with spit.

She looked at me viciously.

"And to think I once thought you were one of my dearest friends."

I said, "But Marjorie, I hope I still can be. Let's not allow a silly little hiccup like this to ruin our relationship."

Marjorie sneered. Then she dug in her handbag and pulled out a creamy-white envelope. She pushed it at me.

"Some hopes," she said, and "There," pushing the envelope at me, "for your very close and dear friend. And I hope she chokes on it."

I took it.

"I trust you're satisfied, Emma," she said, in a voice that seemed to me to be ever so slightly over-dramatic, "I really trust you're happy to know that you have ruined two lives."

Then she turned and she swept out, just like that.

I immediately went round to see Tricia. I took my short route, cutting across the churchyard and round through the back field behind her cottage.

On the way past the church, I saw on the notice board, in

large, hastily scrawled letters: "Service Suspended Indefinitely." Oh dear. I hoped nothing serious had happened to Geoffrey. Perhaps, who knows, some problem with the Hall. Because the Bishop is very close to Sir Richard. They went to school together, I seem to remember. Dear me. Such a nice Vicar and so well-liked. It was a real shame, because this meant that on Sunday, we would have to go over to Saint Chrysostom's in Welding. It's quite a nice church, but it must be said that their vicar has a palate that is not entirely uncleft, which leads to some chillingly impenetrable sermons and the occasional unseemly hoo-ha at the baptismal font.

I walked though the grassy back field to Tricia's cottage, let myself in the back way, as usual, and went through into the front room.

Tricia was at the window, staring through the lace curtains.

"Come here, come here," she said.

I joined her at the window. Across the road, outside the Major's house, there was an ambulance and a knot of people consisting of the usual official nosey-parkers.

I said, "What's going on?"

Tricia grinned at me.

"There's all hell breaking loose," she said.

I leaned over her shoulder to part the curtains. She stopped me.

"Doesn't do to show too much interest." The little crowd opposite had swelled slightly, if anything. Then, a stretcher came out of the house, carried by two paramedics. Just behind them came Bernard Heptonstall. I watched him very carefully. Was he swaying? Yes, and then he stumbled slightly. Surely he couldn't be – no, not at this time of day. It wasn't possible. But, he did appear to be unshaved, and his shirt was open at the neck.

I watched the Major being loaded into the ambulance, and Doctor Heptonstall standing by, swaying, (yes, I had to say) drunkenly.

"Well," Tricia said, "something is up, isn't it? He must have had one of his heart attacks. I wonder what brought *that* on. And oh look, here comes Marjorie."

And here, indeed, came Marjorie driving her car, which was crammed with suitcases and boxes. As she passed the circus on the other side of the road, she slowed down. At that moment, Doctor Heptonstall turned and saw her. Some sort of silent exchange took place between them, and then Marjorie, her face set, revved up and accelerated away, heading in the direction of the main London road. Doctor Heptonstall's head drooped and he turned away.

Tricia turned to me.

"Dear me, looks like someone's moving house," she said. "All right, let's have a look at it."

I opened the envelope and there was Camilla's invitation. Sir Richard and Lady Pamela Ffiennes have pleasure in inviting Miss Camilla Battersby etcetera, etcetera.

"Not bad," said Tricia, "though I say it myself."

"You didn't do anything," I said, indignantly. "I had to do everything."

"No," she said, "I mean the workmanship. Who do you think designed this thing for them?"

I looked more closely at the invitation and, yes, now that she mentioned it, I recognized Tricia's script which is, I have to admit, rather beautiful.

"She doesn't deserve this, you know," said Tricia, "she really doesn't."

"No, she doesn't," I said, "but what can I do? I'll have to give it to her."

"Well, be sure to get that recording off her when you do," said Tricia.

"I'm not that silly."

"Silly enough to get caught stealing chick-peas." She was speaking absently, looking at the invitation.

Then, she went to her desk and sat down. She laid the invitation in front of her, and then reached for a large steel-nibbed pen. She also opened a bottle of Indian ink.

"What on earth are you doing?" I said. I was horrified. She was going to spoil everything.

Tricia grinned. "Don't you worry, Emm, it'll be undetectable."

She bent over the invitation. At the bottom, where normally it would say Evening Dress but doesn't because everyone knows it's evening dress at the Fur and Feathers, Tricia began to write. I couldn't see anything until she leaned back with a satisfied sigh.

"There," she said, "that should slow her down a bit."

I looked at what she had written. In the same beautiful script, indistinguishable from the printing above, she had put:

Fancy Dress Theme – Your Favorite Film Monster

I couldn't help smiling.

"There you are, Emm, your own little time-bomb. All you have to do is wait for it to go off bang."

I thought of the scene under the glittering chandeliers of Monkby Hall, the assembled toffs in full fig, all the jewels and medals, all the freshly-shaven cheeks, the snow-white linen, the silver and the crystal, the ball-gowns and corsages, of course, for the ladies. It was absolutely vile, what Tricia was doing, and it was exquisitely delicious.

"You're terrible. But you're brilliant," I said.

Tricia didn't answer. She was staring out the window.

Then she said slowly, "No, this is too good. This I have to see."

"What?" I said.

"I have to be there, Emma. When it happens, when she arrives. You can't deny me that."

"What do you mean?" I already had a nasty empty feeling in my tummy.

"You have to get me an invitation to the Fur and Feathers, Emma. I have to be there when she arrives."

I was aghast.

"I can't, Tricia, I can't! No, it's impossible. Look at the hell I've been through already. And the Ball's on Friday, for God's sake!"

Tricia said, "That still gives you three days. That's plenty of time."

"I absolutely can't, Tricia!"

"Yes, you can, Emma." Her tone had become hard. "I realize the Major's out of the loop, and apparently the Vicar, but there are others."

"Tricia, believe me, I can't do it."

She was looking at me very steadily.

"Emma, you're my best friend. I've never asked you for anything before, but this I *must* have. It would be a pity if

James and everybody found out what you've been up to, now wouldn't it? I don't know who on earth would tell, mind you, but these things get around, don't they?"

She was staring at me,. Her eyes were very, very bright, and there was a little smile hovering round her mouth.

"Think about it," she said.

I gaped, yes, I gaped at her. I could find no words to say. My dearest friend in all the world was actually blackmailing me.

I had a sudden feeling of dizziness, as though I were standing on the brink of an enormous cliff. I stared around that cluttered room, looking for inspiration, looking for a way out, desperately trying to get my brain to work. I thought about the agony of the last few days. I thought about Camilla and Marjorie and the Doctor, I thought about the Major and the Vicar, and I thought about James and me and Tricia, my dearest friend, all of us in a circle, all going round in my head, round and round, faster and faster and faster in a hellish dance that was never, ever going to end.

All I wanted to do was scream and scream and *scream.* But of course, I didn't.

Well, the Fur and Feathers was an *enormous* success; James and I had a wonderful time. It was slightly marred, but also enlivened, by the arrival of Camilla Battersby who, for reasons unclear to the host and hostess, had decided to come dressed as Frankenstein's Monster, completed with a bolt through her neck, and who was invited politely but firmly to go home again, which she did, in the same taxi that had brought her.

But, I must say, the gaiety was somewhat muted this year, since the entire community is still in a state of shock following the murder in Handlebury three days before. James says that no one is safe these days, when a woman can be hit over the head in broad daylight in her own home with one of her own golf clubs. A Number Seven iron, at that. He had a chat with the Chief Constable at the Ball. Apparently the police are completely baffled and *there's* a novelty. They simply have nothing to go on. There are no clues. No one was seen entering or leaving the murdered woman's cottage, but there was a medical emergency happening across the road at the estimated time of the murder, so that's hardly surprising. They're said to be working on the theory that it was an itinerant maniac.

I, of course, am completely devastated, and everybody has been very kind and gentle, knowing how close Tricia and I had always been. James, especially, has been wonderfully comforting. He says it just goes to show the appalling things that can lurk beneath the surface of even the loveliest English village.

And how right he is, because one thing that is definitely still lurking is Camilla Battersby. I saw her in the High Street the other day and she gave me the nastiest look, a sort of smug, *knowing*, you-wait-and-see look. I know she blames me for her public humiliation at the Ball, and I've no doubt that she is out for revenge, but what's behind that look? What can she be cooking up in that nasty little mind? She's quite capable of starting some sort of whispering campaign about me, not that anyone should ever listen to lying, unsubstantiated gossip, but one never knows in a place like Handlebury. Well yes, one *does* know actually: they'd lap it up.

So, I'm wondering if she still plays early-morning golf as poor, dear Tricia once said. Well, if she does, she's being very foolhardy: those deserted links could be extremely dangerous with a killer on the loose. Especially, yes, now I think of it, that short seventh hole, which is surrounded by dense woods. I should think absolutely *anyone* could get into those woods. And out again, without ever being seen.

I think she'd better watch her step because, as James says, the cost of playing golf these days can be absolute murder.

But then, Camilla runs a shop and she of all people should know that the cost of *everything* is going up. And that includes chick-peas.

Not Too Far From the Tree

Paula J. Matter

"You ain't nothin' but a big baby, y'know that, Jimmy? Just a big old whiny crybaby. Now, c'mon before it gets dark and Mama starts hollering for us."

Kenny was always calling me a big baby just because he was four years older than me. He was always talking about being older and how things was before I came along. Mama told me to ignore him, and how I was the apple of her eye, her baby. And how Kenny was just like Daddy. Except she sounded sad when she said that.

He grabbed my arm and pulled me hard, leaving a big old red mark. I stuck my tongue out at him and said, "Knock it off, Kenny, or I'm tellin'."

"Oh, yeah? You tell Mama and I'll tell Daddy what a big wuss you are. Y'know what he'll do then, don't you?" Kenny had that stupid smirk on his ugly face and I hated his guts even more. He always knew what to say and do to scare me real good. Yeah, I sure did know what Daddy would do.

"Now, c'mon."

So I went.

We'd been at Potter's Creek just about all day fishing and swimming and complaining about having to go back to school in another few days. Kenny was going into the middle school and he was acting all tough and like a big shot. Kept telling me how I was only gonna be in third grade at the baby school. That's all he talked about the whole summer and Mama told me to not pay any attention, that now he'd be the baby in the big school and he'd find out what it'd be like. She told me to just wait and see, that sooner or later Kenny'd find out he was too big for his britches. Then we laughed.

Mama and I shared secrets like that all the time. It sure did make me feel good and Mama said having me to talk to just about saved her from going crazy. She always seemed not as sad when it was just the two of us.

The saddest I'd ever seen Mama was when she lost the baby. She said it was a girl and how I would've been a real good big brother. I still ain't sure how the accident happened but it took a long time before Mama stopped crying all the time. Even after all the bruises wore off, she still kept crying. Mama said she's too sore to walk up the stairs so I guess that's why she's still sleeping on the couch. Daddy ain't real happy about that, but he acts nicer to her since the accident and doesn't say too much. Mama said guilt is an amazing thing. I don't understand that, but I reckon Mama knows what she's talking about.

"C'mon, you little wuss, hurry up!" Kenny hollered at me. I was going fast as I could seeing as how I was carrying both poles and the bucket. We hadn't caught any fish and I reckon that's why Kenny was meaner than usual. He knew Daddy would be mad 'cause he was counting on having fish for supper that night. So I stumbled along after him trying to catch up, the bucket bumping my leg as I hurried.

Before I knew it, we were getting nearer to Old Man Dunhill's apple orchard. Kenny knew I hated going through that place, but he always said it was a shortcut, so we took it.

Kenny said Old Man Dunhill would never shoot at us, that he only liked waving his old shotgun around to scare us. Daddy said those stupid No Trespassing signs wouldn't stop his boys from cutting through that stinkin' old orchard, that we'd been living there lots longer than that old fart and he couldn't stop us from using the shortcut. Mama said just to be careful.

All I wanted to do was get on home, but Kenny stopped at one of the trees. He had that mean look on his ugly face. I tried to move on by him, but he grabbed my arm, the sore one that he'd hurt before.

"Uh-uh, wuss, you ain't going nowhere. I want an apple

and you're gonna get me one." I hated it when his eyes looked like Daddy's. All squinty and mean, and I knew it was best to just do what he wanted when he looked like that. I was only eight years old, but I sure wasn't stupid. Mama said I was the only one in our family that got any brains when the good Lord was passing them out. She said that was one of our secrets and to never let Kenny and Daddy know she had said that.

If our secrets helped Mama from going crazy, they helped me from getting beat up more by Kenny. It was bad enough, but I was smart and I knew when trouble was coming. Any time Kenny was whipped by Daddy, I knew it was best to run and hide.

My brains told me to not run that time, that I'd better just get the stupid apple for him. I dropped the poles and bucket, looked around for Old Man Dunhill, took a real deep breath and climbed the tree.

I grabbed the closest one to me and tossed it down to Kenny. He took a real big bite out of it, then his eyes became all squinty again.

Holding onto a branch, I waited.

"Get one for yourself, wuss. A big one."

I figured maybe I'd get away with just picking one and bringing it home. Maybe he wouldn't make me eat it right then and there. He knew what eating apples did to me and I sure was praying while I looked for one. I reached up to pick an apple and down below I heard Kenny.

"Uh-uh. That one ain't big enough. Reach on up higher, wuss. Go on now, do as you're told."

That was when we heard the first gunshot.

I swore later I had felt the bullet whoosh by my head, but Mama said that couldn't be 'cause Old Man Dunhill was too far away. Besides he probably wasn't really shooting to kill, he was just doing it to scare us. I jumped out of that tree right quick enough 'cause I wasn't taking any chances.

Even Kenny looked scared and we took off running forgetting all about the poles and bucket. It wasn't until we were in our bedroom that I saw the apple in my hand. Hoping Kenny hadn't noticed, I tried to hide it somewhere. But, sure enough, he'd seen it.

My brain was working real hard and I figured I'd just eat the apple real quick then go right away into the bathroom and put my finger down my throat before anything bad could happen.

Kenny must have been thinking the same thing 'cause he said, "Okay, wuss, you eat that real nice and slow." He kept shoving me until I landed in the corner, my back against the wall.

"And you ain't gonna go to the bathroom and upchuck this time. I'm gonna stay right here and watch you eat it. Then I'm gonna make sure you don't go anywhere. You sure ain't gonna go tell Daddy I ran from that old fart Dunhill, y'hear me, wuss?"

I tried really hard to not start blubbering 'cause I knew that'd just make it worse. Eating the dang apple was the only thing I could do.

The apple was real wormy 'cause Old Man Dunhill never sprayed his orchard. He didn't really do nothing with all them apple trees anymore. He'd just grow 'em and then let 'em rot.

Mama said it was a waste and how she missed getting apples from Sophie Dunhill all those years. Back in those days the apple orchard was taken good care of. The trees were sprayed regularly to keep the bugs and worms out of them. Mama said Miss Sophie was good about cleaning any apples she gave us. Mama was a real stickler for clean fruit and vegetables, though, so she always washed 'em again no matter what Miss Sophie said.

Mama always laughed when she talked about the first apple pie I'd ever eaten. I didn't remember it 'cause I was only a little kid, but I sure did know now what would happen when I ate this apple.

Within minutes I'd get itchy bumps. Hives is what Mama said they were. Mama said she was sorry I'd 'herited that from her. She sounded even sorrier when she talked about what Kenny had 'herited from Daddy.

Mama didn't know about how I'd heard her praying for forgiveness 'cause of how she felt about her oldest boy sometimes. How she didn't have the love in her heart like she did for me. And how she sometimes wished that Daddy would leave and take Kenny with him. Mama didn't know I heard all that and I guess I was keeping that as a secret for just me to know.

I started praying for the same thing and I reckoned the good Lord might just listen harder if both of us asked.

So far He hadn't.

Kenny shoved me again and my head banged into the wall. At least I didn't dent the wall like that time Kenny did when Daddy threw him across the room. Daddy said he wasn't gonna fix the hole 'cause it might teach Kenny to remember who's boss in this house. Seems to me that Kenny only gets mad when he sees the hole.

"Eat it, wuss. Right now."

I didn't see no worms, just holes where they had been. The holes were all brown and gross and when I bit into the apple, juice dribbled down my chin.

"Chew it up real nice and slow, wuss."

I tried eating with my mouth open so some of it might fall out, but Kenny jammed his hand against my chin so I had to swallow. I could feel the itchy bumps starting already. Mama said later that was just my 'magination, that the bumps didn't start all that quick. But it sure did seem like it at the time.

That was when we heard the second gunshot.

Kenny forgot all about me and ran over to the window that looked out over the orchard. I spit out the apple, then squeezed in next to him to see what was happening.

Old Man Dunhill stood by the tree closest to our fence, shaking his gun at our house. We watched him pick up one of our fishing poles, wave it in the air, then he snapped it in two and threw it over the fence into our yard.

Before I could even get mad, Kenny grabbed me by the shirt, pulled me real close to him and shoved his ugly face into mine.

"That better be your pole and not mine, wuss. You stupid little jerk, why'd you leave –"

I reckon we both heard Daddy at the same time and Kenny let go of me. Looking out the window again, we saw Daddy standing by the fence shaking his fist at Old Man Dunhill.

"Man, oh, man! That old fart's in for it now! He'll be sorry he ever messed with us. I'm gonna go get closer."

About a minute later I saw Kenny running through the yard toward the fence. He bent down and picked up the broken fishing pole. He smiled and I knew then that the busted one was mine. In a way I was glad 'cause that meant I wouldn't have to hide from Kenny later. He'd be madder than a wet hornet if it was his pole that was broke.

I still can't believe what happened next. And I never would if I hadn't seen it with my own eyes.

Daddy grabbed Kenny by the neck and waist and threw him over the fence. He landed right next to Old Man Dunhill, and just sat there looking up at him. I couldn't see real good but I bet Kenny's old squinty eyes grew real big when the old fart pointed his shotgun right at him.

I about jumped out of my skin when I felt something on my shoulder. Mama had come upstairs.

"Hush, child. Let's see what that good for nothing son of a gun's going to do next."

I wasn't sure if Mama was talking about Daddy or Old Man Dunhill. Her hand squeezed my shoulder while we watched and waited.

I looked up at Mama and saw she had her eyes raised toward the ceiling. Her lips were moving and I reckoned she was praying. I wondered what she was praying for. She must've seen me looking up at her 'cause she lowered her eyes and stopped moving her lips.

When we looked out the window again we saw Old Man Dunhill still had the shotgun pointed at Kenny and Daddy was laughing. The old fart looked really ticked off, but sort of confused too. It was like he wasn't sure what to do next. Then I looked at Kenny.

I'd seen that look plenty of times whenever I've looked in a mirror. Downright fear. And hate. I don't think Daddy saw the look 'cause he was laughing so hard and yelling stuff at Old Man Dunhill. I couldn't hear all the words, but it sure seemed like Daddy was challenging him to pull the trigger.

I wondered what it'd be like without Kenny around anymore. I guess Mama wondered the same thing 'cause she suddenly pushed me aside and leaned her head out of the window.

"Y'all stop that right now, y'hear?" She backed away from

the window without even waiting to see if they'd listened to her. I reckon she knew they had. "Enough of that. I have supper to fix. Vegetables to wash, peel and cook."

When she was heading toward the door she saw the apple and the chewed up apple pieces I had spit out on the floor, and without looking at me, she said, "Jimmy, clean up that mess." Then she walked out.

Before I cleaned it up, I looked out the window again. Old Man Dunhill was gone and Daddy was walking back toward the house. Kenny was standing by the apple tree, looking after Daddy. He must've been crazy because of what he did next.

He bent down, picked up an apple and raised his arm like he was gonna throw it. Daddy must've sensed something 'cause he stopped walking, then turned around and saw Kenny. I felt like I was watching that Gary Cooper movie I'd seen on our old black and white downstairs.

I wished they did have guns so they could have a shootout. But the only weapon Kenny had was that stupid apple and he was going up against Daddy, so he didn't stand a chance. I reckon he realized that 'cause he dropped the apple. Daddy said something to him, then he turned away and came into the house.

Kenny picked up the bucket and his fishing pole and tossed them real hard over the fence, then he followed after. He picked up the pole, then kicked the bucket hard as he could. It bounced and clanged across the dusty yard. Boy, he sure did look mad.

I knew it was time to hide.

Heading toward the door, I saw the apple on the floor and remembered Mama told me to clean it up. Dang it. Kenny would be up any minute and I knew I didn't have time to hide and clean up the mess. I'd never not done what Mama told me to do, so I wasn't real sure what to do.

I figured I'd hurt Mama's feelings if I didn't listen to her, but Kenny would hurt me real bad if I didn't hide. Maybe Mama would understand just this once. I crawled underneath my bed just in the nick of time.

I was laying on my belly with my head turned toward the door when I saw Kenny stomp into our room. I realized I'd been holding my breath and let it out slow and quiet. I started praying real hard, but I wasn't sure if the good Lord would listen 'cause I wanted to keep my eyes open to watch Kenny's feet. I ain't never prayed with my eyes open before and I didn't know how it worked.

Kenny stopped at the apple mess on the floor, and he swung his foot back. I heard him grunt, then his foot hit the apple and it left the floor. Next thing I heard was glass breaking. Man, oh, man! He was sure in for it now.

I watched his feet run toward the door and could hear loud stomping coming up the stairs. Kenny's feet stopped, seemed stuck to the floor. Then I saw Daddy's feet. More than anything I wanted to shut my eyes, but I was too scared.

Kenny didn't have time to say a word. Daddy must've picked him up and thrown him across the room like he done that other time. I'll never forget the sound Kenny made when he slammed down on to the floor. Then I did close my eyes. The only sound I heard was Daddy going back downstairs.

I waited forever to see what'd happen next. I opened my eyes. It was quiet and I couldn't even hear Kenny. I wondered how bad hurt he was this time, but I sure wasn't gonna leave my hiding place yet.

Slow and quiet, I scooted over to get a better look at Kenny. He lay all crumpled up against the wall; his one leg twisted real funny under him. I held my breath to try to listen harder. No sound came from him.

Moving like an army man crawling under barbed wire, I inched myself across the floor a little ways. Just in case Kenny was faking it, I stopped a few feet away from him. No way was I gonna let him jump up and scare me. I stood and tiptoed over to him.

Still no sound coming from him. Figuring he couldn't keep from hollering if I touched his broke leg, I nudged it. Still nothing. Both his arms was under his belly, so I thought I'd have time to run in case he tried to grab me. I moved closer.

I could tell from all the blood that Kenny wouldn't be grabbing me. Not then or any time.

I didn't want to look at Kenny any more, so I looked out our bedroom window instead. That's when I seen Old Man Dunhill spraying the apple tree closest to our fence. The one me and Kenny always picked apples from when Daddy wanted one of Mama's pies. She always had to make two pies 'cause Daddy said he could eat one all by himself. Mama said it was a good thing we was both allergic 'cause between Kenny and Daddy there wouldn't be enough for all of us.

Old Man Dunhill was wearing yellow gloves like the kind Mama uses when she's washing dishes. He had a funny looking mask over his mouth and nose, and he just kept on spraying.

A sick feeling hit my stomach and I didn't want to watch the spraying any more. Plus I didn't want him to catch me watching. I backed away from the window and nearly stepped on Kenny's foot.

"Jimmy, that's far enough." Mama's voice stopped me. "You go on downstairs. Now. Tell your Daddy to come up."

I took another quick look at Kenny, then raced down the stairs. Daddy was in on the couch in front of the TV, and I told him real quick Mama wanted him in our room. He cursed and I wasted no time getting out of there.

Old Man Dunhill wasn't by the tree when I went out on the front porch. With him gone and Mama and Daddy upstairs it was real quiet and I didn't know what to do with myself.

I wondered what it'd be like now what with Kenny dead. I reckoned the good Lord had answered Mama's prayers. I sure wish Daddy hadn't done that and I wondered if he was sorry too. I remembered how he kept telling Mama he was sorry after her accident, and I wondered if he was saying the same thing now about Kenny's accident. I knew that's what Daddy would call it.

Mama said Daddy had a way with words and for getting out of trouble. Like that time Kenny had all those bruises and the teacher sent him down to the office. We all knew how he got them bruises, but when that man and lady came to our house asking questions we all said Kenny had fallen down the stairs by accident. Kenny even said that, so the man and lady left.

Daddy was real careful after that and didn't punch Kenny in the face no more.

I wondered if I'd be the one having accidents now that

Kenny wouldn't be around. 'Course it turned out later I didn't have to wonder or worry about that. But before that, while I was standing on the porch wondering about accidents and Kenny and stuff, it hit me.

It wasn't no accident when Mama lost my baby sister. Daddy must've stopped punching Mama in the face, too. I was glad I finally figured it out, but madder'n a hornet at the same time.

I had to help the good Lord answer Mama's prayers. Kenny was gone now and all Mama wanted was for her and me to be together. I had to make Daddy go away.

I remember that time when the man and lady were here asking questions Kenny told me that he shoulda told the truth. That maybe they'd take Daddy away for a long time for what he done to him. Kenny said there was lots of men in jails for hurting little kids. But then he figured when Daddy got out he'd come looking for Kenny, so we never told nobody the truth.

I didn't want Daddy to ever come back.

"Jimmy! Open the door, son," Mama's voice hollered to me. I turned and looked through the screen door. Daddy and Mama was carrying Kenny down the stairs. I opened the door right quick.

"Open my car door, boy. Be quick about it, y'hear?"

I jumped off the porch and ran fast as I could to Daddy's car. The door was heavy, but with two hands, I could pull it open.

Looking through the window, I seen Daddy and Mama lay Kenny down on the seat. He looked so little. His eyes was open and I swear he looked right at me. Then he cried out.

"Be careful, Ken, he's hurt real bad this time," Mama said, then backed away and stood next to me. With her arm around my shoulder, we watched. Real careful, I closed the door.

Daddy ran around to the other door, hopped in and started the engine. "I'll call you from the hospital."

Me and Mama stood there a long time even after we couldn't see the car no more, just the dust clouds off the road.

"Well, then, that's that. I'm going to finish getting supper ready. Your Daddy will be hungry when he gets home."

"Mama –"

Mama was looking at the apple trees and not paying much attention to me. I tugged on her dress. "Mama, what's gonna happen? I mean with Kenny?"

Still looking at the trees, she said, "It looks like a broken leg. All the blood was from a little cut on his head – they always bleed real bad, but it looks worse than it is." Mama looked down at me, smiled and said, "Jimmy, how about you go pick some apples for me? I'd bet Daddy would like a nice pie after supper."

"But, Mama –"

Mama pressed a finger against her lips. "Go on, son, do as you're told." And she went back into the house.

The way Mama said that made me remember that I hadn't listened to her and cleaned up the apple mess. Maybe if I had Kenny wouldn't be on the way to the hospital. He wouldn't have had that apple to kick, then the window wouldn't have broke.

This time I would listen to Mama right away.

"Jimmy, you be careful, y'hear?" Mama hollered from the screen door. "And get just enough apples for one pie."

Using my brain, I knew I oughta get some gloves to wear because of all that spray. I wondered if that's what Mama meant or did she just mean for me to be careful not to get caught by Old Man Dunhill.

I went into the shed and found Daddy's gloves he wears when he's chopping wood. They was way too big for me, but they'd do just fine. Going out back into the yard, I saw the bucket me and Kenny had used earlier, the one he'd kicked real hard. I picked it up.

I went to the fence, tossed the bucket over, then climbed over after it. I didn't hear or see Old Man Dunhill anywhere and I wanted to get this job over and done with quick as I could. I climbed the tree.

The smell was pretty bad and I wished I'd used my brain to get a mask of some kind. I reckoned I just better hurry and started picking apples. Each one I picked, I threw down to the ground trying to toss 'em into the bucket. Some of 'em made it and some landed near it.

When I figured I had enough, I climbed down the tree and put all the apples into the bucket. It took some doing, but I finally made it back over the fence into our yard with the bucket.

The bucket was kinda heavy and I carried it with two hands and went into the kitchen. Mama wasn't there and I figured she was upstairs in our room cleaning up the blood and maybe the apple mess.

Putting the bucket on the table, I saw two of my favorite cookies sitting on a napkin. It was like they was waiting for me, and I knew it was Mama's way of telling me we had another secret to share. Mama always hid the good chocolate chip cookies from Kenny and Daddy, saying they was just for me for being a good boy. Whenever me and Mama had a secret, she gave me two of my favorite cookies. I pulled off the gloves, sat down at the kitchen table and started eating. I heard the water running upstairs and that gave me an idea.

I picked up the heavy bucket and rolled the apples into the kitchen sink. Then I closed my eyes real tight and prayed to the good Lord to forgive me for what I was gonna do. I hurried back to my chair when I heard Mama coming downstairs.

Mama came into the kitchen. She was wearing her yellow dishwashing gloves except they looked kinda pink. Smiling at me, she went over to the sink.

"Mama, I, um, already washed those apples for you. All you gotta do is slice 'em for Daddy's pie. I swear." I looked up hoping the good Lord wouldn't strike me dead on the spot.

Nothing happened, so I looked over at Mama. She nodded, then took out her cutting board and her good knife.

She picked up an apple and sniffed it. Her nose wrinkled a little bit and I figured I wasn't gonna get away with it.

Without looking at me, she said, "You did fine, son, just fine."

I reckon this was our biggest secret of all.

Hidashar

Tom Sweeney

Rashid Halah heard his wife's footsteps clicking in the hall and quickly flipped the channel from al-Jazeera to the early morning CNN news show, then winced as the TV voice changed from a deep-throated Saudi newscaster to a high-pitched and frantic-voiced ad for cheap long-distance rates. Four-year-old Ahmed, playing with a set of multi-colored wooden blocks a few feet to the right of the television, looked up at the sudden change in sound. Apparently seeing nothing of interest, he returned to the tower he was constructing.

Memphis stopped in the doorway and wiped her hands on the dish towel tucked into her waistband. She gestured toward the television set. "You're watching it again, aren't you?"

Rashid knew she didn't mean CNN or the long distance service ad, but what was wrong with watching al-Jazeera? Was he supposed to be ashamed of his race? He chewed on his lip, biting back a response that would only generate another futile argument, and nodded.

Memphis moved to sit on the ottoman in front of him and his resentment melted away. She was beautiful as only an Egyptian woman can be beautiful. The luckiest man ever he was, to be blessed with this wife and gentle mother.

Yet so Americanized. There are no pure blessings, eh? Memphis had been born in Los Angeles of wealthy expatriate Egyptian parents, and often seemed to him more American than Egyptian. Even now he marveled that she had moved with him here to Newark, the one place in America where

Muslims could most truly be Muslim. He knew she would be happier living someplace less . . . ethnic. Her parents constantly encouraged her to move back to southern California to be closer to them.

Memphis carefully spread the towel on her lap before speaking. "You made out a check to *The Palestine Children's Fund.*"

"We can afford it."

"It was for five hundred dollars, Rashid."

Rashid nodded toward Ahmed, still constructing his block tower. "It was for him. And Hidashar," he added, waving in the direction of their daughter's bedroom. In the sudden silence, her low murmuring could be heard through the closed door. "She is lucky she can plan her ninth birthday party knowing that all her friends will be able to come, not having been killed in the short week between now and then."

Memphis dismissed his response with a wave of her hand. "Don't prevaricate. The check was written for you, not them. You don't feel Muslim enough, and so we live in this unpleasant place where there are no decent schools for Ahmed and Hidashar and you can send money to murderers."

The unfairness of this staggered him. "No! I sent money to help children whose parents had been murdered."

Memphis blinked at the force of his words and Rashid realized that he was leaning forward in his chair. He forced himself to relax. He was so quick to anger lately. His world was on edge, about to tumble out of control, and whatever he did to stabilize it only made it worse.

Memphis switched to Egyptian. "Is this about my not being Muslim enough for you? Do you wish me to cover, wear a veil?"

The words were dutiful but the tone was mocking. The challenge hung in the air while Rashid sought a response. In the tense silence, Ahmed's block tower toppled to the floor. A single block fell from the pile and rolled between Rashid and Memphis.

Rashid slowly picked it up and tossed it back to their young architect-engineer, using the time to think, to frame a reply to Memphis. It wasn't her fault her parents were so Americanized, nor was it a fault of hers to want the best for their children. The schools certainly were bad in Newark.

But she was correct: she was not deeply Muslim. She observed Ramadan and daily prayers, but beneath it all she evidenced little respect for their culture. It showed in many ways.

The naming of Hidashar for instance.

When Rashid spoke, it was in English. "Is it wrong then, to try to make the lives of all children better?"

"You are playing with words as the PLO is playing with our money. You know that most of the money goes to purchase guns."

"But not all."

"They are criminals and sending them money is a crime, Rashid."

"But such a small crime, no? And a crime against whom? It will have no effect on us except a slightly smaller bank balance. We can afford it. For what do I commute to New York every day?"

Memphis rose from her seat. "Yes, we can afford it. You have a fine job. But ask yourself why you are doing these things, why you have some of the friends that you have." She walked to Hidashar's door and raised her voice. "Time to go to school. Are you ready?"

An hour later the challenge thrown to him by Memphis still rankled. His friends were his friends. A man *is* entitled to have friends, is he not? And entitled to send money to help orphaned Arab children. Which is exactly what he had done.

Of course he did. He walked to the train station trying to unjumble his thoughts. Was he truly attempting to bolster his own average life by associating with those who answer to a higher calling? Every boy imagines himself to be a warrior, a hero, at some point in his life. Those who hang on to that dream are the ones who fulfill their destiny. Others merely exist. Why could not he, Rashid, be a hero?

He worried the subject all day and that night dreamed he was the protector of his neighborhood, driving off the gangs that lately ventured from their slum strongholds in search of easier, wealthier prey. In his dream, he single-handedly bested a carload of inner-city punks who were robbing a Chinese market.

Rather than being thankful, though, the owner of the market was angry, so angry his face became an unrecognizable blur. He reached behind his back and pulled out a metal wand. It sparkled, catching Rashid's eye, and he wasn't prepared when the man swung the bar viciously. Rashid caught the blow full in the mouth. He felt teeth shatter, and blood spilled down onto the front of his shirt.

With the reality found in dreams, he suddenly was in a hospital, dressed in a clean business suit. He sat on a gurney, waiting for someone. A doctor entered the room and motioned for Rashid to step before a large, ornate mirror mounted on the wall. Now covered only by a hospital robe, Rashid did as directed.

The doctor, who had become Hidashar, indicated for him to open his mouth. He did and looked in horror at the gaps where he had lost teeth.

"My teeth are gone," he cried.

Hidashar nodded with child-like mock wisdom. "You have lost eleven," she said and disappeared, dissolving into the air.

Rashid woke with a yell, wet with perspiration. He grabbed Memphis fiercely by the shoulder. "Memphis. I've lost Hidashar!"

She bolted from the bed before realizing that Rashid had but dreamed. She sat back down and put an arm around the still-quivering Rashid. "It was a nightmare," she said. "Go back to sleep."

"I lost a tooth in a dream," he said.

Memphis slipped back between the sheets and jerked the covers to her shoulders. Rashid easily imagined her rolling her eyes. "We live in a modern city in the New World, Rashid," she said, speaking slowly as though explaining an important lesson of life to young Ahmed. "Omens that were entertaining in the eighth century have no meaning now. No one will die because you lost a tooth in a dream."

"I lost eleven teeth. I lost Hidashar."

"Rashid, go back to sleep."

He couldn't. He lay rigid, staring at the ceiling but seeing

Hidashar in a white hospital uniform, watching her melt into nothing, reliving the dream over and over.

He lost his daughter because he sent money to Palestine, that much was clear. Memphis was right. He had not saved any Palestinian children, and now he was going to lose Hidashar.

Friday his dream caught up with him.

Rashid's neighborhood had once been mixed-ethnic residential, just far enough from the center of Newark to escape most of the problems yet close enough to benefit from the city's rich culture.

Over the last few years, the more affluent neighbors moved farther west and were replaced by the less fortunate who were fleeing from the hell that inner Newark had become. They brought with them their small shops and specialty stores. And crime. Begging was common near the train station, and Rashid encountered it more and more often on the five-block walk to his home.

This evening, four days after his dream and four days before Hidashar's birthday, a Chinese beggar accosted him as he left the train station. A light, gritty rain was falling and Rashid had opened his umbrella for the short walk home. Waiting on the sidewalk with a crowd of commuters for a traffic light to change, he felt a tug on his left sleeve.

He turned to see a middle-aged Asian man, dressed incongruously in a bulky overcoat and worn woolen suit and a red-and-green tam. Annoyed at the brazenness of the beggar, Rashid shrugged him off. "I have no change," he said, and crossed the street with the rest of the crowd.

Halfway home, the crowd having mostly dissipated, Rashid sensed someone behind him. He whirled to confront the Chinese beggar, who held up a hand, as though to say *Stop.*

"We thank you for your check," the man said, and Rashid suddenly recognized him as Hu Wang, who ran a Taiwanese food market several blocks away on what was rapidly becoming a business strip.

"We?" asked Rashid.

Hu Wang smirked. "Not all Muslims were born in Egypt, no matter what Egyptians might think."

The man was daft. Rashid turned to leave, but Hu Wang held his arm in a tight grip. "Not too fast. You sent money to the Palestine Children's Fund?"

Rashid recoiled, sensing forces at work behind the words. Though posed as a simple question, Hu Wang's words evoked images of buzzards circling in the desert. Rashid ran a tongue across his teeth. The omen in the dream circled above him.

Wang was still speaking. " . . . and find ourselves needing help from outside our group. You are close and known to Jabbar."

"Jabbar? Who is Jabbar?"

"Jabbar is . . . Jabbar. He is impatient." Wang reached into his misshapen overcoat and pulled out a thick envelope and what appeared to be a large shoebox wrapped in brown paper. "This one," he said, placing the shoebox in Rashid's hand, "you will deliver to this address." He pulled a yellow note from the envelope and stuck it on the box.

The package was surprisingly heavy, perhaps seven or eight pounds, much more than a pair of shoes might weigh. The yellow sticky had a Bayonne address with which Rashid was not familiar.

"These checks," he said, opening the envelope and riffling a two-inch-thick wad of checks, "are to be cashed and the money delivered to the same address."

Rashid stepped back. Whatever this was about, he had no intention of becoming involved.

He pulled his hand away when Wang tried to give him the envelope. Wang smiled. "You have no choice," he said.

Rashid held out the shoebox. Wang hesitated, but took the package. "You know where my market is. I will keep the packages there until nine o'clock. Then I must return them to Jabbar. But I think I will see you in a few minutes. I know how much you love children."

Wang tucked the envelope and box back into hidden inner pockets and scurried away, greasy coat swaying in the breeze, right side hanging lower with the weight of the shoebox. Rashid rubbed a hand over his eyes and turned homeward.

He sensed a commotion before he reached his side street

and hurried his pace. The sight of two police cars, blue lights flashing mutely in the rainy mist, caused him to break into a run.

The police told him little, but within five minutes, Rashid knew more than they did. The police knew that Hidashar had been walking home from school with three friends when a maroon van pulled alongside. Two masked men jumped from the van and threw Hidashar inside. They jumped back in themselves with the van already in motion. No one noted the license plate number, but the van was found a dozen blocks away and was quickly determined to have been stolen. The police did not know why Hidashar had been singled out from the group of girls or why she had been taken.

Rashid knew why, but knew that telling them would cost Hidashar's life. He had to get to Hu Wang by nine o'clock.

The fool police acted as though they believed Rashid had kidnapped his own daughter. They carefully recorded the name and address of his employer, telephone numbers of fellow bond traders who could verify that he was at work at the time Hidashar was kidnapped. And still they questioned him as time slipped away, asking the same questions over and over. Finally, with only fifteen minutes left of the time that Wang had given him, they appeared to be finishing. Rashid dared not wait any longer.

"If you are finished, I need some air," he said, and left the house.

He forced himself to walk, albeit briskly, to the corner. Once out of sight, he broke into a run.

He reached Wang's market in time, but Wang was not in sight. A Chinese man, Wang's age but even thinner, stood behind the counter and eyed him suspiciously. "You look for my brother?" he asked.

"Hu Wang. Yes."

The man behind the counter nodded his head toward a curtained doorway. Rashid took a deep breath, pushed aside the curtain and entered.

The room smelled of old incense, as though the furniture had been saturated with the sweet scent. The place was dimly lit, with packing boxes and crates stacked haphazardly about. In the far corner, a desk lamp showed a man hunched over a cluttered desk.

The man turned. Before Rashid could move or speak, Hu Wang slid a shiny pistol out from under a sheaf of papers on the desk.

"Jabbar trusts you. I do not. Your errands are there." He waved the pistol toward the opposite corner. "Deliver them at four o'clock tomorrow afternoon."

"My daughter." Rashid clenched and unclenched his hands.

Wang shrugged. "I know nothing of your daughter. I am sure that Jabbar will make everything right." The tight smirk again crossed Wang's face. "If you do as you are told."

The police cars were still in front of Rashid's house when he returned carrying the shoebox and the envelope of checks. He entered through the kitchen door and hid the packages under the sink before entering the living room.

The police seemed suspicious that he had left the house. Dealing with them was difficult, but after their departure, Memphis turned on him. "Where did you go just now?"

Rashid hung his head. She had the right to know. He sighed and told the story.

"This is all your doing," she said. "You and your Palestine Children's Fund."

"It may yet be made right. I think that Hidashar was taken only to ensure that I do Jabbar's errands."

"You think? You *think?*"

"What do you want from me, Memphis? I can't turn back the clock. We must go forward."

"Go –"

A high pitched wailing came from Ahmed's room. He was too young to understand what was happening, but must have known something was wrong. He'd never before heard his parents shout at each other.

Memphis shot Rashid what could have been a glare or a look of resignation, and left to comfort Ahmed.

Rashid sat at the table and looked again at the checks. All were made out to the Palestine Children's Fund and all had been endorsed to him. They totaled ninety-five hundred dollars, and from somewhere Rashid knew that ten thousand dollars was some sort of trigger for bank officials.

He could cash the checks. That wouldn't be a problem at his bank in the morning. The package, though . . .

He picked it up again and hefted it, turning it over in his hands. The brown wrapping paper was crudely fastened with transparent tape. He and Memphis had argued about opening it. She hadn't wanted to disturb anything for fear that the kidnappers would know.

Rashid picked at the tape. It pulled easily off the cheap paper and the ends opened. Rashid finished the job, carefully pulling the tape from the other end and removing the paper.

It was a simple grocery bag, pulled apart to lie flat and turned to put the store name on the inside. The box was yellow and black and held, or had originally held, steel-toed work boots.

Rashid lifted the cover and saw a machine pistol stuffed within a handful of wrapping paper. A gasp behind him told him that Memphis had been watching. "Is it an Uzi?" she asked in a hushed croak.

"I don't know," Rashid said. "Issa could tell me."

"Him! He is another one to stay away from."

The two of them stared at the gun without speaking, then Memphis slumped into a chair beside Rashid. "You can't do this thing," she said.

Rashid blinked at her. "They have Hidashar. What choice do we have? I must."

"What will this gun be used for, Rashid? Who, how many, will die if you deliver this gun?"

"Hidashar will die if I don't."

Memphis stared at him with flat eyes. "Sometimes I wonder if I know you at all," she said.

Rashid stared at the gun. To deliver the weapon was to sign death warrants for people he didn't even know. Could he save his child and then wonder how many lives bought hers every time he looked at her? Could he refuse, knowing that to do so would kill his daughter? What if he did all he was told to do and Hidashar was murdered nevertheless?

Memphis shifted in her chair. "You cannot do this thing,"

she repeated.

Memphis was right. He must rescue his daughter, but he must not be responsible for the deaths of others, even indirectly. He put the cover back on the box. There was one thing he could do, one thing to keep his conscience clear and maybe save his daughter. "Issa can fix the gun so that it will not fire. I'll take it to him."

"Issa is evil, Rashid. No good can come of it."

"He can fix the gun so that it will not fire. Jabbar will not know until after we have Hidashar back. He will not even know it was I who did this."

"No good can come of this, Rashid. You should never have sent the check."

Rashid placed a hand on hers. "You are right, but now I must do this. I cannot deliver a working weapon to murderers, and I cannot sit idly by and allow Hidashar to die. Issa is my only hope."

"And if it doesn't work?"

"Issa will fix the gun. I will deliver it as directed. The rest is in the hands of Allah."

Issa was a heavy-set, bearded Saudi. He held a finger to his lips, pointed to the interior of his house, and quietly led Rashid into the basement. They passed through a paneled room and stopped before a heavy wooden door. Issa unlocked the door and motioned Rashid inside. He closed the door and turned on the overhead lights.

Two walls of the low-ceilinged basement room held racks of guns, gun parts and assortments of cellophane packages, cans, and bottles. A counter with drawers built underneath took up a third wall and an indoor firing range lay alongside the remaining wall.

"Let's see this gun of yours," he said, taking the box from Rashid's hands. Rashid had left the wrapping paper home as a precaution to keep it as clean and untorn as he had received it. Issa lifted out the gun and whistled. "Nice," he said. "Going into business for yourself?"

"What do you mean?"

"Bring this into a bank and tellers will fall over themselves to hand over their money. You wouldn't even have to fire it."

"I need you to fix it so that it will not fire, but in such a way that no one could tell it had been tampered with. Until they attempted to actually shoot it," he added.

"Why?"

Rashid had debated with himself on the drive to Issa's house and gun shop, trying to decide whether or not to tell Issa what had happened. Since Issa had not mentioned the kidnapping of Hidashar, either he didn't know or he knew but didn't want to say so. If the latter, Rashid would be so far over his head in intrigue that he might never surface.

In the end, Rashid said nothing of Jabbar or Hu Wang, only that he needed the gun fixed. "And I need a working pistol for myself," Rashid added. "A small one. One that I can hide."

Issa raised an eyebrow. "You think you know someone," he said, "and then they come around with automatic weapons and order hide-out guns."

Rashid said nothing. His actions seemed even more out of character to himself than they did to Issa.

"Times change, Issa."

Issa nodded acknowledgment. "That they do," he said, "and never for the better." He looked Rashid up and down. "You want a small one, you said. To hide under your clothing? Where you can reach it easily?"

"Yes," said Rashid, feeling foolish, but biting his lip against the need to explain himself.

"That is easy." Issa opened a drawer and pulled out a small, flat automatic. It almost fit into the palm of his hand. "Not very accurate or especially powerful," he said. "Only .25 caliber, but it will knock a man down from a few feet away and is easily hidden." Issa waved the gun behind his back, then held up an empty hand to Rashid. He spun around to show his back. No gun in sight. He lifted his shirt and the gun butt appeared. He pulled the weapon out and handed it to Rashid.

"Untuck your shirt," he said. "No one will see the gun back there and you can reach it easily. Make sure you stick it there with your right hand, so it will come out ready to fire." He cocked his head as though seeing Rashid for the first time. "You are right handed?" he asked as an afterthought.

The Bayonne address turned out to be the middle unit of a triplex two or three blocks back from the water. The neighborhood wasn't as bad as Rashid had imagined, but it was bad enough. The street was empty, odd for a Saturday afternoon. The rain had stopped and the street appeared clean.

He parked in front of the building and turned off the engine. The gun, carefully repackaged, and an envelope filled with money sat on the seat beside him. The .25 caliber automatic dug into his back. Perhaps he should have put it somewhere else while driving, but he wanted to get used to the feel of it.

The money had been surprisingly easy to obtain. He called ahead to the bank to make sure they had the cash available and was treated to an amused response that they indeed had that much cash on hand. When he arrived at the bank, though, the teller had a problem cashing so many third-party checks and called the manager, who led Rashid into his office and closed the door.

He entered Rashid's account number into his computer station, then spent a few minutes looking over the checks. Finally, he looked up. "You wish to have the total amount of these checks in cash?"

"I only wish to cash the checks."

The manager nodded. "There is a problem –"

"I have much more than that on deposit here." Rashid started to rise, felt the gun catch on the back of the chair, and sat quickly back down lest it fall out. Perhaps he should not have brought the gun into the bank. Did they have metal detectors? Hidden x-ray machines?

The banker smiled. "I see that your account is ample to cover the checks. The problem is an internal one. It is difficult for us to cash such checks without drawing attention." He stared at a pen set on his desk. "Writing reports, if you will."

"Reporting the transactions."

The banker nodded again. "Exactly so. It would be simpler

if you would deposit the checks with us and let our automated system run its course."

"But I need the money now."

"Could you not write a check for the amount? I could cash the check and give you cash – the total is thoughtfully under ten thousand dollars. Your account would be credited within two weeks for the checks." The banker spread his hands and smiled.

Rashid slumped into the chair, ignoring the prod of the gun. Everyone, neighborhood gunsmiths and corporate bankers – everyone – knew more than he did. He had always thought himself to be sophisticated. In fact, he was as a newborn.

The gun had been no more difficult to arrange. Issa had worked with a file for a few moments, then re-assembled the weapon. He placed a round in the chamber and brought it to the firing range. He pulled the trigger. Nothing but a sharp click.

He wiped it carefully and handed it back to Rashid. "Someday you must tell me what this is about."

At home, Rashid had wiped the gun again before he had put it back into the box and refastened the tape. Now, looking at the package on the seat beside him, he couldn't tell that it had been opened.

He checked his watch. Four o'clock exactly. He scooped up the envelope of money and the shoebox and slipped out of his car.

He climbed the crumbling concrete steps to the middle unit. When he reached the top, the door opened. A man wearing a burnoose, his lower face covered, held out his hands.

Tentatively, Rashid offered the packages. "Jabbar?" he asked.

The man took the envelope and shoebox. "Not here," he said. The voice was smooth, like that of a radio announcer, with no trace of accent. "You will be contacted tomorrow."

Abruptly the door slammed shut. Startled, Rashid stepped back, then lunged at the door. It was locked. He hammered at it. "Let me in! Let me in!"

A car started in the alleyway to the side of the left-hand

unit. After a moment of an engine revving, a black compact shot from the alleyway. It slewed onto the street, barely missing Rashid's car, and sped away. Two men were plainly visible in the front seat. There was no child in the car.

Rashid drove back home with only despair as company. He pulled the gun from the small of his back and tossed it in the glove compartment. Fine job he had made of it. All his imaginings, all his day dreams. A man of action. A hero. And he had just lost the only link he had to his daughter.

He dreaded facing Memphis, but she was surprisingly comforting. Prepared for her anger and accusations, her sympathy broke him and he sat at the kitchen table and sobbed.

She agreed that they should not tell the police what Rashid had done. "Nothing good could come of that. If it is Allah's will, Hidashar will be returned to us."

For the first time, Rashid wondered that Memphis might have the deeper belief of the two of them.

It was Sunday evening, a full day after Rashid had delivered the checks and the gun, and two days since Hidashar had been kidnapped. No word had been received. No phone call. No messenger. No communication at all. The strain was breaking the facade that Memphis had put up and Rashid himself was coming undone.

The police had been by again, seemingly more suspicious than before. Evidently Rashid was not behaving in the usual manner of a father whose child had been kidnapped.

There was no hope for that. Rashid feared the police less than he feared that Jabbar would call at a time when the police were in his home. The call didn't come, though, and after the police left, Rashid and Memphis returned to the kitchen table, a phone between them. "We must do something," Rashid said. "*Some*thing!"

Memphis merely stared at the refrigerator. "What? Tell the police?"

"No. Hu Wang is the key." Rashid stood, legs stiff from hours of sitting, waiting for the call.

Memphis did not look up. "Who is Hu Wang?"

"The man who gave me the checks and the gun to deliver. I know where he works."

Memphis looked up, a spark of life showing in her eyes for the first time that day. Rashid was suddenly grateful to be married to her, for all the things she could have said to him but hadn't. When this was over, they would move to the west coast as Memphis had always wanted. His own company had an office in Los Angeles, and if they wouldn't transfer him, there were other bond trading companies in L.A. He squeezed her shoulder. "Wait for the phone call," he said. "I'll be back."

Hu Wang's market was still open. Rashid retrieved the pistol from the glove compartment and placed it carefully behind his back, stuck in the waistband of his pants. This time he would not be taken unaware.

The store was empty, or so Rashid thought at first. Only after looking around did he see Hu Wang's brother sitting at a table, a young man to either side of him. Hu Wang's brother stared vacantly at a wall opposite. One of the young men spoke urgently in Chinese into the elderly man's ear.

Evidently they hadn't noticed his entrance. Rashid cleared his throat.

One of the young men looked up. "We are closed," he said.

"I've come to see Hu Wang."

At the sound of his voice, the brother raised his head. His eyes widened. "You!" he shouted.

The young men spoke at the same time, asking questions in Chinese. The older man answered and both jumped to their feet and advanced on Rashid. Their intent was unmistakable; hatred and anger – outrage – colored their faces.

Rashid drew the gun and aimed it at the man advancing on the left. The other assailant slid further toward Rashid's right side. In a moment they would be too far apart for him to shoot both before one of them closed on him. He must act now, right now, shoot the nearer of the two and then the other . . .

"No! *Zhu shou!*" The old man shouted first in English and then Chinese. He spoke another sentence in Chinese and the two young men took a step backwards. He pointed a shaking finger at Rashid. "You go now."

Keeping the gun trained on the closer of the two young men, Rashid backed from the market. Outside, he collapsed against his car, breathing heavily. What had that been all about? Why the change in Hu Wang's brother? Had something happened to Wang?

And why had he himself been so quick with the gun? Yes, he wanted to be able to access it quickly, and he did, but he had been so ready to kill those boys, themselves hardly more than teenagers. There was no honor, no glory, there. No answering to a higher voice. He had been willing to kill – twice – to prevent injury to himself.

What had he become? He stuck the pistol into a pocket and drove home.

Rashid knew something was wrong as soon as he entered the house.

It was silent, yes, but there was also a presence . . . someone, something was in the house.

He hurried into the kitchen and found Memphis still sitting at the table. Across from her, facing the doorway in which Rashid stood, was a slightly built man, likely Saudi, wearing a pencil mustache and a business suit.

He might have been an insurance salesman. He might have been a detective.

But Rashid knew instinctively who he was: he was Jabbar.

Memphis spoke quickly. "She is safe, Rashid. You must do only one more thing."

Rashid looked from Memphis to Jabbar, wondering why he felt no anger or hatred for the man who controlled his daughter's life.

Jabbar stared at the bulge in Rashid's pants, the outline of the pistol. "Does that one fire better than the one you delivered to me?" he asked.

"What – ?" Rashid ran his hand down to the pocket toward which Jabbar stared. He felt the gun, and understood.

"You know."

"My partner Aswad is more suspicious than I and test-fired it. Or tried to. Someone had tampered with the weapon and it would not fire."

Rashid waited. He wished he'd returned his own gun to its hiding place in the small of his back. He still felt no emotion toward Jabbar, but this night Rashid *knew* he could kill. Kill without regret.

Jabbar continued. "Delivering the gun was a test. Cashing the checks was useful, of course, but we needed to know if you would bring the police. When none chased us from Bayonne, we knew we could trust you."

You can trust me to kill you, thought Rashid, but he maintained his composure.

Jabbar waved a hand negligently. "My partner was angry, but I told him it only meant you were a man of principles, balancing between keeping his daughter alive and not being party to murder himself. There are those who have no principles, only look for profit. They do not live so happily or so long."

"Are you speaking now of Americans or Taiwanese?"

Jabbar's lips tightened in what could have been a grin. "Hu Wang, you mean? Yes, he could not be trusted. Especially as we approach our goal. And so we have dealt with him."

"And I?"

"For you I have a special task." He withdrew a packet of papers from inside his jacket and threw it on the table. Memphis stared at it blankly. Her face was haggard, hollow, with no trace of the innocence or beauty of only last week. She seemed apathetic, overwhelmed. The day that they emerged from this horror would be the day they moved to southern California. They would not spend another night in Newark, but would leave immediately and pay to have their belongings follow them. Memphis could be close to her parents. She'd be happy, their children would be happy. He could be Muslim anywhere.

Jabbar prodded the packet with a long finger. "Here are four sets of identification and four credit cards. Go to a different travel agency and at each purchase a ticket for this flight." He pulled a slip of paper from the packet and placed it on top. "You will return these credit cards and identification, along with the tickets, to the Bayonne address at noon tomorrow. You will show the tickets to the man who will be waiting for you there. He will give you an address here in Newark where you will deliver them."

"Where is my daughter?"

"She will be at the Newark address. When we have the tickets, you will have her."

Rashid took his foot off the gas and braked to a stop in front of the Bayonne triplex. Oddly, there was more traffic on the street on a Monday than the previous Saturday.

The gun was once again in the small of his back. It was loaded and he had test-fired it at Issa's basement range.

He took a deep breath, and tickets in hand, climbed to the front door.

Once again it opened as he reached it. This time, though, it was opened by Jabbar, who motioned him inside.

The room was unlit, but Rashid could see that it once had been a living room. Now it was cluttered with boxes and several cots. He looked at Jabbar. "The Newark address?"

Jabbar made a sign of apology with his hands. "Again, a concession to Aswad. He does not trust you."

As you did not trust Hu Wang, thought Rashid. He wished he'd noticed if Jabbar had looked to see if he had placed the gun in his front pants pocket. Would Jabbar think that he didn't bring the gun? Or that he had it hidden elsewhere? Was there another place to hide the gun besides the small of his back? He wished he had asked Issa. So much that he did not know.

"And you? Do *you* trust me?" Rashid's eyes, now accustomed to the light, took in the room. There were two doorways besides the outside entrance. One, probably leading to a bedroom, had a closed door. The other, wider, had no door and probably led to the kitchen. If Hidashar was in the house, she was probably there. With Aswad the Untrusting.

Jabbar again opened his palms. "You cashed the checks, you delivered the gun. That you made the gun unworkable only displays your principles of non-violence. Yes, you can be trusted."

Jabbar took a few circular steps that brought him closer to the kitchen doorway. Rashid tensed.

"Yes, you can be trusted, to a degree. You have honor, integrity; you hold back your emotions to keep your word. But the dam breaks, doesn't it, when you are betrayed, when your family is injured. A man like you, regardless of your lack of training, is dangerous. Only death would keep you from revenge should we not keep our part of the bargain, no? We must either return your daughter or kill you."

Rashid felt the gun in the small of his back, shifted a hand to rest casually with his thumb in his pocket. "Which do you choose?"

Jabbar turned his head and snapped, "Aswad. Come."

A small dark man, Somalian perhaps, entered the room holding Hidashar by the hand. She had been crying, her face dirty and tear-streaked, and now she tried to run to Rashid. The man jerked her back roughly and Rashid twitched. "Daddy," she called.

Rashid thought of the gun stuck in his pants but his body betrayed him. Unlike either of the men before him, for Rashid action did not come simultaneously with the realization that he must act, and he hesitated. For a moment the attention of both men had been on Hidashar. The moment had passed and with it his chance to take them by surprise.

He took in the scene before him and realized suddenly that this trait – this inability to act quickly, which would be suicide in a revolutionary – had probably just saved his life. Jabbar stood to the side, a thin, amused smile on his lips. The Somalian had no expression, his face so still it seemed that his features had been smudged or blurred.

I was supposed to act, Rashid thought. I was supposed to move, to attack, and then Aswad was to have killed me and Hidashar. The Somalian drew Hidashar close and Rashid tensed. Or perhaps he was to kill only me.

A cold chill grabbed him. To die and leave Hidashar in this man's hands . . . he didn't need much imagination to fear the worst. A trickle of sweat ran down the center of his back. What would happen to Hidashar if they killed him?

No, he could not permit it. Better she die a clean death with him than to live a toy to Aswad and Jabbar.

Jabbar moved again, away from Aswad. Rashid had to back a few steps to keep them both in view. The gun felt hard in the small of his back. He had only a moment to decide his fate and Hidashar's.

Jabbar had one weakness, and therefore Rashid had only one weapon: integrity. His own and Jabbar's. Jabbar had a need to honor his word, and if Rashid could be shown to honor his, then he and Hidashar might yet escape alive.

He looked from Jabbar to the Somalian and realized this thought was laughable. Nothing he did would save his or Hidashar's life. He had a gun, yes, but they would be expecting him to have it. Jabbar knew he had a gun. He could never kill them both – that was too much to consider – but he could kill Hidashar. Would that not be better for her? He could not allow himself to even think what her life would be should they kill him and keep her. She was only one day from her ninth birthday. He could not permit it . . .

What choice did he have?

Jabbar spoke, breaking into the runaway train of thought driving Rashid to desperation. "You have something for me?"

Grateful for the chance to move closer, he said, "Yes," and pulled the envelope with the airline tickets, credit cards, and IDs from his jacket pocket, stepping forward to hand it to Jabbar.

Jabbar didn't reach for it and Rashid stood, right hand outstretched with the envelope. Fool, he thought. Now my hand is occupied and too far from the gun. Wildly, he considered trying to draw with his left hand, somehow turning the gun around and firing it in one motion as though he were some sort of martial arts expert.

But he knew the futility of it and stood still.

Jabbar suddenly plucked the envelope and said from the corner of his mouth, "Let her go."

No one moved, and Jabbar turned to face the Somalian. "Let her go," he said again, no louder and with no more emotion than he had spoken before, but this time with menace. A shadow – fear? – passed momentarily over the Somalian's face and Rashid realized he had judged the wrong man as the more dangerous of the pair.

The Somalian let her go and Hidashar ran to Rashid. He caught her in mid-stride and lifted her in his arms. She clung, arms around his neck, and sobbed violently.

Afraid now to turn his back to leave, Rashid asked, "May we go?"

Jabbar jerked his head in the direction of the entrance door but as soon as Rashid turned, Jabbar grabbed his arm and pulled him back.

The sudden chance at freedom and the quickness with which it had been snapped away drained the last bit of emotion and hope from Rashid. I'm not built for this, he thought. Life and death was beyond his control. As Allah wills it, he murmured under his breath and turned to face his fate.

Jabbar indicated Hidashar with a wave of the envelope still in his hand. "She tells me her name is *Hidashar?*"

Rashid's heart sank. We're not Muslim enough, he thought. Not for Jabbar.

"Yes," he said.

"You named your daughter *Eleven?*"

"She was born on September eleventh. It was her mother's idea." He attempted a smile. "It helps us to remember her birthday. It's tomorrow," he added.

Jabbar tapped Rashid's chest with the plane tickets.

"After tomorrow," he said, "you will never again have trouble remembering your daughter's birthday."

It's Crackers to Slip a Rozzer the Dropsey in Snide

Ted Hertel, Jr.

They say, "Let the punishment fit the crime." If that's true, then why am I here? All I really did was bribe a crooked cop with counterfeit money. Is that any reason to die?

I suppose you could say it all started about a year ago, when I was just a young punk of twenty. I had no family that would claim me, so I had to make my own life. All I wanted was to have a life. 'Course, droppin' out of school four years before that meant crummy jobs that weren't good enough for me, like packin' groceries or parkin' cars. So I did what any decent, upstandin' kid would do: I turned to crime. Crime became my life, my woman, my love. Sure, I did a little time once, but that's just the price ya gotta pay to get ahead.

I wound up workin' for a counterfeiter named Warren Garth. This guy made the best phony money I ever seen and he did it the old-fashioned way. Plates and presses and inks. None of that color photocopier or computer crap that high school kids played with. You could spot that shit from a thousand yards away. Nope, this was the real thing. Garth sold the finished paper to a couple different mobbed-up guys who paid him thirty cents on the dollar for it. Now the stuff was so good, so hard to tell it wasn't real, that I don't know why Garth didn't just keep the junk for himself. He woulda been better off, I thought. But I guess he figured let someone else take the rap if the work was found out. All I had to do was haul the bills around for him. That was my job.

When I wasn't doin' nuthin' at Garth's, I just sat around and read these old *Mad* magazines he had lyin' there. Sure, they were old, but they were pretty funny, too. Get pictures of Alfred E. Neuman, "two for a quarter, suitable for framin' or wrappin' fish." "The usual gang of idiots." That sorta stuff. But there was one I never got: "It's crackers to slip a rozzer the dropsey in snide." In fact, I guess Garth liked that one a lot. He even had a hand-lettered piece of paper hangin' on the wall above the press with that on it. So I asked him a couple times what that meant. But Garth was never much for explanations. All he wanted to do was crank out those bills, so he'd always just tell me to shut the hell up.

One night last year I loaded up a case full of fifties for delivery to a customer downtown. I had the case in the trunk of my car across the street from Garth's and had just started up the engine when a half-dozen black and whites, sirens blarin', lights flashin', surrounded Garth's joint. Cops jumped out faster'n bugs off a hot griddle and kicked open the doors. I got out of there, suitcase and all, before I could see what happened, not that I cared or nuthin'.

See, I figure I didn't need to deliver the goods anywhere. Garth wasn't gonna miss 'em if he's in the slammer. The customer didn't know I got 'em instead of the cops takin' 'em for evidence. Cops didn't know I got 'em, either. Hell, I knew I could always use a few fifties. I hadda have a life, too, right?

Well, now a year's gone by. I been careful with spreadin' the phony dough around town. But there was only 30 Gs in the case and it's almost gone. Time to get another job.

There's this bar in this lousy part of town I visit. It often gets a lotta cash customers along about the third of the month. That's welfare check day, see? Everybody and his partner come in, stand three deep at the long bar rail and buy, buy, buy. Right up 'til 1:00 a.m. when Eagan has to shut the hole down on account of it's the law. Eagan don't take no chances on gettin' busted with all that dough in there, since he's sure that there'll be an accountin' problem later, what with all those cops standin' around with nuthin' better to do than finger a bit of it for themselves. Especially old

Ferguson, the beat cop on the block. Comin' up on thirty years on the force and needin' every nickel he can get his fat mitts on. Too lazy to move up in the ranks. Maybe it's 'cause of his drinkin' problem. Or his shrewish wife. Or his equally shrewish mistress. Or those couple kids in college. Like an old whore, they suck him dry and it's no fun.

So this seems like a perfect set up. I know Eagan's got tons of dough and I know Fergie needs money. On the second of the month, I stop the cop on his beat and ask him if maybe he could use an extra hunnerd, tax-free, this week. No, the slimy bastard tells me, but he sure could use an extra two hunnerd. Fine, I says to him. Tomorrow night, 2:00 a.m. Who does he have to kill, ha ha ha, he asks. Just don't look in on Eagan's spot after we meet, that's all. Done, he says.

Now, I don't care if this scumbag wants two hunnerd or two thousand, 'cause every bill I'm givin' him is fake. I ain't got much more'n two Gs left, but he coulda had it all, since I know for a fact that Eagan must have three, maybe four, times that much in what passes for his safe. How do I know? 'Cause one night I tailed him from the bar rail into the back of his joint usin' the excuse that I had to go to the john, which is also in the back. He's takin' some of the dough the drunks have forked over and stashin' it back there for the night. After he closes up, he's too bright to take it to the night deposit at the bank for fear he'll get mugged. So he takes it there the next mornin'. I watched him do it a couple times to be sure.

Next night, two o' clock rolls around and I meet Ferguson on the corner. No words are exchanged, just the four bills. This happens as we pass each other by, me on the way to Eagan's on the other corner, Ferguson to any place but there.

I've got my gloves and my burglar tools with me. It's nuthin' for me to get in the door, almost like someone opened it from inside. I turn on the mini-flash, head over to the lousy safe, and work on it for a few minutes. And they say prison ain't educational. The safe pops open easy as a woman's legs on the third date.

About that time Ferguson comes bustin' through the front door, yellin' about funny money and how he's called more cops. I got no idea how a stupid jerk like him spotted it.

Probably tried to spend it somewhere and someone with a brain spotted somethin'. Can't figure what, since that dough was perfect, far as I could tell. Don't matter none, though, since the damage is done.

Now, I know he can't tell the other cops about the dough I passed him, so he's gotta be tellin' 'em he came across a burglary in progress. He's so dumb and mad he don't even have his gun out, so I grab my tools and hightail it out the back door, knowin' the fat bum can never catch me, since it would mean actual movin' on his part. I hear sirens in the distance and silently thank the cops for the warning.

When I hit the street at the end of the alley, there's a car sittin' there, lights on, motor runnin', right in front of the all-night drug store. Seein' as how no one's in the car, I open the door, hop in the driver's seat, put it in gear, and get outta there, just as a squad goes flashin' past in the opposite direction.

I ain't gotten more'n two blocks when this god-awful scream from the rear seat makes me jump nearly through the roof of the car. I turn around and in the back is this little kid latched into a baby seat and wailin' its head off. Its ma is gonna come outta that store in no time, notice the car and the brat are gone, and start bellowin' for the cops, most of who are down the block at Eagan's, anyhow. She'll give 'em a description of the car and maybe even the plate number, if she can remember it. So I head down a couple side streets, thinkin' I gotta ditch the car and the kid. Besides, it's makin' me nuts 'cause it won't shut up.

It's now nearly three o' clock and I'm gonna need new transportation. But up ahead a few houses I see some broad lockin' up the door to her place. She's got a suitcase in one hand, on the way outta town, no doubt. I drive by, then stop the car a half block down the street, get out, and close the car door quietly, the kid in the back still makin' noise.

She's thrown the suitcase in the trunk by this time and now she's tryin' to get in the driver's door, fumblin' with the car keys. Got on a very nice outfit, too. Even wearin' gloves. Don't see much of that these days.

Just as she opens the door I come up behind her, screwdriver from my tool kit in hand. I jab the rear end of it in her back, whisper in her ear it's a gun, and don't make a sound bitch if you wanna see the sun come up again. She does as she's told and gets in the car, crawlin' over the console, revealin' long legs and a very nice ass as her skirt rides up and tightens.

I take the keys outta the car door, climb in, and start it up, tossin' the burglary kit and gloves in the back, after checkin' to be sure she ain't planted a kid back there, too. We pass the car with the whiner in it and head off toward downtown and farther still away from Eagan's. We ain't gone more'n a couple blocks when she tells me to pull over and get out. I look at her and see she's holdin' a gun. Seems like a big one, too, at least from the end I'm starin' at. Where'd that come from?

Anyways, now it's my turn to do as I'm told, except in pullin' over, I hit the brakes real hard. The broad goes flyin' into the dashboard, hits her head on the windshield, and drops the gun. Some people just never learn about wearin' seatbelts, I guess. I grab the gun, open her door like any gentleman would, and kick her ass out in the street. Then I toss the gun in the glove compartment. As I squeal away, the door slams shut on its own and I'm home free.

At least for the next fifteen minutes. Then up behind me comes this squad, red lights flashin' on only at the last minute. What happened to that siren warning system they're supposed to use? I pull over. After all, I done nuthin' wrong. I mean, I never even got so much as a buck out of Eagan's safe.

Cops come up, one on either side of the car, and ask for my license. That's fair. I got a license. I show it to them. Next they wanna know if this is my car. I lie and say I borrowed it from my lady friend. We had a little fight over how much she was drinkin' and I was gonna drive her home. Only I had to let her out on account of she was so drunk she was fightin' me to get at the wheel. Not a great story, I admit, but the best one I could think of quick-like under the circumstances.

The cops inform me that the car is registered to one Anthony A. Aldrich, recently deceased, as in murdered, as in within the last hour, so would I please get out of the car, sir? Well, I tell them, I don't know nuthin' about anyone gettin' killed. I was just drivin' Mrs. Aldrich home 'cause she was a souse. Imagine my surprise when they informed me there was no Mrs. Aldrich. Seems someone broke into Mr. Aldrich's house, stole some drugs, and shot him somewhere along the line just for good measure. Neighbors heard noises and called it in, along with a description of Aldrich's car, which had been parked in front of the house but had since vanished, only to turn up in my possession.

While I was explainin' that there must be some mistake, the sharp-eyed cop on the passenger side notices the tool kit on the rear seat. He pulls it out and then notices the gloves. This leads to a totally illegal search of the car, a fact that I point out to them repeatedly. But this don't stop 'em from findin' the .38, which it turns out could be the murder weapon. Things get even worse when they pop the trunk and find the suitcase loaded with dope back there. They close up the trunk and will later pretend to first discover this down at the station, once they get a warrant, the one cop says to the other. But I know all about cops. I figure they're just buyin' themselves some time so they can lift some of the dope themselves.

So I come clean. I bribed a cop, I told 'em, with counterfeit money, tried to rob a bar, stole a car or two, and even gave 'em the description of this broad who was obviously the one they were really lookin' for: tall with good legs and a very nice ass. Very helpful, they said, laughing all the way to the station. We'll be on the lookout for her, all right. I tried to tell 'em my prints ain't gonna be found in the house and the one smartass cop waggles the gloves in my face and tells me he bets they'll be all over the gun. That's when I remember that the broad with the good legs and nice ass was wearin' a pair of gloves herself. They looked mighty swell at the time. Now I ain't so sure.

Not even my lousy public defender believed me. He says he talked to Ferguson. Naturally, the cop denied takin' any bribe. What a liar. There just ain't no honest cops left, I guess. He probably dropped them fifties in the first dumpster he came across. And he said he didn't know who it was in Eagan's. I bet those other two cops, the ones that wanted the dope for themselves, put him up to sayin' that, just to make their story look good. Funny thing, though. I heard later that the cops all said Eagan's got cleaned out that night. Over seven Gs gone from the safe. I know I didn't get a dime of it, but I can guess what fat cop took it all. I hear he's retirin' soon, too.

Further, this public defender, who couldn't have been outta law school more'n a couple weeks, tells me that in spite of the description I gave the two cops who picked me up, they never found that broad I kicked out of the car. Probably never even tried, the lazy bastards.

So that's why I was convicted of murder, when all I was tryin' to do was make a life for myself. Yeah, they set a date to kill me, but that crummy lawyer tells me no matter what, it'll take 'em at least fifteen years before they stick the needle in, what with all the appeals I got comin' to me.

While I'm sittin' in this cell today, who walks past but my old boss Warren Garth, the guy who got me into this spot in the first place. If he hadn't trusted me with that phony dough like he did, why I wouldn'ta had none to give to old Ferguson. So, while I see it all as his fault, I don't hold no grudge against him. It's just part of the price you gotta pay.

Then, at what passes for lunch in this joint, I get a chance to talk to him. He don't hold no grudge against me, neither, for walkin' off with that 30 Gs. Maybe it's 'cause he found God in this hellhole and God told him to forgive me. But, more likely, it's 'cause he don't know I done it in the first place. No point in askin', I figure.

So, anyways, we get to talkin' about the old days over this crap they call food. How he always made the best dough around. The dough was so good, they shoulda put him to work in the prison kitchen, I say, laughin'. He don't find it too funny, but that's okay. I can see he might be a little bitter.

Then I tell him how I wound up here and ask him how could that stupid cop spot the fake bills so easy. Well, Garth says to me, ya gotta be careful. See, while each bill is perfect itself, it is also perfectly identical to every other bill, right down to the serial number on it. That don't change. So, by givin' Fergie four bills, someone with a good eye might notice they was all the same.

Now, see, right here is where I coulda decided to hold a grudge. But I ain't that kinda guy. I probably shoulda spotted that myself. Still, Garth really shoulda filled me in on that. Again, I see it's Garth's fault I'm here. I mean, all I did was bribe a cop. I don't deserve what's comin' in fifteen years.

As we're finishin' up, I remember somethin' from my days with Garth, so I just gotta ask him. What's that sign mean in the shop, I say? What sign, he asks, like there was more'n one there? That one on the wall, I say. That one I asked you about a couple times, "it's crackers to slip a rozzer the dropsey in snide."

Oh, that, he laughs. That just means ya gotta be crazy to pay off a crooked cop with counterfeit money. He laughs again.

Now I begin to hold that grudge.

Pick Six and You're Dead

Dorothy Rellas

Let's get one thing clear. I am not an alcoholic. I have a drink now and then, but after sixty plus years, I know when I've had enough. Tonight – a couple of Jack Daniel's. Okay, maybe four. When I stomped out of Harry's Bar on Hollywood Boulevard, I wasn't drunk. Furious? Hell, yes. Right now, I'm tap city, so broke that my daughter Toni is up in a small town near Fresno playing the piano in a biker bar. I'm a P.I., and Toni works for me. When things are tough, we do what we gotta do. Toni gets a gig. Me, I try to collect on our delinquent accounts or find a job as a bartender. That's what I was doing at Harry's Bar.

I told Harry that I'd make it short, but he insisted we sit at a table near the stage where a combo was sending out lyrical lines. He waved away my offer to pay for my drink. That should have alerted me. And when he began tapping his fingers fast on the table all through a mellow arrangement of "The Nearness of You," the bells and whistles should have started. But I just sat there sipping my free drink, listening to the music like a rube.

The musicians filed off the stage, and I turned to Harry. "You owe me a grand from the last mess I got you out of. I need something on account – or at least a job behind the bar."

"Michael, things along the Boulevard have come to a standstill. Another misguided campaign to clean up Hollywood has been launched. The LAPD is driving all the customers away. Business –"

"Cut the shit, Harry. You owe me ten C-notes. I need the money."

Harry Singakou is Asian, a tall, good-looking guy about my age whom I've known for years. Moxie gleams through his inscrutable expression, and his persona has always been cool and smooth. Tonight, there was a slight tremor in his tightly clenched lips, and he still tapped his fingers on the table. Finally, he crinkled his brow.

"There is something you might be able to help me with, Michael. A minor problem I'm having with Alonso Lucchesi and his associate, Sam Giancarlo. Both very connected."

I knew they were connected. What I didn't know was how Harry had gone from the relatively benign intrigues of Hollywood politics to the big-time machinations of the Las Vegas mob.

"A slight difference of opinion with Mr. Lucchesi over a real estate transaction. I was with him for a short time this afternoon – trying to reach some kind of concordance. Unfortunately, the horses interfered with our negotiations –"

"Horses? Where the hell were you?"

"The racetrack – the first two races at Santa Anita." Harry frowned at me. "Surely you, Michael, of all people are cognizant of the commotion at a race –" He stopped, tension practically oozing out of his pores, staring at a dapper man and two goons who had just come in and strode to our table.

"Sam Giancarlo," he whispered.

Giancarlo was stocky with olive skin, a big nose and wearing an exquisitely tailored suit. He pulled a chair away from an adjoining table and sat down. The bodyguards stood behind him, as cool as college professors out for some good jazz instead of two gorillas whose guns bulged under their jackets.

Harry introduced Giancarlo – then, always with the good manners, the thugs.

"Connie." He nodded to the one wearing a sheen of perspiration on his face and a long, broad-shouldered jacket that hadn't been in style since the '40s, "And Stan."

Stan looked almost normal until you noticed that one of his eyes didn't focus, which made me itch to smack it into position.

Jake walked out from behind the bar and hovered just a few feet away.

"Jake, a drink for Mr. Giancarlo – and another one for Michael."

Sam shook his head. "No drinks. Mr. Lucchesi wants the deed of trust."

"Nothing for me, either, Jake," I called to the retreating figure and had pushed my chair back when Harry's hand clamped down on my arm.

"This is my associate, Michael O'Donnell," he said to Sam. "He will be talking to Mr. Lucchesi tomorrow. Everything will be cleared up."

I had the feeling that the balance of worry had just shifted from him to me. I wrested my hand free. "Harry, I –"

Jake shoved a glass into my hand. Giancarlo stood up, took a card out of his jacket pocket and sailed it across the table. "Mr. Lucchesi's address."

I waited for the card to go off the edge and land on the floor, but it stopped in front of me.

"I'm not getting mixed up with you and the Las Vegas godfathers," I said as soon as Giancarlo and the two men had left.

"I will pay you what I owe plus two thousand more – just for a short conversation with Lucchesi."

I took two fast gulps of my drink. "Make it three thousand more. I want a thousand for this job, up front, tonight."

I watched his smile harden. "I doubt I have that much cash." He stood up. "Let me check."

He disappeared through the green curtains to his office. Jake brought me another drink, and I settled down to listen to the combo that had come back on stage. They segued through a half-dozen tunes before Harry reappeared.

"Unfortunately, Michael, I am a little short tonight," he said. "Here's a hundred. I will have the rest tomorrow, after you talk to Lucchesi and this impasse is brought to a conclusion."

I stood up. "Stick the impasse up your ass." I put the hundred dollar bill in my pocket.

I strode to the bar's front door, gave it a big shove and

stumbled. Didn't fall, you understand, just lost my footing and hit my ankle on the heavy damned door when it swung shut. I limped to my car in the alley, backed out onto the Boulevard and was waiting for an opening in the traffic when there was a tap on my window. I rolled the window down. One of Hollywood Division's finest stood there looking scornful as hell.

"Sir, would you please drive back into the driveway and get out of your car?"

I eased back into the alley and slid out of the car. "What's the problem, officer?"

"Can't let you drive in your condition. License, please?"

I handed him my license and popped a mint into my mouth. "You think I'm drunk?"

"Like I said, you shouldn't be driving, sir."

"I've had three drinks. I am not under the influence –"

"I could give you a ticket, but if someone can pick you up –"

To make a long, miserable story short, he had me walk a straight line, which was pretty hard to do with an ankle that was probably broken. I explained that my daughter was out of town, and at midnight I wasn't about to call anyone else to drive into Hollywood. Then I thought of Harry. This entire complication was his fault, after all. But when the cop and I went back inside the bar, Jake said Harry had just left. Probably for the best. I'd get a ticket, for sure, when the cop had to pry my fingers from around Harry's neck.

When we were outside again, I explained that I'd once been an LAPD cop working out of Hollywood Division just like him.

"Then you should know better. Now, let's find you a cab." He turned, and wouldn't you know, a cab was passing at that moment.

Normally, you could stand on the Boulevard until they made you one of the Hollywood Redevelopment projects before you'd find a cab.

"What about my car?"

He took my arm and led me to the cab. "As one cop to another, I'll keep an eye on it." He closed the taxi's door and slammed his hand down on its top as though he was giving the okay for a squad car to take me to Parker Center.

The cabbie half turned. "Where to, Mac?"

I mumbled my address. "Up there." I nodded to the Hollywood Hills north of the Boulevard. "I'll direct you."

"I know where it is."

I sat back and closed my eyes. In the big scheme of things, it was just a little inconvenience. A ticket for DUI would have cost more than a cab. In the morning, I'd call Harry and he could pick me up on his way to his bar even if it meant I'd have to beat off his pleas to take his case.

I'd kind of dozed off when the cab stopped.

"Here we are, Mac."

I paid the fare and then watched the cab disappear while I tried to plow through the cobwebs in my brain. I turned. That's when the situation registered. Maybe the cop had been right and I was drunk, seeing pink stucco elephants shaped in a new, funky style. Or rather white ones in the shape of a new, glass and wood house with a blaze of lights inside. Which was pretty funny considering that I lived in a redwood frame ranch that was fifty years old.

I looked around just in case someone had moved my house across the street or up the block. They hadn't. A street light shone down on the mailbox that sported a bunch of numbers and a street name. The numbers were off by a few hundred and the street name wasn't even close.

I was wondering where I was and how long it would take me to find my own house when the front door flew open, and a blonde came rushing out. The door slammed shut with such force that it banged open again. All I could tell about the woman was that she was young and wore a sheer, light-colored dress that accentuated every curve. I was so mesmerized, I almost didn't notice she was almost past me as though she was running away from something. Not an irate lover, I hoped, chuckling. I'd had enough excitement for one night.

"Pardon me," I called after her. "You wouldn't happen to know where Dolorosa Circle is, would you?"

She stopped, stared for a few seconds, turned and ran to a dark Jaguar parked on the street.

I jogged behind her. "Okay, how about a lift down to Hollywood Boulevard?"

"Screw you, Pops," she said in a low, husky voice. She clicked the car door open and slid inside.

"Only if you can change a five dollar bill," I yelled after the departing car. Pops?

I fumbled in my pocket but couldn't find my cell phone. I remembered – it was at home, recharging. When I reached the still wide-open front door, I stepped inside. "Hello, anyone here?"

There was no answer – and no phone visible, either. I passed the curved stairway, aiming for the sunken living room. Every light seemed to be on, accentuating the large, magnificent room that was sleek and white – from the grand piano in front of a gigantic picture window to the half-dozen leather sofas and chairs. Even the fancy bottle of fingernail polish knocked over on a white end table looked expensive and classy. The disarray around a large white leather chair, as though someone had been searching for something, didn't take away from the room's elegance. My poplin pants, wild-patterned orange and blue Hawaiian shirt and tweed jacket seemed out of place.

"Hello," I said again when I was at the end of the living room. I walked through an open sliding door that led to a pool and an incredible view of the Los Angeles basin stretching to a foggy void in the distance. The illumination from the lights in the pool and the light standards that peeked out of the shrubs around it gave the scene a soft, surreal glow.

After I'd gotten used to the lack of bright lights, I made out more clutter. Bottles of lotion, empty glasses, a pair of dark glasses and a couple of what looked like race track programs lay on a low table. On the floor were beach towels pushed to one side and a mass of newspapers. I recognized the *Daily Racing Form* on top.

A man lay on a chaise in front of the pool. His paunch and sparse hair put him at least in his late fifties. And from the big diamond ring on his right ring finger, I figured he was the lord of the manor.

A sudden eerie sense of gloom spread over me. Being Irish, I was steeped in the superstitions and myths I'd learned as a kid. Over sixty-some years, I'd come to believe in them. I'd already disregarded my inner voice which had screamed caution when I'd let Harry orchestrate the agenda at the bar. Now, it was telling me to get the hell out of this house. Instead, I walked closer to the man.

"Pardon me, sir," I said, taking off my Dodger cap and holding it in one hand. "Your front door was open, and I needed to use your phone –"

I stopped abruptly when the reflection of light on the water spotlighted a small, messy hole in his forehead. There was no sign of life when I touched the artery in his neck. Sir was dead.

I turned around, ready to make a fast retreat, and stumbled over a pair of sandals. One of them skittered across the slippery tile. I reached out and retrieved it before it fell into the pool. When I put it down, a piece of white paper that had been stuck to the bottom fluttered to the ground. I picked it up and held it down toward a pool light in front of me. It was still too dark to make out what it was, but the texture of the paper had a vague familiarity.

"Okay, turn around and put your hands on top of your head."

I jumped, stuck the paper in the inside band of my cap that I still held in my hand, plopped the cap on my head and turned. A cop. Again. Actually, two cops. They walked over to me, patted me down and stopped searching when they found the gun in my jacket pocket.

A model citizen all of my life, I'd just gone from suspicion of drunkenness to a probable charge of murder. I spent the night in a cell with a dozen or so other men, most of them at some stage of inebriation. It was after eight in the morning when I was finally led to an interrogation room and Dave Bannon walked in carrying a file folder.

Dave and my daughter Toni have an on-again-off-again relationship. Although he lacked a sense of humor, I'd always felt there was a certain rapport between us – neither of us could figure out Toni.

"Dave, you know me. Think I could kill anyone?"

He sat down, the usual dour look on his face. "We find

Alonso Lucchesi dead and you with a gun in your pocket," he said. "You were a cop once. What would you have thought?"

I stared at him. "Lucchesi? The mob guy from Vegas?" In spite of a killer headache, you should pardon the expression, and a queasy stomach, I figured that one out fast. I'd just fallen for one of Harry's cons.

Bannon opened the file. "We have two witnesses who say Harry Singakou hired you to do some serious negotiating with Lucchesi – who has a rep for playing rough. What happened? He push the wrong button?"

"This is a set-up, Dave. First of all, I didn't agree to take Harry's case." I gave him my story. "Check with the officer who put me in the cab – and the cab driver."

"Too early to corroborate either one," he said.

Before I could say more, a uniformed cop opened the door and gestured to Bannon.

"Wait here," he said, as though I had a choice.

When Bannon came back he said, "You can go. Your gun wasn't the one used. The preliminary report puts Lucchesi's death between six p.m. and ten. Harry and the bartender put you at the bar at that time. But don't go far. We'll know better when the official autopsy results are in."

Harry had given me an alibi. He truly was all heart.

It was almost nine when a cop drove me to my car and warned me about parking in a No Parking zone. Yeah, that was all I had to worry about.

I drove home – to my own cozy, dilapidated house and crawled into bed. When I woke up, I took cereal and coffee outside to the deck. It was an incredible January day, sunny and clear. The houses rising up a hill over an adjacent canyon didn't make as dramatic a picture as Lucchesi's view, but I felt no envy. Unlike Lucchesi, I would be going to Santa Anita again – which reminded me of the piece of paper that was still in the band of my Dodger cap.

It was the previous day's Pick Six ticket from Santa Anita. I found the results in the paper's sports section. Like most big betters, Lucchesi picked more than one horse in each of the six races – sometimes a lot more than one. But this time he'd hit the jackpot. Three long-shots had come in, which made him the lone winner. For a bet totaling around thirty-five hundred dollars, he'd won over eight hundred thousand. Except for the bullet hole in his forehead, he'd had a great day. Which brought me to Harry.

When I walked into the bar, the bartender nodded toward the green curtains. "He's in his office."

I didn't knock—just opened the door and walked in. Harry was slouched in his chair with an uncharacteristic look of doom on his face. I almost felt sorry for him. Almost.

"Okay, Harry, how did you work it? Set up the rent-a-cop-and-phony-cabby routine while I was waiting for you to count your money? Your scheme back-fired. Lucchesi was dead when I arrived at his house – in case you didn't know."

He sank lower in his chair. "You must find out who killed him, Michael, before Las Vegas decides I am responsible."

Harry—always thinking of the other guy. "I plan to, Harry. Because your buddies have my number, too, along with the cops who haven't dropped me as their prime suspect." I sat down in a chair in front of his desk and told him what had happened – at least most of it.

"Now I want addresses. Lucchesi's, the blonde who came rushing out of his house, your pal Giancarlo and the dozen or so other thugs who might want Lucchesi out of the picture. First, though, what about this Mickey Mouse real estate scheme of yours?"

"Michael, I admit I talked to a cop friend and set up the trip to Lucchesi's house, but I swear, I had nothing to do with the gentleman's death."

"The story, Harry."

He sighed. "I have an interest in an apartment complex near Western and the Boulevard. Lucchesi decided it would be a good area for an upscale condominium complex. He approached me, and we entered into an agreement—of sorts."

I could imagine how that had gone. Two grifters trying to cut each other's throats.

"He tried some legerdemain. When I called him on it, he was insulted by my accusations. I was not about to be taken advantage of so I gave him an ultimatum." Harry sank down farther in his chair.

"Any threats?"

"Veiled."

"How's Giancarlo involved?"

"Second in command to Lucchesi in California. A very dangerous man. It's best not to make him your enemy."

"Is he aiming for a higher position?"

"We are all interested in bettering ourselves."

"I'd say with Lucchesi dead, Giancarlo has scooted right up to the top of the ladder."

"From your description, the girl sounds like Zelda Nolan," Harry went on. "I don't understand why she would be visiting Lucchesi. She's Giancarlo's fiancée – lives in a condominium in Pacific Palisades. A lovely young lady, gracious, very refined."

She hadn't looked very gracious or refined last night. But who was I to argue with Harry, whose fame as a playboy was second only to his reputation as a con man.

Harry took cards from his Rolodex and jotted down addresses on a piece of paper. "You shouldn't have any trouble finding Lucchesi's house again. Giancarlo lives in the Hills near him."

"One thing puzzles me," I said. "I didn't see any security around. The mob's big power in Los Angeles, and he's sitting there, a big, fat target marked 'Shoot Me'? Seems like he'd have someone hovering within yelling distance."

"He has an elaborate security system in his house," Harry said. "He and Giancarlo share the two main bodyguards – Connie and Stan. There are others. I don't know why no one was with him last night. Except that Lucchesi was always very secretive. Especially when it came to his personal life."

"What's the story about Connie and Stan?"

"Connie is an ex-fighter, still very conversant with the art of fisticuffs. Stan? An enigma. Related to someone important, but relegated to a minor position. The reason? I don't know."

Harry reeled off the names of a few of the wiseguys in Southern California's mob picture, wrote down the name of the bar in the Valley where I could find most of them and handed me the paper.

A half-hour later, I was standing next to my car on Ventura Boulevard near the bar. I punched the bar's number on my newly-charged cell phone. Of the two wiseguys, I decided it was safer to take my chances with Connie, sweat and zoot suit notwithstanding. When I had him on the line, I told him that I was waiting in front to take him to Mr. Giancarlo. Then I called my daughter Toni at her hotel, asked her to call me in exactly ten minutes and disconnected before she could ask any questions.

A few minutes later, Connie came out, wearing the same out-of-style suit. He looked up and down the busy street.

"Mr. Giancarlo's waiting," I said and nodded toward my car.

"Why'd he send you? Whyn't he call me direct, like always?"

"He doesn't make his own calls anymore what with his new job. Let's go."

I prodded him forward with the gun I had in my jacket pocket. He frowned for a second and then walked with me to my car.

"Get in," I said and walked around to the driver's side.

"We gotta talk first," I said when we were inside the car. "Why weren't you and your buddy Stan at Mr. Lucchesi's house, watching out for him last night?"

"Hey, wait it a minute. I know you. You're the old guy works for Harry Singakou. We heard it was you offed Mr. Lucchesi."

Old guy. I gritted my teeth. "You heard wrong. I was at Harry's Bar when Lucchesi was shot."

"It's Mr. Lucchesi to you, pal," Connie said. "And we were at the bar, too, remember?"

"Then we're all off the hook." If the ME's hours were correct, Giancarlo or either one of the wiseguys had plenty of time to shoot Lucchesi before they showed up at Harry's Bar.

"Who had a grudge against *Mr.* Lucchesi?"

"A lot of guys. He was important – involved in maybe a dozen deals."

Connie reached inside his jacket and I brought my gun up.

"Give me a break," he said and took out a white handkerchief. He blotted the sweat off his forehead. "It's hotter'n hell in here."

"Okay, another question," I said, lowering the gun. "What was Zelda Nolan doing at Mr. Lucchesi's house?"

His eyes opened wider. "You musta seen wrong. Too much to drink last night maybe."

He smirked, and I clenched the gun tighter.

"She and Mr. Giancarlo are engaged," he said quickly and loosened his tie. "How about putting a window down."

"I'm almost finished. You at Santa Anita yesterday?"

"Sure. When the boss plays the ponies, I go along."

"Who else?"

"Mr. Giancarlo, Ms. Nolan, Stan." His eyes narrowed.

"Giancarlo'll probably take over as number one, which means everyone moves up a notch. You, or Stan, in line for a promotion?"

"Not Stan for awhile, but me, maybe."

"Why not Stan? I understand he's connected."

Connie shrugged. "He's what you call on probation. Sometimes he acts before he thinks. His uncle needs to make sure he's over that kinda bullshit."

"His uncle being?"

"The main man in the Chicago family."

I nodded, and gestured toward the car door. When we stood outside, I said, "Thanks for the information, Connie, but some advice. Don't sell yourself short. You belong up there with the power players." I flicked an imaginary piece of lint off his lapel. "Get yourself a better tailor, keep the handkerchief handy and you can go as far as you want."

"Where you planning to go?"

Stan had come out of the bar. He looked from Connie to me and back again – I think. With that crazy eye it was hard to tell.

I was debating whether I should ask him any questions now or wait until later. Then my cell phone rang.

"Dave Bannon just called," Toni said. "I'm gone for three days, and you're already involved in a murder –"

"Can't right now," I said, looking at the two men and turning.

I lowered my voice, but not enough so they couldn't still hear me. "The cops'll be outta the guy's house this afternoon. Gotta get up there and find the ticket I told you about."

"Double-talk. Okay, I understand."

"Can't remember exactly where." I gave a weak little laugh.

"I was a little – you know – under the weather last night. My memory is kinda hazy."

"Remember, Dad, you'll be six feet under if you try to set something up and it backfires."

I heard the two men behind me shuffling around.

"Gotta go," I said and disconnected the call.

"You find something at Lucchesi's house last night?" Stan asked when I dropped the phone in my pocket and turned around.

"*Mr.* Lucchesi." I grinned and walked around the car, waved to the two men and opened the door.

I drove to Zelda Nolan's condo – located in a small, expensive complex in the Palisades – figuring I'd drop in on Giancarlo on my way home. There was a security phone in the vestibule of Zelda's building. Before I decided what to do, a well-dressed woman came out. I slipped into the main lobby while she stared at me, not sure what she'd done.

Three minutes later, I was standing in front of Zelda Nolan's door, taking out the appropriate tools from the pouch I carried. A couple of seconds and I was inside her apartment.

The first thing that hit me was the smell of cigar smoke. The second was something hard, like the butt of a gun, cracking me across the back of the head. When I came to, Giancarlo, a cigar clamped in his mouth, motioned me to stand up and pushed me into a chair. He sat down on a sofa, a gun aimed at me.

"What are you doing here?"

"I'm Mike O'Donnell –"

"I remember who you are."

"I want to talk to Ms. Nolan."

"What about?"

I was just about to explain when a key turned in the lock and Zelda Nolan breezed in carrying several large packages. In her elegant tan suit and striped blouse, she looked different than she had the night before. She dropped the packages on the coffee table in front of Giancarlo.

"I need a drink. That traffic –" When she turned toward the portable bar, she noticed me. "Who's the old duffer?"

"This is the guy who found Lucchesi. The cops think he

killed him."

"I'm the guy who staggered out of the cab when you were leaving."

"I don't know what he's talking about," she said, looking at Giancarlo.

"I know you were there," he said, a nasty smile on his face.

"And not the first time. You kill him?"

She swallowed a couple of times and then huddled down on the sofa, away from Giancarlo. "Do I look like I have a death wish? Mr. Lucchesi was already dead. I just went up there to –"

"Save it," Giancarlo interrupted. He turned to me. "Okay gramps, whatta you want?"

First old duffer and now gramps. I was trim and still had most of my hair – salt-and-pepper which gave me a certain rakish quality which more than one woman had found appealing.

I stood up. "I've got something to sell. I stumbled over a ticket last night, which might be worth a lot of money." I tried for my weak laugh. "If I can find it."

Giancarlo stood and dropped his gun in his jacket pocket. "That's funny. Something to sell, but you lost it."

"Not lost it, exactly. I just don't remember where I put it when the cops walked in."

I turned and started walking toward the door, Zelda behind me. She walked out into the hall.

"I'm sorry about last night." She smiled. "I was very rude, but I was – so scared." She gave a nervous little laugh.

Maybe Harry was right and she was lovely and gracious. I glanced past her. Giancarlo sat glowering on the sofa.

"You gonna be all right?"

"I can take care of him." She stood up very straight, an expression of supreme confidence on her face.

I had no doubt of that.

As soon as I walked into my own house, I fixed a drink. I'd just settled down on the deck to do some thinking when Toni called.

"Dad, I want to know what's going on."

I told her. "I figure someone at the races with Lucchesi knew about that Pick Six ticket. He went to Lucchesi's house and confronted him. They went out to the pool. It was dark and when Lucchesi dropped the ticket and it stuck to the bottom of his damp slipper, the killer didn't notice. He killed Lucchesi then couldn't find the ticket and started ransacking the place. Maybe the Nolan woman interrupted him before he'd found what he was looking for. She panicked when she saw Lucchesi and ran out just as I arrived. The killer must have called the police at the same time. I just set up the two wiseguys and Sam Giancarlo."

"And you've called Dave to tell him about the ticket and your theory."

"I was just about to do that very thing."

"I'll be home in two days, Dad. The case better be in the hands of the police by then."

"Of course, Darlin'."

A half-hour later I raised the yellow police tape and let myself into the Lucchesi house. The place was even messier than the night before. I walked through the living room and out to the pool area. The view today was incredible – clear enough to see downtown clearly. Even the ocean was visible – if you used your imagination.

I went back to the foyer, opened the big front door and pushed a chair behind it – and sat down to wait. The way I had it figured, the murderer had been at Santa Anita with Lucchesi. All three men – Giancarlo, Stan, Connie – undoubtedly looked forward to the time when Lucchesi was out of the way. Gamblers had to tell someone when they'd won big. Maybe Lucchesi hadn't announced that it was the Pick Six ticket specifically, but he'd undoubtedly hinted to someone that it was a big one. The added reward of a bettor's winning ticket gave one of the three men the impetus to make it all happen at once.

It was getting dark, and I'd begun wondering if my brilliant deductions were so brilliant after all when I heard a noise coming from the living room. I frowned, walked to the entrance and peered around the corner. Nothing.

The voice came from behind me. "Okay, gramps, where is

it?"

I turned. It was the second time that day that someone had called me gramps – and was aiming a gun in my direction. Zelda Nolan this time.

"Let's head for the pool. You can show me where you hid the ticket."

I walked out to the deck, aware of the gun still aimed at me.

"Is that how he lured you up here? Showed you the ticket at the race track?"

"We'd been having a little – let's call it flirtation. He promised me part of the ticket – probably a payoff to keep me from feeling guilty about two-timing Sam Giancarlo."

Seeing the cold, steely look in her eyes, I doubted there'd be much chance she'd feel guilt.

"But the time of death was earlier. It was around midnight when I ran into you –" I stopped talking. I'd been so sure that Lucchesi's death was part of the desire for everyone to move up in the hierarchy. That Zelda's nervousness last night was due to having just discovered Lucchesi. It had never occurred to me that she'd killed him hours before, gone through each room – searched and looked everywhere – except the bottom of one of his shoes – finally given up and been on her way out when I arrived.

"Ahhh, you've figured it out. Too bad, because now I have to kill you, too." She raised the gun.

"Drop it." The voice came from the living room. I wasn't sure who I expected to see walk out – Giancarlo? Connie? Stan? Not Dave Bannon.

"You okay, Mike?" he asked me.

"Great. Toni called you, didn't she?"

He nodded. "Good thing. You were this close –" He held up two fingers almost touching.

"I had it worked out. Another few seconds and Zelda was going for a swim."

"Remember the perfectly centered bullet hole in Alonso Lucchesi's forehead? Zelda Nolan is a crack shot. She might have gone into the water, but you'd have gone with her. Except while she swam, you'd sink to the bottom."

Bannon held out his hand. "I know you were planning to

hand over the ticket."

"Almost slipped my mind," I said, dug it out of my pocket and dropped it into his palm at the same time Bannon's cell phone rang.

I stomped out to my car. Guaranteed his call was from Toni. My daughter had solved the last case we'd worked together. She'd saved my life on this one. And she'd told him about the ticket. Toni was annoying the hell out of me.

My cell phone rang just as I reached my car.

"I'm so proud of you," Toni said.

I opened the car door and slid inside.

"Dave just told me you set up that woman for him," she went on. "How did you ever figure out Zelda was the one?"

I sat up straight. "It was just a matter of eliminating the obvious, Darlin'." My mind raced. "And the bottle of nail polish sitting on the table in the living room – that's what gave her away. Gotta give the cops a statement," I said and clicked off before she had time to think about it.

Little Nancy Curran

Kevin Egan

For two days in August of that year, emergency repairs to the county courthouse lobby blocked access to the judges' private elevator. Rather than muck in with the lawyers and litigants who crowded the public elevator bank at 9:30 in the morning, the judges climbed to the second floor, where, deep in the back corner of the Commissioner of Jurors Office, they could catch their elevator and ride to the rarified air of the courthouse tower.

One of the judges who passed through the office during those two days was Judge Henry Johnston. Every judge has a shtick, and Judge Johnston's shtick, a relic from his two successful judicial campaigns, was to acknowledge literally everyone who passed before his eyes. He didn't merely nod or wave his hand. He didn't merely say hello or how are you. He would stop and engage the person in conversation. He would tell someone, "You're doing a great job." He would tell someone else, "Everything I said about you, I take some of it back." He would tell yet another, "Don't listen to what everyone's saying about you." And if Judge Johnston knew the town where the person lived, he might embellish this last statement with, "Don't listen to what everyone in {town name} is saying about you."

Most people, even people meeting Judge Johnston for the first time, recognized this shtick as a shtick. A few people, the credulous or the naive, swallowed the act for a day or two before catching wise. But no one bought the act so completely as Nancy Curran.

Nancy was pleasantly nondescript except for a husky voice that didn't quite fit with her diminutive height and robust figure. Forty-ish, she had come to the Commissioner of Jurors office after the only employer she ever had known, the village justice of Milton, collapsed during a DUI bench trial. Nancy was neither credulous nor naive. Her years in the Milton village court taught her to read all kinds of people: the drunks who spent freezing winter nights in the town lock-up, the stockbrokers who believed parking ordinances and speed limits didn't apply to them, the kids who acted like juvenile delinquents but probably just were confused or unloved. Yet there was something about judges that set them apart in Nancy's mind. They were the ultimate authority, the final arbiters, the men (or women) charged with the task of deciding questions no one could answer or untangling problems no one could solve. When they spoke, Nancy listened as if they spoke *ex cathedra.*

Judge Johnston took his time passing through the jury clerks office during those two days in August. The office was a large warren of cubicles, and the jury clerks all were female. The Judge stopped at every cubicle, telling "the girls" what a great job they were doing. The clerks smiled and laughed and thanked him for his compliments. Nancy Curran smiled as well. She remembered her first week on the job, when Judge Johnston had come to her with a friend's jury summons. She helped arrange the deferment, then basked in Judge Johnston's shower of praise.

Judge Johnston fed his elevator card into the slot and pressed the up button. Inside the shaft, machinery whirred. As he waited, he glanced back toward Nancy Curran's cubicle, and though he already told her she was doing a great job, his eyes alighted as if seeing her for the first time. A bell chimed. The elevator door opened, and before Judge Johnston stepped in, he called back, "Everyone here is very proud of you, Nancy. Don't listen to what they're saying about you in Milton."

Nancy held herself together for the rest of the workday. She hunkered down in her cubicle and worked as hard as she knew how, keeping one ear tuned hopefully to the office banter. Was everyone as proud of her as Judge Johnston said? Did any of the other clerks have friends in Milton? And, she wondered, did anyone *not* laugh when Judge Johnston spoke to her?

She was tempted to go up to his chambers and ask him exactly what the people in Milton were saying. Her old boss had been a neighbor, a friend on a first name basis before his election. She could walk into his office and say, "Now look, Tom," and he wouldn't flinch, wouldn't retreat behind his title, wouldn't demand that she address him as Judge. But the judges here in county court were cold and distant, even someone who seemed as accessible and as down to earth as Judge Johnston.

So she waited in her cubicle, hoping a chance came her way, thrilling each time the bell chimed. But Judge Johnston never stepped off the elevator, not for the rest of the day. And that evening, after Nancy returned to her apartment and closed the door behind her, she succumbed to her nerves.

"I knew this would happen," she wailed. "I knew it, I knew it, I knew it."

She had believed right from the start that running for office was an absurd concept. Her name on posters, her face taped in shop windows, lashed to telephone poles, crumpled in trash baskets along Merchant Street. Little Nancy Curran, shy Nancy Curran. Never had a boyfriend, never went out on a real date. Absurd.

It started in June, on the flight back from England with the rest of the Legion of Mary. Their guide, a Knight of Columbus who had been stationed in England during the war, settled beside her after the flight attendants had cleared dinner.

"We're fielding a slate in the village elections this fall," he said. The *we* needed no gloss. "The spot for receiver of taxes is open."

"I'm a Republican," she said.

"It's a simple matter to change parties."

"But I don't belong."

"Who says? People know you from your years in the village court. You are well-respected. You have credibility."

Maybe it was the sherry from the wide-mouthed plastic airline cup. Maybe it was the visit to Canterbury and the story of Thomas à Becket. Maybe it was the realization, the kind that hits during a vacation's heightened sense of awareness, that if she ever were to do anything with her life it had to be now. She looked out the window, dreaming the possibility. Small clouds hugged the slate surface of the Atlantic as the plane chased the sun toward home.

"I can't campaign," she said.

"There is no campaign," he countered. "Not in the traditional sense."

"No one digging into my life?"

"For what?"

She grinned her tight grin.

"I promise you," he said. "No debates, no speeches, no interviews with editorial boards or the League of Women Voters. No one takes us seriously. That's the luxury of being a single-issue party."

After dinner, Nancy phoned her friends in the Legion of Mary. "What are these people saying about me?" she wanted to say. Instead, they spoke the usual news about the ministry to the sick and the menu for the communion breakfast and next summer's pilgrimage to Rome. Was everything okay with her, they asked. Yes, she answered, fine.

She phoned her campaign manager, that same Knight of Columbus from the flight. "I told you so," she wanted to say. Instead, they spoke of printing costs for posters and the flow of contributions and the give-away buttons for the Labor Day parade. He assured her once again that there would be no stumping, no door-to-door, no interviews with the editorial board of the local newspaper. The luxury of a single issue party, he reminded her. Nancy's laugh rang hollow. Was everything all right, he asked. Yes, she answered, fine.

But later, in the darkness of her bedroom, horrible scenarios played out in her mind. The drawback of being alone, she told herself. She knew exactly what Judge Johnston would have heard; how many different ways could someone say it? The horrors were in the effect. Embarrassment? Definitely. Ostracism? Yes. Criminal charges?

She whipped off the sheets and crept to the window. Below, a lamp shrouded in the leaves of a maple cast familiar shadows on the paths criss-crossing the co-op's quadrangle. Crickets chirped. In the distance, traffic whined on the Interstate. Close by, the sudden ignition of a car engine startled her. She crept back to bed, quivering with the fear that no possibility was too remote.

The next morning, the repairs to the lobby were complete. Nancy sat in her cubicle, listening to the whir of the private elevator as the judges rose to their chambers. By noon, she could take it no longer. If she couldn't talk to Judge Johnston, she had a better idea.

Nancy paused at the foot of the driveway. The bus she caught outside the courthouse had dropped her several blocks away, and the heat of the afternoon and the exertion of the walk squeezed the sweat from her pores. Barbara's car, a German convertible with a gunmetal luster, was parked where the drive curved close to the front door.

They had been unlikely friends for a brief spell in high school, and now, almost thirty years later, the divergent arcs of their lives had swept them into parallel universes. Barbara lived in this huge Tudor in a leafy neighborhood with a wealthy husband who indulged her passion for liberal causes. She held fundraisers in her garden, hosted visits from candidates of national stature, appeared weekly in the Sunday society section of the newspaper. In the flesh, Nancy saw Barbara only on rare occasions – at the ten o'clock Mass when Nancy missed the simpler, more sparsely attended eight, or noodling in the gourmet shops along Merchant Street as

Nancy dragged her groceries home from the A&P. They always spoke when they met, suitably cordial for a friendship now removed in time and space. But invariably, and this was not Nancy's imagination, it would descend upon them as if it had been hovering overhead, waiting for them to meet. I remember, Nancy wanted to say. But as the words bubbled up in her throat, Barbara would back off, claiming some excuse for giving her the dodge.

No one answered the door, and Nancy drifted around back. She had been to Barbara's home only once, several years earlier for a reception to welcome a new bishop. She had a brief conversation with Barbara that night about a sideboard she recognized as similar to one she remembered in Barbara's childhood home.

"It's the same piece," Barbara had said. "Just sanded and refinished."

Like you, Nancy had thought but did not say out loud.

She found Barbara kneeling on a pink cushion at the edge of a flower garden, her hands plunged into huge canvas gloves. Barbara stood up at the sight of Nancy, smiling a smile that was half pleasure, half confusion.

She wore shorts and a shirt knotted above two inches of flat belly. She still had her high school figure, thin legs without spider veins. In contrast, Nancy felt blunt and heavy.

"Hi," said Barbara, tugging off one big glove.

Nancy answered with a roundhouse to the jaw.

In the kitchen five minutes later, Nancy blubbered while Barbara, leaning over the sink, gingerly pressed an ice pack to her swollen cheek.

"I'm sorry," said Nancy.

"You'd better be more than sorry," said Barbara.

She lifted the ice pack away and ran her tongue along the salty inside of her mouth. "You'd better have a good reason for socking me like that."

"I do," said Nancy.

A long, dramatic pause followed. Nancy opened her mouth, but nothing came out. She started to blubber again, her entire body shuddering.

"Oh great," said Barbara. She dropped the ice pack and probed the numbed thickness of her cheek. "Lovely."

Nancy took a deep breath and stiffened herself. "It's out," she said.

"What's out?"

"You know."

"I certainly do not know," said Barbara.

"Me. Running for office. Do I need to say it?"

"Nancy, I don't know what you're talking about."

"Yes you do. You arranged everything."

"Arranged what?"

"You even came with me."

"Came where?"

Nancy made a digging motion below her waist.

"That? Oh, Nancy," said Barbara. She gathered Nancy into her arms. "I'm sorry for being so obtuse. But what do you mean it's out?"

"People are talking about it."

"What people?"

Nancy shrugged against Barbara. "One of the judges at the courthouse told me. He said not to listen to what people are saying about me in Milton. What else can they be saying? I mean, that, and the party I'm running for. It's like a bad joke."

"But no one's saying anything, Nancy. I certainly haven't heard anything, and I hear everything in this town." Barbara pushed Nancy away. "Nancy?"

Nancy looked at the floor.

"Nancy, do you think I'm doing the talking?"

"Well, it made sense. The people you support. Me, my party. The hypocrisy of having me run."

"People I support? Hypocrisy? Nancy, you were my friend. Do you think I would deliberately hurt you for, for what? The receiver of taxes?"

"I guess that does sound a little silly," said Nancy. "Doesn't it?"

Barbara nodded. "Want some iced tea?"

"Sure," said Nancy.

She could feel the beads of sweat gathered above her upper lip, and, as Barbara ducked into the refrigerator, she unstuck her blouse from her shoulders.

She really didn't know what to think. Was Judge Johnston joking or telling the truth? If he had heard people talking about her, the topic could only be the one newsworthy event in her life. But at the same time, she believed Barbara, believed her as she had believed everything Barbara told her in high school. Nancy seemed to advance through the different stages of life as a recurring neophyte. Yet, at each stage, she always latched onto a more sophisticated friend to show her what she needed to know, to teach her things that, looking back, she could not have survived without knowing. Barbara had been such a friend.

They moved to the kitchen island and sat on opposite stools. Barbara placed the iced tea before Nancy, tall and cool with a slice of lemon hooked onto the lip. A perfect presentation, as was everything Barbara did.

"I'm glad I came here," said Nancy.

"So am I. We should stay in better touch." Barbara gently patted her own cheek. "Just not this way."

"I'm sorry. I've been in such a state since yesterday. You have Bill, and I'm not saying this out of envy, but when you are alone with no one to talk to, your mind can run wild. I felt this close to a nervous breakdown." Nancy pressed her thumb and forefinger together.

"Forget it," said Barbara. "Maybe I deserved that punch."

"For what?"

"Falling out of touch."

"Now you forget that," said Nancy. She took a sip.

The flavor of the tea burst on her tongue, reminding her of the glass milk bottles Barbara's mother set out on the back stoop on summer mornings.

"Is this sun tea?" she said.

"Yep," said Barbara.

Nancy felt her sweat recede. Whatever Judge Johnston might have heard, if he heard anything at all, seemed far away.

"He must have been kidding," said Barbara.

"Who?" said Nancy.

"That judge. The one you spoke to. What was his name?"

"Johnston," said Nancy.

"Oh yes. He was here once for a cocktail party. Bill knows him. He seems quite the character."

"He always has something to say."

"Well, there you have it. People who talk a lot are bound

to hit on something. After all, you and I were the only two who knew." Barbara unhooked the lemon from her glass. "Nancy? Something wrong?"

Nancy stared through her drink. Something Barbara had just said struck her. It was as simple and as immutable as a mathematical principle, like the associative or commutative rule. If Barbara and the Judge are both telling the truth, then . . .

"Nancy?" said Barbara.

But Nancy did not hear. Her mind was too busy making connections.

"Nancy," said Barbara. "Are you all right?"

Nancy could feel the sweat heavy above her lip.

"Nancy," said Barbara, nervously now because of the strange look on Nancy's face.

"One other person did know," said Nancy.

"Why does that matter now?" said Barbara.

"Because it was –" Nancy's eyes locked on Barbara's across the table, then broke away.

"Bill?" said Barbara. "Are you saying it was Bill?"

"I'm sorry."

"You're saying it was Bill, aren't you?"

Nancy said nothing.

"You are, aren't you? Well, I don't believe you."

"It's true," said Nancy. "Chris Booker's party. The boathouse. You went home sick to your stomach. I stayed."

Barbara cocked her head, searching her memory.

"Why should you remember any of that? It was just another night for you. It wasn't for me."

"I don't believe you."

"It's the truth."

"The only truth I see is you, Nancy. You never accept your share of the blame for anything. My husband did that to you? Right. Even if I believed that, which I don't, I doubt he'd be spreading rumors to sink you. He doesn't care about the politics of this little town. He has bigger fish to fry."

"He has a birthmark midway below his navel."

Barbara charged around the island. She knocked Nancy off her stool and fell upon her, clutching at her throat. Nancy broke the grip and turned turtle, crawling away. Barbara crawled after her. Nancy got to her knees and then to her feet. She absorbed Barbara's blows with her elbows and her shoulders. Nothing hurt. Barbara's tiny fists felt like the hands of an expert masseuse, kneading away the tension of the last two days, the guilt of the last thirty years. This was why she had come here, she realized, not to talk but to fight.

Nancy grabbed Barbara in a bearhug and lifted the lighter woman off her feet. She felt the flatness of Barbara's stomach against her own, the pricks of her icy little tits. She tightened her arms against Barbara's bony spine, squeezing harder and harder each time Barbara tried to draw another breath. Nancy jumped, like she once saw wrestlers do on television. Barbara groaned. Nancy jumped again. A twig snapped, and Barbara's eyes rolled back in her head.

During their brief friendship in junior year, Nancy often spent Friday nights at Barbara's house. Barbara's bedroom was in the attic, and they could stay up until dawn, listening to records and talking about boys and plotting their wonderful futures. How convenient it was, then, that the chosen day fell on a Friday, when Nancy could lie groggy in Barbara's trundle bed, her insides raw and leaking into pads that Barbara tied into plastic garbage bags and surreptitiously dumped into the neighbor's trash. They never talked about it afterward, not the next day, or the next Friday, or any other time as their friendship slowly trailed off. Nancy rationalized what she had done, what Barbara insisted she had to do, and as the weeks passed her rationalizations erected a conceptual maze that prevented her from reaching the truth. She had been sick, she began to believe. Something foreign had been growing inside her. It had to be removed or else it would have taken her over and killed the person she had planned to become those Friday nights in Barbara's attic.

Now, back in her apartment, her clothes churning through a second cycle in her washer, she went about all her usual business. She phoned her friends in the Legion of Mary and spoke about the ministry to the sick and the communion breakfast menu and next summer's pilgrimage to Rome. No one asked if she was okay before she rang off. She called her campaign manager and spoke of printing costs for posters and the give-away buttons for the Labor Day parade. She even volunteered to go before the newspaper's editorial board for an interview. It won't be necessary, he told her, the luxury of being a one-issue party. She laughed, and was pleased to hear that her laugh didn't ring hollow.

Later, after dark, as she sat by the window and stared down at the quadrangle, she heard distant sirens and knew that Bill had just returned home. Feeling as if a circle had closed, she went to bed and turned on a window fan to drown herself in white noise. She couldn't have planned it better, she thought. Taking the bus, walking through a neighborhood where the homes sat well back from the roads and the residents rarely looked out their windows. There was no blood, no murder weapon.

Nothing for her to destroy or throw into the waters off Poningo Point. Her fingerprints were on the iced tea glass, and her fingerprints were on file in the Office of Court Administration with those of every other court employee. But who ever would think to match them up? If the police ever constructed a list of Barbara's acquaintances, she would be near the bottom. As Nancy drifted off to sleep, with her arms crossed on her chest and their tiny hairs standing pleasantly erect in the chill from the window fan, the words perfect crime formed in her mind.

The next day, the murder of Barbara Cobb was the talk of the office. Nancy stood in her cubicle, listening to the other clerks and making all the appropriate gestures and sympathetic but inane comments.

The discussion reminded her of the days when *Roe v Wade* came up at the dinner table at home, and she would fold into herself, saying nothing one way or the other until the topic passed.

Just before noon, a bell chimed and Judge Johnston stepped out of the private elevator. He held a jury summons in his hand, and Nancy immediately apprehended he needed a deferment for a friend. He walked past, but then stopped and fixed his eyes on Nancy as if remembering something important. A chill ran through her, not at all like the pleasant chill she felt as she drifted off last night, but a sharper one with a jagged edge. The chill ended at her arms, which heated up with the feel of Barbara's chicken ribs pressing against them. She thought she would wet her pants.

"You're doing a great job, Nancy," said Judge Johnston. "Don't listen to what they're saying about you in Milton."

And before Nancy could stop herself, she confessed.

The murder was just the start. As the other clerks silently converged around her cubicle, she confessed to everything she had done in her entire life. She was sobbing about Bill and Barbara and that day thirty years ago when the police arrived to take her away.

Pleasant Drive

Chelle Martin

Sam Winters walked behind his lawn mower, periodically stopping to check the football scores on the radio. The air was crisp, and the ground already began to accumulate multicolored leaves. During pauses, he would sip a beer, taking pleasure in knowing this was the last cut of the season. Up and down the street, he caught glimpses of his neighbors working to keep Pleasant Drive as picturesque as the name implied.

"Hey, Sam." Adam Cutler waved as he stepped off his porch and headed to his new Mercedes, the envy of the neighborhood. Black and shining, it sat in his driveway so everyone, including Sam, could drool over it.

Cutting the engine, Sam grabbed what was left of his beer and strolled over to his neighbor's yard. He almost leaned against the car, then caught himself. Now that the old Chevy had been replaced, there would be no leaning. "Taking her out for a spin?" he asked.

"Going for a paper. You want anything?"

"Nope, but thanks anyway. Jessie isn't going with you?"

Adam laughed. "Jessie's on another one of her tears. If it isn't one thing, it's another with her. Thank God I've got my baby here so I can escape." As he spoke, he slid behind the wheel and shut the door.

Sam motioned for him to roll down the window. "You aren't going to leave it running in the parking lot like you did with the Blazer, are you?"

Adam grinned, but didn't answer. "Don't you have a game to watch?"

"I'm telling you, buddy, someone's going to make off with her one day. You're just lucky no one grabbed your SUV in all these years."

"That's what insurance is for," Adam said, rolling up the window.

As Sam watched the Mercedes pull away and head up the street, he remembered that he was supposed to ask Adam for his missing nine iron. Sam should have been forewarned weeks ago when Adam had talked about an upcoming business outing at the driving range with several prospective clients and bigwigs at his firm. Adam, ever the social climber. Sam was sure his neighbor "borrowed" it since Adam had a habit of sneaking into Sam's garage through the back door on occasion and making off with a tool or piece of sports equipment. Technically it could be deemed stealing if it weren't for the fact that Sam eventually received his property back. Sam shook his head. Adam could afford a Mercedes, but not a set of golf clubs.

Sam wheeled his mower into the garage, went into his house, and plopped in front of the television. His team was winning.

On Monday morning Sam heard the Cutler's garage door open and close around six and was glad he didn't have a long commute to work. He couldn't understand how Adam would want to drive into Manhattan every day. Of course, the answer was simple, money.

While Sam reasoned that he could probably be making considerably more if he hadn't opted to stay local and work in the town factory, to him it wasn't worth the loss of sleep and daily aggravation of sitting in traffic to be part of the suit and tie crowd. He might never be able to afford a Mercedes, but Sam was happy with his two-story home, his nine year old Oldsmobile, and knowing that all his bills were paid.

As he rolled over for another hour's sleep, Sam heard voices carrying from down below. Apparently, Adam and Jessie were at it again. While he couldn't make out what was being said, the tone and volume were enough to tell him, and the entire neighborhood for that matter, that the Cutler marriage was less than pleasant. Sam was about to go to the window, when he heard the Mercedes' engine gun, followed by squealing tires and a heavy foot on the accelerator. Jessie slammed the front door and so ended another morning at the Cutler residence.

It wasn't until eight thirty that Sam backed his own car out of the garage and ambled out to manually lower the door. At that moment, Jessie stepped off the front porch, house keys in hand, and her purse slung over her shoulder. As always, she looked crisp and freshly showered, but it was obvious that she wore a forced smile.

"Hi, Sam," she said. "Would you be able to drop me off at the market? My car isn't working, and it's on your way."

Sam smiled. "Sure," he replied, motioning for Jessie to jump in the passenger side while he brought the door down. He found Jessie a likeable, practical woman, and wasn't sure how she wound up with someone as power-hungry and pretentious as Adam. Not that Adam couldn't be a fun guy when he let himself go, but Jessie deserved better.

"I really appreciate it," she said. "He'll have a fit if I don't have dinner ready for him on time."

He knew it wasn't his place, but Sam asked just the same, "Why do you stay with him, Jess?" From the corner of his eye, he could see her staring ahead, and he wasn't sure if she had heard him, or if she simply chose not to answer. But then he realized she was struggling to fight back tears. She raised a hand to her mouth and through trembling fingers, simply said, "I don't know."

Sam hadn't even made it out of the development when he pulled over to console her. So he'd be a few minutes late for work. He felt he had to do something other than just deposit her at the market and drive off pretending that nothing was wrong.

He put the car in park and began to turn to her, but Jessie was already reaching to hug him. As his arms circled her, she sobbed heavily. "Why does he hate me, Sam? Why?"

Sam had never been married, and he hadn't made any women cry that he knew of, so he wasn't quite sure how to handle the situation. He just held on and let Jessie pour out her troubles while he stroked her soft, brunette hair. He wondered why Adam didn't just divorce her and have it over and done with. Surely he could find someone as upwardly mobile as himself at the big corporation where he worked.

When Jessie had calmed down, Sam drove her to the market. He hated leaving her there, upset as she was, but what more could he do?

"You going to be all right?" he asked.

"Yeah," she said, and smiled weakly. "I'll grab a cab back. I'm sorry to dump this on you, Sam." She dabbed at the few stray tears that pooled in the corners of her eyes. The motion erased any last trace of makeup she had been wearing.

Sam watched her disappear into the store, then headed off to work.

Despite worrying about Jessie, Sam had been surprised at how fast the day had gone. Before he knew it, it had been break time, then time for lunch, followed by his afternoon break, and quitting time. Unions could be a good thing, he reasoned. Breaks were an essential part of the job. Granted, he didn't get golf outings like Adam, but he and the guys played on weekends just the same. Speaking of which, he made a mental note to again ask Adam for the club he'd borrowed. His usual foursome already had a tee time reserved for this Saturday. He needed it back before then.

Sam was home in no time. He pulled into the driveway, opened the garage door, then drove the Cutlass inside. He brought the door down from within and locked it, opting to enter the house from the pantry door. Before going in, he glanced at his set of golf clubs in case Adam had sent Jessie over to return his nine iron. It was still missing. Sam knew he could prevent his neighbor's unlawful entry by simply locking the back door to the garage, but in case he locked himself out, he liked to know he had an alternative. He kept a spare key hidden in the garage, which he felt was safer than leaving one under the front doormat, the first place a thief would look.

His search of the refrigerator produced a container of leftover spaghetti, which he promptly tossed in the microwave. While waiting for it to heat, Sam went to retrieve his daily newspaper and mail. In the mailbox were the usual magazines and junk mail, but apparently his paper carrier had passed him by. Not the first time. Sam wondered why he even bothered to have the thing delivered in the first place, when he enjoyed a nightly walk to Munchito's and could easily pick one up there.

As soon as he finished dinner, Sam cleared the dishes and left them in the sink. He grabbed his keys, locked the front door, and started down the front walk when he remembered his nine iron. The Cutler house looked deserted, but he decided to ring the bell anyway. When no one answered, he walked around back. Sometimes Jessie liked to sit on the deck, and she'd always said she could never hear the doorbell from there. But when Sam reached the backyard, Jessie was nowhere in sight. He was about to walk away, when he spotted his golf club leaning against the back porch. Sam smiled. He took the opportunity to return it to his golf bag in the garage before setting out again for the convenience store.

Munchito's was only a few blocks away, open twenty-four hours, and had been in business since he was a kid. As Sam walked through his housing development, he realized it seemed deserted. Then he remembered there was supposed to be a home owners meeting tonight at the development's club house. He'd completely forgotten. That would probably explain where Jessie and Adam were. Well, no matter, he had no intention of going there now. He'd just have to get filled in on what transpired by his neighbors or read about it in the monthly newsletter put out by the housing board.

By the time Sam reached Munchito's, it was completely dark, despite Daylight Savings Time being in effect for another couple of weeks. To his surprise, there was only one car in the parking lot. When Sam realized the Mercedes was left unoccupied with its engine running, he had no doubt it belonged to Adam. And from where he stood beneath a darkened streetlight, his suspicions were confirmed when he spotted Adam through the window, surveying the store's liquor section. The clerk was situated at the other end of the store watching the television mounted above the counter.

Adam had to be the most careless person he knew. It didn't matter that no one was around. There was always a chance someone could happen by. Look how easy it would be for him to steal Adam's car with no witnesses in sight.

Sam watched from the safety of the shadows a while longer. Adam and the clerk were still both in the same spots they were earlier. He moved closer to the driver's side of the car where he could see Adam's set of keys dangling from the ignition. Perhaps he should slip inside and surprise his neighbor when he returned with his purchase. But what good would that do? Adam wouldn't think twice about it. So, Sam had waited for him in his car. The car, after all, would still be there.

Another glance into the store. Both men still preoccupied. Sam grabbed the door handle and cracked it open. The leather interior was inviting. The dash was aglow with lighted controls and trimmed in rich walnut. He got in and closed the door. Sam noticed right away how the seat molded to his body, how smooth the steering wheel felt in his hands. How could Adam take a chance with such a beauty? Then again, he didn't take good care of Jessie either. Maybe Sam should throw a good scare into him, starting with the car. If he could make Adam think it was stolen . . .

Sure that no one was in sight, Sam put the car into reverse and eased it out of the parking lot. The headlights hadn't been facing the store, so it wouldn't arouse anyone's attention. By the time Adam came outside, he would be blocks away.

The car ran beautifully. He could picture how it must handle on the open highway, how it would accelerate, and how it would take the curves. But he wouldn't get a chance to find out. All he wanted to do was park the car somewhere nearby, but in a deserted enough spot to throw a little scare into Adam. And it had to be relatively close enough for him to walk home.

Sam remembered a dead end that had been cleared for construction, with only a few homes built toward the upper part of the street. He negotiated the few blocks it took to get there and headed for the far end of the street. Once there he turned off the ignition and slipped out of the vehicle, keys in hand. Maybe he should walk home with them and tell Adam about the prank. After all, it wasn't like he hadn't warned him. And he hadn't really stolen the car. So the guy might be annoyed for a few days. He'd get over it.

On the other hand, he could wipe off the steering wheel, the keys, and the door handle, and let Adam wonder who had made off with his precious possession. While he pondered his decision, he twirled the key ring about his finger. He thought perhaps he would have heard a police siren in the distance by now, but the neighborhood was quiet.

Before he could decide, the keys slipped off Sam's finger and landed on the gravel strewn road. The impact of the remote caused the Mercedes' trunk to pop open. The unexpected motion startled Sam, and he jumped. Then he realized what had happened. So much for ever really stealing a car, he thought. He just wasn't cut out for it. And now to boot, he couldn't see the keys on the dark street since the street lights only went as far as the constructed homes.

He dropped to one knee and started groping around in the dark, but came up short. Still, the keys couldn't have been thrown far. He'd find them, but decided to close the trunk before someone up the street was alerted to the light. He stood and went to the back of the car. But as he reached up to grab the lid, he made a horrifying discovery. Wrapped in a blanket, head and face covered in blood, was Jessie. Dead.

A wave of nausea hit Sam, and he had to steady himself against the car. His heart beat wildly in his chest. Oh God! Adam must have killed her. Yet he looked so calm walking around Munchito's. Had he made a stop there before heading off to dispose of her body?

Sam quickly sobered up when he heard the faint wail of sirens approaching in the distance. Then it dawned on him. The car would surely have a tracking device. All the better ones did these days. He quickly removed his T-shirt and used it to wipe his fingerprints from the trunk. Then he returned to the driver's door and did the same there, inside and out. Hurrying, hands shaking, he ran the shirt over the steering wheel, and could see flashing lights a street over in the development. He used the T-shirt to close the car door, and then took off running through the vacant building lots, heading for the solace of the neighboring streets where he could blend in with society.

By the time Sam had turned the corner for Pleasant Drive, he could see several police cruisers parked in the Cutler driveway and at the curb. He had to walk past them to get to his house. One officer was outside, preoccupied with a phone call. Adam was nowhere in sight, but the Cutler's front door was ajar, indicating that Adam must be inside with another policeman.

Nervously, Sam unlocked his front door, but before he could open it, he heard, "Mr. Winters?"

Sam froze, and then turned to the policeman approaching him. "Yes," he said, looking past the cop toward the Cutler house. "What happened, Officer? Was there a break in?"

"I'm afraid it's worse than that, sir. There's been a murder." He then produced his identification and introduced himself as Detective Rafano.

"Who? When?" Sam wondered if he sounded guilty, scared, or reasonably upset at hearing such disturbing news.

"Jessie Cutler. Her body was found a short while ago."

Before Sam could comment, the Cutler's front door flew open and an angry Adam came tearing across the lawn.

"It was you, wasn't it?" he shouted, his fist waving in the air. "You killed Jessie! When did the affair start, Sam? When? God was I an idiot. John Gaffney saw you with her this morning. Saw you embracing in your car!"

An officer had followed Adam out of the house and grabbed him by the shoulder before he could reach Sam. "Affair? There was no affair, Adam!" Sam shouted back in reply. It was obvious to Sam that Adam was trying to set up an alibi for himself. "How can you . . . ," he started to say, but just then another police car arrived at the scene. Its driver approached them with a paper in hand.

"Here's the warrant you asked for," he said.

Hours later Sam Winters was greeted at the police station by his lawyer. "Thank God you're here," Sam said, as he shook the man's hand. "When can I get out of here?" he asked.

"Well first, Sam, perhaps you better explain a few things to me. Like how Jessie's hair was found in your car. How traces of her blood were found on your nine iron. Why your fingerprint matched the one on the key to Adam's Mercedes. And how your shoes were covered in the exact dirt from the location where the car was found."

Adam had forgotten about the key he'd lost in the dirt. But all he could think to say was, "What about Adam's fingerprints?"

"Oh, sure. His prints were in the car and on the key as well. After all, they do belong to him."

"What about the nine iron? He borrowed it. Obviously to kill his wife and blame me for it."

"The only prints on the murder weapon were yours. The DNA confirmed the hair and blood as those of Mrs. Cutler."

Just like Adam, Sam thought, to wipe everything clean. To erase any evidence that would convict him of killing his own wife. Which again confirmed what Sam had already known about Adam – he'd do anything in the drive to get ahead. Or in this case, to eliminate a woman he never deserved.

Deep Doo-Doo

Gary R. Bush

On Monday morning William DeMora stepped in dog shit.

Billy Dogs, as he was often called, loved canines, but hated to see dog shit on the sidewalks and in the parks. He had hated it in Brooklyn, where he had made his bones, and he hated it here in Tucson, where he had retired. All he wanted to do was walk his dogs, sit by his pool, play a little golf with his retired associates and indulge his wife of 40 years, Mia. And, of course, screw his mistress, Carolee.

Every morning at seven, before the heat of the day, Billy would walk his dogs – the Greyhound, Sonnyboy, and the little Yorkie, Pepper. When the dogs defecated, Billy would scoop it up and put it in little bags he carried. "You clean up your mess, whether it's dog crap or a stiff," he told his bodyguard, Michael "Mickey the Moose" Incardona.

On Mondays, Billy would walk the dogs to the park, then continue a few more blocks to the home of Carolee, a 30-something real estate agent.

Mickey would stay in the kitchen with the dogs, drinking coffee, while Billy and Carolee would retire to the bedroom for an early morning mattress mambo.

On this particular Monday, as they were walking, Billy was haranguing Mickey about Greyhound racing, which he despised.

"The dogs are treated badly and some are just killed after their racing days are through. I hate the damn sport."

Mickey just nodded. He had heard the rant a thousand times. "That's why I got Sonnyboy here," Billy Dogs continued, patting the big hound. "Greyhound Rescue. Of course he had to be trained to interact with people and not to chase little dogs like Pepper. He and Pepper are buddies now and . . . Son-of-a-bitch!" Billy had stepped in a pile of dog shit that lay in the middle of the walking path.

"Oca! Damn!" he cursed. "Who the hell didn't clean up after their dog?" Mickey and Billy looked around, but saw no one. "I'm gonna be late for Carolee. I gotta go home and change shoes. I want to find the *figlio di puttana,* the sonofabitch, that did this. It's against the law, you know."

"A misdemeanor, Boss," Mickey said.

"A damn crime against the environment is what it is!" Billy steamed. "Tomorrow we're going to be here at six and if I see the *arruso,* the asshole, who don't clean up his dog shit I'm gonna . . ."

"Boss, don't do nothing rash," Mickey admonished. "You gotta keep a low profile."

"I'll low profile the *arruso* who did this." Mickey saw the look in Billy's eye and kept his mouth shut. They went home. Billy tossed his handmade, elkskin-walking shoes in the garbage, which made him even angrier. A Mexican shoemaker in Nogalas had charged him five hundred dollars for those shoes.

Now he had to call Carolee to tell her he'd be late. This would not be easy, for she had power over him, a power different than any other women he had ever known.

Carolee had the power of sex. She could do things for him that no woman had ever done in his nearly 70 years.

Carolee was unhappy and Billy knew it was going to cost him. Maybe a new bracelet or worse, a trip to Vegas. The jewelry he didn't mind, but he hated Vegas. He spent too many years there and couldn't stand being in the casinos anymore. But if Carolee wanted Vegas, Vegas it would be. Right now she was too angry to demand anything, but she told him he couldn't come over today and no matter how much he apologized, she remained firm.

"Merda," he said, slamming down the phone. "Tomorrow we find the *arruso* that doesn't clean up after his dogs. There

are laws . . ."

By six the next morning Billy and Mickey were in the park. They had left the dogs home to be walked by the maid. "Boss, are you sure you want to do this? I mean it's pretty drastic."

"I'm going to rub his face in it. If he don't clean up after the dog, I'm going to rub his face in it."

"What if it's a broad or a kid?"

"A broad or a kid, I'll make them clean it up. But I'll give you odds it will be a guy."

A few people were walking their dogs and cleaning up after them. "I don't know, Boss," Mickey said, "these people seem all right."

Before Billy could answer, a man with a shaved head, beard and wearing a sleeveless T-shirt, blue jeans and cowboy boots, came walking down the path. He had a brindle dog with a large head and clipped ears on the end of a stout leash. The dog was harnessed to a set of steel drag chains. Billy pulled Mickey off the path and they ducked behind a couple of large saguaro cacti. The dog stopped, squatted and crapped. The guy tugged the leash and he and the dog continued on their way.

"What the hell's with the chains?" Mickey asked.

"Pit Bull," Billy spit. "That *arruso* is training a Pit Bull. The chains build up the dog's muscles and make it easier to control. He doesn't want his dog attacking other dogs or people in the park."

"Do we go after the guy?" Mickey asked. "Do we rub his face in dog shit?" Now Mickey was angry. You couldn't be around Billy long without having affection for dogs yourself and what Mickey saw made him want to beat the hell out of the dog's owner.

"New plans, Mickey," Billy Dogs answered. "I want you to follow the guy, but not too closely and stay clear of the dog. Find out where he lives. I want to know what he's doing in this neighborhood. Guys like that don't hang around multi-million dollar developments here in the foothills."

"What about the dog shit?" Mickey asked.

"I'll take care of the dog shit, and that ain't all, I'm going to clean up. I'm going to clean up that ugly *stronzo,* that turd, too. And if there's one guy breeding dogs to fight, there will be more. I'm going to destroy them all."

"How you gonna do that, Boss?" Mickey asked. "You call the cops or the Humane Society?"

"No. They'll get a slap on the wrist, a fine, maybe community service, a year at most in the county lockup. No, anyone who abuses animals don't get a break. Now get going."

Mickey nodded and took off. Billy Dogs took out one of his bags and cleaned up the pile that the pit bull had dropped.

Billy Dogs returned home to find the household in turmoil. Mia was comforting the maid, who was hysterical.

"What's the matter with Soledad?" Billy asked.

"Oh, Mr. DeMora, a man he tried to . . ."

"Rape you?"

"No."

"Rob you?"

"No."

"What then?"

Soledad started to wail again and Billy turned to his wife. "Mia?"

"Some bastard tried to steal the dogs."

"What the hell. Are they all right?"

"Calm down, Bill," Mia said. "The dogs are OK."

"Sí, Señor DeMora," Soledad said, reverting to Spanish. Then in English: "I was walking the dogs down by the road, just beyond the gates. A few minutes ago, maybe ten, a van pulled up and a big man with a shaved head and tattoos on his arms, got out and took little Pepper from me. But Sonnyboy bit the man and I kicked him in the *cojones,* grabbed Pepper and ran like hell. By the time I got back to the gates to tell security, the man drove off. And Mr. DeMora – that guy he had other dogs in the van. I heard them barking."

Billy Dogs took Soledad's hand and in a calm voice said, "Good girl. Can you describe the van?" He already recognized the man's description.

She nodded. "A blue Chevy, maybe '96 or '97. My cousin Roberto has a van like it, only his is brown. I got part of the license number – 349. Sorry I couldn't get anymore. I just grabbed the dogs and ran like hell."

Billy Dogs put his arm around Soledad. "You did good. You get a raise for this."

Mickey came in, saw Soledad in distress and asked what happened. Both Billy and Mia knew Mickey had a thing for the Mexican girl and she for him. They were an odd couple – Mickey six-six and three hundred pounds, Soledad five-one and maybe 98 pounds.

Soledad turned on the tears, probably to get a rise of Mickey, and told the story again.

"Damn, Boss," Mickey said. "I followed that guy like you said. He got into a blue '97 Chevy van. Vanity plate, *349 Bull.* The van was headed back this way, but because I was on foot I couldn't follow him."

"I know what this is about," Mia said.

They all looked at her.

"What?" Billy asked.

"Dogs have been going missing all through this area. I've seen posters at the mall and on lampposts. I saw a poster for a missing Labrador. Most people think coyotes are killing dogs and dragging them off. Coyotes might kill an 80-pound Lab but they won't drag it off where it can't be found."

Billy nodded. "I'll take care of it. Soledad, Mia, if you walk the dogs, you stay within the gates. We have security here. Mickey, you inform the gatehouse to watch out for the van."

They all nodded. No one was going to disagree with Billy Dogs.

Billy and Mickey retired to Billy's den. "Call Phoenix, get our contact in the DMV to run those plates. I want this *arruso* real bad."

By the next day Mickey had the name and address of the driver of the van. "Lingley, Frederick Lingley. He lives between St. David and Tombstone."

"He comes a long way to steal dogs," Billy said. "Probably got too hot for him south of here."

"Why the hell does he steal dogs?"

Billy shook his head with disgust. "So his Pit Bulls can practice killing other dogs before matches."

"A big dog like a Lab?"

"Labs aren't fighting dogs," Billy explained. "A Pit Bull could take one down and kill it. They begin training on little dogs like Pepper."

"What's the plan, Boss?" Mickey asked.

"We get to know Mr. Lingley. We show interest in his dog and take it from there. Tomorrow we go back to the park and hope he's there. Otherwise we'll have to track him down." Billy began to tell Mickey their cover story.

By six the next morning Billy and Mickey were in the park, where Lingley showed up, walking his dog. His hand was bandaged and he was limping slightly.

"Hey," Billy called out. "Good-looking dog. American Pit Bull Terrier?"

Lingley pulled up and eyed Billy and Mickey with suspicion. Most people gave him a wide berth. He was big and bearded, with a shaved head and prison tats on his bare arms.

"Yeah, so what?" He looked Billy over. A gray-haired geezer of middle height. Healthy looking, but still a geezer. Mickey, on the other hand, was formidable and even bigger than he was.

"I had a dog like that back in Brooklyn. A big brindle and white dog. He went 60 pounds of pure muscle. Best damn Pit Bull I ever owned. His name was Caesar. Shit, I doubt there was a dog on the East Coast could have taken him. Great animal."

"Yeah?" Lingley asked. "What happened to him?"

"The damn Humane Society and the cops."

"Took him?"

"Yeah, then they put him down. Said he was a menace. Hell, that dog was good with kids. I let him play with my grandchildren, he never harmed them." He turned to Mickey. "Ain't that right, Mick?"

"Sure is, Uncle Bill."

"People get the wrong impression about Pit Bulls," Fred Lingley said, more relaxed now, and bending over to pet his dog.

"They do," Billy agreed. "By the way, my name's Bill DaCosta. This here's my nephew, Mickey." Billy stuck out his hand. Fred Lingley hesitated for a moment and then took it.

"I'm retired. I was in the tire business back in Brooklyn." It was true that Billy was in the tire business, but DaCosta was his wife's maiden name.

"Fred Lingley, I'm from Tombstone."

"The town too tough to die," Mickey said, shaking hands with Lingley.

"As long as the suckers keep coming looking for the ghost of Johnny Ringo or the Clantons."

"What brings you up our way?" Billy asked innocently.

"I'm visiting my brother in Tucson, but I thought walking the dog up here would be cooler. I got to take care of this boy." Lingley gave his dog an affectionate pat.

Billy nodded and bent to pet the dog. "Careful – Seven don't take to strangers."

"Seven?" Billy asked, as he scratched the dog under the chin and got a tail wag for his effort.

"Yeah. I just give them numbers."

"You got seven dogs?" Mickey asked.

"Twelve, but Seven here is a champ." He looked at Billy and his dog. Billy was petting the dog and the dog was wagging his tail. "I can't believe he took to you like that. He's usually wary of strangers."

"I got a way with dogs. I'd like to get another Pit Bull. This one for sale?"

"Not Seven. But I got a littermate of his, a real comer, I call him Ten. I could let you have him for two grand."

"I'm from Brooklyn, not East Podunk. Before I shell out two large for a dog, I'd have to see him in action."

Lingley laughed. "There's a match tomorrow at my place, 8 p.m. I'll put Ten in the ring against any dog, except Seven. You can see him fight. If you like what you see you can buy him. And if you don't like him, there will be a dozen other handlers and breeders there. You could check out their dogs. But I damn near guarantee Ten will whup any dog there. Or, I have one puppy left out of a litter, male, about ten weeks old. He comes from top bloodlines. I was thinking of keeping him, but I can see you love dogs. So if you like the pup you can have him for the same price as Ten – two grand."

"Sounds good, but I can't make it tomorrow," Billy said. "When's the next match?"

Lingley rubbed his head and said. "Monday, if you're serious."

"As serious as a heart attack," Billy replied. "Tell me what time and how to get there. Even if I don't buy, it'll be good to see a match."

"We start letting spectators in about 7:30 in the evening. Matches start around eight. and here's how you get there . . ."

"How did you know so much about Pit Bulls, Boss?" Mickey asked after they had returned home.

"When I was a kid, my Ma rescued a Pit Bull. His name was Caesar. She told me about the business of fighting dogs. You should have seen her break up the matches. We had adopted dogs all over the house. Nobody gave us any trouble – Ma was a tough cookie and my old man was a capo."

"Lingley seem to be genuinely fond of his dog," Mickey said, wondering. "And he was willing to sell you a puppy, because he saw you were a dog lover."

"He probably loves his dogs, but it's a perverted love. He and the rest of the pit fighting community are all perverts. We're going to take him down and anyone else that's involved."

"We're going to need a big crew. That's cowboy country down there and I'll bet most of them are armed," Mickey cautioned.

"Yeah, that's why I want you to go down and scope the place out."

Mickey nodded. He had been a Marine in Desert Storm and reconnaissance was his game. "I'll go tonight and look it over. Then I'll watch what happens at the match tomorrow night."

"I'm going to call Fatass in Vegas," Billy said. "I'll give him a list of guys I want. And he can get the equipment we need."

"Tell Fatass to get Moe Skillion," Mickey said. "He was an Army Ranger."

"Good choice," Billy said.

Sunday afternoon, Billy's recreation room was crowded with people. Fatass Goldberg had brought down a six-man crew: Frank Almy, Charlie Gibbs, Alberto Santos, Peter Lasala, Lou Macheca, and Moe Skillion.

As he shook hands all around, Billy said, "I'll give you the set-up and if anyone wants out, they get a grand and they can leave. Take the job and I'll pay you each five grand plus expenses."

When Billy finished, he asked, "Any questions or who wants out?"

No one wanted out, but Moe Skillion asked, "How about the layout?"

Billy turned to Mickey.

Mickey walked over to the pool table, where he had set up little cardboard cutouts as a makeshift topographical map. "Just south of where highway 80 meets highway 82, there's this little dirt road to the left. A mile and three quarters down that road is a turnoff for Lingley's ranch. You cross a cattle guard and come to a gate. The gate is manned by two guards who won't let you in unless your name is on a list. The ranch buildings are about a quarter of a mile up the road, over a little hill and around a bend. So you can't see the gate from the buildings."

"The dog handlers began to arrive around six, no later then 6:30. The spectators aren't let in until 7:30 and they wander around looking at the dogs. Betting goes on the whole time. About eight, they begin to gather in the barn here," Mickey said pointing to a cardboard shape. "I got in early and climbed into the hay loft and saw it all. I wanted to puke." Mickey looked up, waiting for anyone to challenge him. The men knew Mickey's reputation and said nothing.

Mickey continued. "There are bleachers around a pit. The dogs are brought in and fight until one is defeated or is killed or the owner pulls his dog. Back here behind the barn are the kennels. It's a surprisingly clean cinderblock building with runs behind it. Earlier, I saw Lingley working a dog. The dog was dragging tires around the yard. Then he brought out a small dog, maybe a Poodle, tossed it in with the Pit Bull, and in less than a minute the little dog was dead. The Pit Bull had ripped it up."

Mickey looked around the table, as did Billy.

"Ah," said Peter Lasala. "I bought my daughter a little Poodle. I want these guys."

The others nodded.

Lou Macheca asked, "How soon do we take these assholes down?"

"Tomorrow night," Billy answered. "Fatass will get two vans and he's got guns for all of us."

"Uzis. They're small, pack a lot of firepower, and these are untraceable," Fatass said.

"Good," Billy said. "Pete, you and Frank take over the main gate. Your job will be to let the dog handlers in and keep the spectators out. Frank, you need to come up with disguises, so the spectators won't be able to identify you later."

"My specialty. I got something in mind," Frank Almy replied.

"Fatass and Alberto will drive the vans. Moe, I want you and Mickey to enter the ranch from the other side. Mickey knows a way in."

Moe Skillion smiled. "I guess I can work with a jarhead."

Mickey gave him the finger but smiled too.

"Remember, these guys are not pushovers," Billy said. "They're tough, ex-cons, bikers, ranchers and most are armed. We need to hit them hard and fast."

They went over the plan several times before they broke up.

Billy Dogs called Carolee to cancel their Monday morning tryst. He needed all his energy for the raid.

"I can't believe you're not coming over, Billy. That's two weeks in a row. Why don't you forget next week too?"

"Carolee, honey, I've got business. I'll make it up to you."

"A trip to Vegas, and not some joint where you're connected. I want the Bellagio, a suite."

"Anything," Billy agreed, but mentally gritted his teeth.

"Next week, I'll take off from work," Carolee triumphed.

Billy Dogs hung up the phone and under his breath, said, "Shit!"

The crew showed up on time and went over the plan for a final time. Frank Almy and Pete Lasala were wearing straw Stetsons, old denim jeans, shirts and jackets. They wore large wrap-around sunglasses and beards and wigs that looked real. Pete's was red and Frank's was dirty blond with a streak of white.

"Good disguises," Billy said.

"My wife was a hairdresser," Frank said. "You should see the stuff she's done for me when I hit banks."

They got into the vans and headed east on Interstate 10, and then south on Arizona 80. Mickey, in the lead van, signaled the turn-off to the county road that led to Lingley's ranch.

Mickey and Moe got out and made their way cross-country.

The vans pulled off the road and into a clump of cottonwoods and waited. Soon Billy's phone rang. "Boss?" Mickey said. "The gate guards are in position."

Billy nodded to Fatass and the vans drove down the road to the ranch gate. He gave the guards his name. "I see your name on the list, but who's this other guy?" one of the guards asked.

Fatass got out of the driver's side and walked up to the other guard. "I'm invited," he said.

"By who?" the guard demanded.

"By him," Fatass answered, pointing to Billy Dogs. The guard turned to look and Fatass smacked him across the throat.

The other guard turned and yelled, "Hey," and reached for his pistol. But before he could draw, Billy shot him in the head with one round from his Uzi. Fatass dispatched his guard as well. Both bodies were thrown into the back of the lead van.

Frank and Pete took up their stations at the gate.

"Remember, only let dog handlers in. Turn everyone else away. Tell them the match has been canceled. If they ask why, tell them you heard the Humane Society was going to make a raid," Billy said. "That should scare them away."

"Got it," Pete Lasala said. Frank Almy nodded.

They drove the vans over the little hill and parked on the side, behind some brush.

Pete called and warned Billy that the first handlers were coming through. By 6:30 he called again to say that all handlers on the list had passed through.

"Any trouble?" Billy asked.

"No, a couple of guys asked where Stan and Howie were. We told them they were off tonight and that we were filling in."

"Good. Now keep everyone else out."

"Shouldn't be a problem. No spectators are here yet, so

they didn't see any handlers go through. Gotta go, here comes a pick-up."

They waited for Mickey's call and when it came, Billy called his crew together. "We're going in. Stick to the plan. Fatass and I in the first van, Charlie, Lou, and Alberto in the second van."

Dog handlers were taking their crates into the barn as the two vans came roaring into the yard. Mickey and Moe came from behind the kennel with guns drawn. One of the dog men went for his pistol and Mickey cut him down with a short burst.

Billy's crew piled out of the vans and began herding the handlers into the barn.

Lingley went for his sidearm, but Billy Dogs smashed him across the face with his Uzi, breaking Lingley's nose.

"What the hell!" Lingley howled, as Billy kicked him into the barn. There were 14 dog handlers in all, including Lingley and a couple of his hands. The dead gate guards and the guy Mickey had shot were dragged into the barn and tossed into the pit.

Mickey had taken charge inside, disarming those who were carrying. He had forced them into the pit, as Billy's crew stood around the bleachers pointing their machine pistols at the men.

"What's this about?" Lingley whined through a broken nose. "I thought you were a dog man."

"I am, you *figlio di puttana.* I love dogs," Billy spat.

"I love dogs too," Lingley said.

"You're all a bunch of sadistic sons-of-bitches. You love dogs. Do you think that by pitting them against one another that you love them? Do you think that by feeding someone's pet to your dogs, you love dogs? Don't bother trying to answer, I'll tell you what you love. You love to get your rocks off while your dog mauls another dog. You think that that makes you tough, that makes you a man? You ain't shit."

"What are you going to do?" one of the men asked.

"One at a time, I want you to bring your dogs back to the kennel and put them in the runs with food and water."

When the dogs were kenneled, and all the handlers were back in the pit, Billy gave his orders. "Fight, fight until you can't stand anymore, fight." They stood around looking at one another until Billy fired a burst over their heads. "Fight!"

Fourteen men began to slug it out. Ten minutes later, four were still standing but barely, including Fred Lingley.

"Now you know how the dogs feel," Billy said.

"What are you going to do?" Lingley panted.

"What any lover of dogs would do when his dog is too beat to go on."

"You'll go to Hell for this," Lingley swore. Then he pleaded, "Don't do it."

For the next week, the papers were full of stories about "The Tombstone Massacre." The Cochise County Sheriff's department, answering an anonymous tip, found 17 dead men in a dog-fighting pit on the Lingley ranch just north of Tombstone. They had been beaten and then shot to death with automatic weapons.

They also found a number of fighting dogs, ten dogs of various breeds and a mound out behind the barn. When the mound was excavated, the authorities discovered the carcasses of dead dogs buried and covered with lime to keep the coyotes away.

A number of the pit dogs had to be destroyed, but the Southern Arizona Humane Society felt that at least five of the dogs could be rehabilitated.

Billy gave Carolee a new diamond and ruby bracelet, and a brindle and white American Pit Bull Terrier pup, which he named Little Caesar. But he didn't get off so easily. It wasn't exactly Hell, but a week in Vegas for Billy was damn close.

The Newspaper

Tim Wohlforth

It was seven a.m. when I trudged out of my house on Cedar Avenue in Oakland, California, determined to find a newspaper. Just moved into the place and the paper delivery hadn't begun. And I had to know. The radio had said Barry Bonds hit two home runs last night. I needed the details. Read a blow-by-blow description. Savor the historic significance of the event as I sipped my coffee. I faced a three-block hike to a newspaper vending machine. Well worth it.

A cool crisp spring morning. The walk would do me good. Get to know the neighborhood. Force myself to leave the house. Been hiding out there, avoiding friends, ever since my wife and I split up. Not quite up to people yet.

Cedar Avenue was peaceful at that hour. Lined with small one-story cottages, neat fenced-in lawns, flower gardens. I passed a holly tree filled with chirping blackbirds. A pale-orange tiger cat with chewed-up ears scurried out from under a parked car. A little unreal. Like a set for a mid-fifties movie.

I took my time. Nothing to do that day. I had been laid off the preceding week. Was expecting it. The company started cutting and I knew I'd end up on the lay-off list. Not that I don't do a damned good job. I'm just not good at the politics of it. Never say a word in meetings unless called on. Refuse to mumble the latest company mantra. Invisible.

Good severance package. I was months away from needing to worry. All the more reason to pick up a paper and spend the morning reading.

I passed a gray stucco house with peeling paint. It stood out among the modestly comfortable houses around it. The lawn was a wheat field, the flower garden a patch of weeds. A rusted fence secured the decrepit place from possible predators. Bars on the windows, like its inhabitants were under siege. A misfit of a house.

I felt drawn to the place. Was I also a misfit in this neighborhood? In three months would I look like the house? Need a haircut? New clothes? The place was unnaturally silent. No birds, no cat, not even a squirrel. Was the property occupied? Probably not.

I caught a spot of yellow in the matted grass. Plastic bag. I knew it contained the *San Francisco Chronicle.* Just sitting there. No one around to mind if I borrowed the paper, read the sports page, and then returned the package an hour later. Borrowing isn't stealing. Save a three-block walk. I salivated as I thought of the *Chronicle's* Sports Green resting inside that wrapper, wasted, unread. Just a few feet away.

I reached over the spiked fence. No luck. The yellow bag was two feet beyond my grasp. To hell with it. Pulled myself together and walked past the iron gate to the property. I stopped. I was drawn back to the gate as if the paper contained some powerful magnet and I was made of iron. I stood in front of the place and checked out the windows. No sign of life. I stared at the bag. Did I expect that under my gaze the paper would levitate and be drawn to me? I gave in to temptation and pushed open the gate.

I walked up the path of cracked cement slabs a few feet and reached the paper. I leaned over and grabbed it. A wailing siren blasted away from somewhere deep inside the house. The damned gate was wired to an alarm with a delay. I froze for a moment trying to decide whether to drop the paper and run or just run. I turned toward the sidewalk. Too late. I was spotted.

A woman came out the front door, holding a shotgun, pointed directly at me. Short, platinum blonde hair, full red lips, pink bathrobe with fuzzy white trim. She wore nothing underneath the robe. Cleavage to challenge Mt. Rushmore. A thirty-year-old Dolly Parton.

"You steal a paper every morning?" she asked, laughter in

her voice. Redneck accent. "Can't afford the twenty-five cents?"

"It's not like it looks."

"Trespassing, stealing," she said. "That's what I see."

"I was just going to borrow the paper to check out the Sports Page."

"Where I come from, people ask first before they borrow."

"I was headed up to the door," I said. "To ask."

"That why I found you turning to go out through the gate? You make a lousy liar."

She had me there. She was right. I really stunk as a liar. That's how Judy and I broke up. Every time she asked me what I was thinking, I stupidly told her the truth. And she asked a hell of a lot. No marriage could survive so much truth-telling.

"You going to call the cops?"

She started to laugh. Loud, crude. Her body shook. A breast popped out from under her bathrobe, exposing a nipple. I looked. How could I not? She saw my eyes and covered herself up. Very slowly. She lowered the shotgun.

"Why don't you come on in and we'll talk about it? Bring the paper. I'll fix us some coffee while you read."

Well, why not, I asked myself. This lady was definitely not my type. But she had two things going for her. She had a figure to die for. Her other attraction was in my hand. Legal possession of a newspaper containing a blow-by-blow account of Barry Bonds' two homers.

"I'm Jimma-Lee," she said, as she poured water into a stained Mr. Coffee machine.

I could see the outline of a shapely posterior pressed snuggly against the robe. She wiggled as she worked, humming a country tune to herself. The sink was piled high with dirty dishes. Yellowed wallpaper, that once pictured roses, was stained with decaying food waste by the sink and grease behind the old chipped-enamel stove. Her shotgun lay on the counter next to the sink.

"I'm George," I said.

"Well, Georgey, you just read that paper I've lent you. I'll take care of everything else."

I did just that. I got so involved in the sports section that, for a moment, I forgot where I was. I felt a nudge by my left hand. A cup of coffee. I looked up. Jimma-Lee hung over me, bathrobe now wide open. I dropped my paper.

God I wanted that woman. Lips. Breasts. Thighs. To be inside her. I didn't think. I could only react. Ache for her.

"You stay just where you are, Georgey, honey." She knew she had me. "I said I'd take care of everything."

She loosened her robe and lowered herself into my lap. I buried my face in her voluptuous breasts.

"Jimma-Lee, you horny bitch," a voice called out from behind her, "get offen him."

She pulled herself up.

"You could knock, you know," she said.

I looked into the hostile gaze of a massive man. Shaved head, small beady eyes, wide shoulders, muscular arms. Red plaid shirt, greasy jeans. He held a large package, wrapped in brown paper. He glowered at me.

I couldn't think of a damn word to say. All I ever really wanted was a glance at the sports page. Wouldn't fly as an explanation. When he barged in, I wasn't reading.

He turned from me in disdain and stared at Jimma-Lee.

"I'll knock the shit out of you," he said to her.

He dropped his package on the floor and rushed toward her. He hit her in the face with his massive hairy fist, before I could even get out of my chair. She fell to the floor, blood pouring out of her nose and mouth. He kicked her with his heavy cowboy boots. Then he jumped on top of her, hitting, smashing, bashing away with his fists. She shrieked in pain. Jimma-Lee would die if I didn't stop him.

I threw myself on him. With one powerful sweep of his massive arm, he flung me across the room. He was just too damned strong.

The shotgun. I ran to the counter and picked it up. I swung around and faced him.

"Leave her be," I said, "or I'll shoot you."

He stood up, hands bloody from beating on Jimma-Lee, and faced me.

"No, you won't," he said. "You haven't got it in you. Give me the gun."

He walked toward me, bloody, hairy hands extended. Jimma-Lee quivered behind him, bruises covering her body, moaning from pain. No woman deserved such treatment.

"Stop," I said.

He kept walking. I saw murder in his eyes. Once he had finished off Jimma-Lee, I would be next.

I fired.

Jimma-Lee returned from the bathroom. She had washed her face, put antiseptic and bandages on her wounds. Added a touch of make-up in a futile effort to bring life back into her face. Still looked like shit. A huge black and blue mark that make-up couldn't hide covered the left side of her face. She winced as she hobbled toward me. Yet a surprisingly cheery grin. She was a survivor.

"Who was that guy?" I asked.

"A friend."

"Didn't seem very friendly."

"He won't be missed."

"I'm calling the cops," I said.

"You crazy?"

"I shot him in self defense and to protect you."

"He had no gun. You expect the cops to believe you?"

"You are my witness."

"Wait a minute, Georgey Boy," Jimma-Lee said. "Don't expect me to hang around here until the cops come. They stick my name in that computer of theirs, and I'm in deep shit. You call, I go."

"So what am I going to do?"

"Don't worry. I'll help you. We'll dump the body. We can come back here. Clean up a bit." She paused and smiled. "Then we finish off what we were doing before we were so rudely interrupted."

Jimma-Lee had lost all her sex appeal. A murder before nine in the morning can do that to you. And I didn't trust her. But what was I going to do? Without her as a witness, I would have a hell of a time convincing the cops it was self-defense. Her plan did make some sense.

She sensed my hesitation.

"Remember you killed him, not me."

"Where do we dump him?" I asked.

"Up in the hills off Skyline Drive. We'll find a quiet spot and drop him in a gully. My car's outside."

Jimma-Lee drove her BMW up Snake to Skyline. We had wrapped the body in an old tarp she had found in the garage. She stressed the importance of not getting her new car bloodied up. He was a heavy bastard. But Jimma-Lee proved to be quite strong. The whole project didn't phase her. The kind of lady who expects the worst to happen and is rarely disappointed.

"Where'd you get this car?" I asked.

"Like it?"

"Must have cost a fortune."

"I have a piggy bank," she said. "You keep on stealin' papers in the morning and in time you, too, can afford a new car."

"A lot of quarters."

We drove on in silence, except for her humming. Rather mellifluous. Jimma-Lee didn't need a car radio. Made me think she grew up in a shack in the hills somewhere out of electricity's reach.

The redwood houses along Skyline used roofs as parking areas and clung precariously to the down side of the hill. We turned a corner and came to a deserted stretch. No houses. Eucalyptus trees enshrouded the street, blocking out the sun.

"Perfect," I said.

Jimma-Lee pulled the BMW over to the side of the road. We got out of the car and walked to the rear. She pushed a button on her key chain and the trunk popped open. I glanced up and down the road. No one. But someone would come. We had to act swiftly.

"Now," I said.

She grabbed the feet and I his shoulders. We lifted the massive mound of deadweight muscle out of the trunk. I heard a car coming. Fast.

"Quick," she said.

We heaved the body down the embankment. A Mercedes convertible sped around the corner. It swerved to miss us, but blessedly didn't stop.

"Let's get the hell out of here," I said.

"Not so fast. You better go down there and cover him up with branches."

I looked down the embankment. She was right. The body lay in plain sight. The tarp had torn loose during the fall. But it sure in hell looked steep.

"Okay, but you keep watch."

"You can count on Jimma-Lee."

Not very reassuring. But I had no choice. I started my descent. Slowly. Trying to hold on to little bushes and an occasional bared root to keep from falling. Useless. I started to slide. Faster and faster. Tumbling over and over. I landed right on top of the corpse.

I looked up the steep slope. Jimma-Lee was on a cell phone. Who the hell was she calling at a time like this? Then she disappeared from view. Damn it. I had to get back up there.

I brushed myself off and set to work as fast as I could. I covered the body with dead eucalyptus leaves and branches. The dirtiest damned trees. Constantly dropping leaves and old branches. A disaster when fire struck the hills. But handy for my purposes.

I started my ascent, moving slowly, digging each foot sidewise into the dirt. Like I was wearing skis and making my way in soft snow. I lost my balance and slid right back down onto the body. No way would I make it straight up. I decided to crawl up on my hands and knees zigzagging in switchbacks as I went. Worked. But slow. So damned slow.

Fifteen minutes later I crawled, exhausted, onto the level roadbed. I looked around. No car. No Jimma-Lee.

Shit.

Jimma-Lee was determined to screw me, one way or another. I preferred the other way. I hadn't quite figured her out. She could have walked out of that house on Cedar Avenue. Instead she talked me into carting the corpse up here in the woods, dumping it. Then she dumped me. There was something more involved. She was a blonde, but not a dumb one. She had a plan. And I knew I would be its victim.

I couldn't waste time trying to figure her out while I stood fifty very steep feet from a corpse. Had to get as far away as possible. I started to hoof it down the road. I was a good hiker and knew, in time, I could walk the seven miles or so back to my house. Maybe Jimma-Lee would be waiting for me down the street in the house where it all started. Somehow, I felt that was unlikely.

I reached the stretch of the road with houses. No one about. Was there ever anyone about? I figured the inhabitants were either on their hidden redwood decks enjoying fabulous views or already in San Francisco on Montgomery Street earning the monthly house payment.

I heard the motor of a car coming around the bend in the road. An Oakland black and white police car cruised slowly toward me. Shit. I looked down and continued to walk. Like I was on an innocent morning stroll. The cop car stopped. A young black officer stuck his head out the window. Thin. Earnest looking.

"Where you headed?"

"For a walk."

"You live around here?"

"Down the hill a bit."

"Where?"

"Cedar Avenue."

"That's more than a bit. Hop on in the back. You can help me check out a ravine up ahead. I'm Officer Edward McCoy. You are?"

"George Kiernan. I'm new to the area."

"Just happened to wander up here?"

"Something like that."

I climbed into the back as directed. Hard, molded-plastic seat. No handles on the door. Thick glass partition, reinforced with wire. A shotgun was strapped into a holder next to McCoy in the front seat. Didn't bring back pleasant memories. I heard a click. I was as effectively locked in as if I was in a cell.

He started the engine and drove me back to the deserted portion of the road. Shit. They had me now. Goddamn Jimma-Lee. She must have used her cell phone to call the cops. And gave them a description of me to boot. There was no way I could lie myself out of this one. And, as Jimma-Lee had noted, lying was not my forte. But I intended to give lying another try. The truth defied credulity.

The patrol car slowed to a crawl. Then stopped. McCoy had spotted the mound I had made. Wouldn't have, except he knew what to look for. He called in for back-up and a forensic team. He came around and opened the back door for me. This time he held a police revolver in his hand.

"Take a look."

He continued to talk in a friendly, matter-of-fact manner. Why not? He was in charge. And he had me dead to rights.

"I don't see anything."

"That mound. Those marks on the side of the hill where somebody recently crawled back on up."

"What's that got to do with me?"

"We received a call from a woman who claimed to have passed by this very spot. She saw a man, looking very much like you, drag a body out of the back of a new black Mercedes convertible and roll it down that slope. Then the man headed down the embankment. She figured to cover up the body."

"Where's the car?"

"Good question. Give us the name of your accomplice and I assure you I will do my best to find the guy."

"It wasn't a guy. It was the woman who phoned you. And the car wasn't a Mercedes convertible. A BMW sedan."

"You better explain."

I told him the whole story. He didn't believe a word of it.

I sat in a drab dirty-green interview room in the Alameda County Superior Courthouse on Lake Merritt. Robyn Steiner, from the Public Defender's office, sat across from me. Perhaps thirty, curly blonde hair, tailored striped gray pants suit. Thin, pretty. Certainly seemed competent. I had just finished telling her my story. The same one I had told McCoy and then repeated to two detectives from Oakland's homicide squad.

"I read your signed statement," she said. "You were aware you could have refused to say anything without the presence of an attorney?"

"I know. But I wouldn't have said anything different. It is the truth."

She looked at me for awhile, without speaking. A weary look. Too weary for such a young woman. How many tales had she heard? How many of them were lies? Was there any belief left in her?

"George, I am afraid that you, like most people, think the justice system is concerned with truth." She spoke as a tired mom would address her young son. "It concerns itself with what can be proved. Evidence. Witnesses. Testimony. The noble end, of course, we all work toward is the truth. Blind, impartial truth. Evidence, however, is the means. It rules. Truth, hopefully, is discovered as we travel down the evidentiary trail."

"So you say what really happened doesn't matter?"

"What matters to the judge and jury is what we can prove to have happened. So far you are doing rather poorly when it comes to evidence. Consider that famous statue of Justice holding a scale. On one tray sits the county's case composed of virtually all the evidence. On the other tray we have this statement of yours. Do I need to tell you how the scale is tipped?"

"What does the prosecution have?"

"They searched the gray house. Covered with the victim's blood. A footprint of yours in the blood. The shotgun has your prints on it. No sign that anyone other than the victim lived in the house. No woman's clothing, cosmetics. Nothing. Someone had gone over all surfaces and wiped them clean of fingerprints. The crime scene people found the brown-paper wrapping of a package on the kitchen floor. Like the package you said you saw in his hand. Traces of cocaine. The victim's name is Frank Carbone. Well-known hood with several past drug-related arrests."

Now I understood why Jimma-Lee wanted me stranded up

on that hill. So she could get back to the house, clear out any signs she had been there, and take off with the cocaine. I would be charged with Carbone's death and she would be able to make her payments on her BMW. Also, the alarm on the gate and bars on the windows. All to protect drugs stashed within.

"Any sign of Jimma-Lee?"

"None. They don't list felons by first name and you didn't have a last name. You didn't have the tag number of the BMW. None of the neighbors had seen anyone outside of Carbone go in or out of that house."

"So what am I to do?"

"The DA offers you a lesser plea if you come up with your partner and the cocaine."

"So you don't believe my story."

"I'm only a messenger when it comes to the plea. The problem is that without the name of the accomplice the DA is not willing to plea at all."

"So what will happen in court?"

"The prosecution will make the case I outlined above. I will put you on the stand to tell your story. That lap dancing business is not going to go over too well with the jury."

"Then what?"

"The jury will surely vote to convict you. The DA's going for the death penalty. Unless, of course, you come across with the accomplice and the stash."

Who was she working for? Me? Or the District Attorney? She seemed determined for me to make a deal.

"I'm telling the truth."

"I'll try for life in prison," she said.

If only I was guilty.

Truth or Lie

Jack Bludis

I finished the easy part of the job in less than six hours, and I didn't need a gun.

"You look positively stunning," said Patrone, the elderly effete who owned *Silk and Lace,* a Fifth Avenue boutique that specialized in lingerie that reminded me of *Frederick's of Hollywood.*

It was 1973, and both on and off my P.I. working hours, I often wore shirts with huge flower or jungle prints, but so did most other men. The wide, creased-to-the-floor, pink trousers and ruffled pink shirt were too extreme for me in both color and style. I preferred my trousers with a modest flare at the cuffs, and my shirts without ruffles.

"When they go into the dressing rooms, you are to count the garments going in and again when they come out. If there is a discrepancy, you let me know and *I* will decided what to do," Patrone said.

I thought he was paying too big a fee for the upscale Klass Investigative Services until I saw that there wasn't a single piece of intimate silk or lace in the store that cost less than fifty bucks.

"Yes, sir," I said. I think he liked the "sir," because he giggled when I said it.

During the morning there was rarely more than one customer in the store. After noon, there were rarely fewer than a half-dozen.

A tall, dark woman, with big sunglasses, and a bright green

babushka moved slowly along one of the counters, inspecting bras and panties and occasionally stuffing one inside her large shoulder bag.

I stayed far away from her until she started for the door. By the time she stepped outside, I was immediately behind her, and I took her arm.

"Would you step back into the store please?"

"Of course, I won't. Who the hell are you?"

"Then I'll hold you right here for a policeman."

She glanced up and down Fifth Avenue. Then her whole body went limp. Her "OK" barely came out with her breath. As I led her through the store to Mr. Patrone's office, I knew that I had seen her someplace.

"Would you explain what this is all about?" she said to Patrone who sat behind his large desk. Two "real" salespeople ran the store while we talked.

"So it's you again," Patrone said.

"Yes. It's me again," she said, raising her chin. "I'm sure we can work something out . . . again."

"You'll *not* get off so easy this time, Ms. Holloway."

That was it. She was Jenny Holloway, an actress and a long-time panelist on the syndicated game show, *Truth or Lie.* She was wearing a dark wig.

"I was just coming back to pay for my items, when this *young man* prevented me from getting into the store."

I was twenty-nine, and I think "young man" was intended to insult me.

"I don't think you were," Patrone said. "Please put your bag on my desk and be seated. We'll wait for the police before we look inside."

"I'll pay for these right now."

"Leave them in your bag."

"I'll sue you from under everything you own."

"The line shan't work, Ms. Holloway. Not this time."

She looked at me. "Are you his lover?"

"I'm a private investigator working for the Klass Agency."

"I know Kate Klass. I'll have your job for this."

I didn't think Kate would fire me, but I decided not to be confrontational.

After almost a half-hour of questioning by Patrone, two

uniformed cops came in. They put *me* through a third degree before they even started to talk to Ms. Holloway. By the time they excused me, they still hadn't even looked in her bag. They were treating her like a celebrity rather than a shoplifter.

She looked better than she did on TV. She looked younger too, and that surprised me.

The next morning when I climbed the stairs to the Klass offices on West 72nd near West End Avenue, I wondered if she had run on hard times. She was still on *Truth or Lie,* but I hadn't seen her in a movie in years, and I didn't think she was doing plays on Broadway anymore.

Kate Klass, a tall blonde in her mid-thirties, looked down her nose through her new contact lenses. She did a great job of making up her model-like face, but she was a bit too voluptuous to be on the cover of a woman's magazine. *Playboy,* maybe. *Penthouse,* definitely.

"You weren't smoking anything were you?" She wasn't talking about cigarettes.

"No, and I wasn't doing anything else illegal, immoral or stupid." I hadn't been working as a P.I. very long, and I had already done at least one each of those things, but not this time.

"You have to keep your head clear about what happened. TV news says Patrone was murdered in his store last night," she said.

"You're sure?"

"And his advance bounced. He had more money than God, but only God suspected that he kept it in his safe until he was murdered. I didn't worry about our fee until I learned that he was dead."

"How was he killed?"

"They didn't say, but that's over. Hold on." She reached into her middle drawer and took out a manila folder. "I've got another divorce case for you."

"That's it? He's dead? Forget it and do another divorce?"

"We can chat about it over coffee sometime. You know by now that this work is not like you see on TV. Trying to track down his cash would cost more than we'd get out of it, and we'd be lucky to get a 'thank you' even if we found out who killed him."

She was right, of course.

I closed out the Patrone file and did some preliminary work on the new case. I still had time to kill, so I called down to Midtown North and got shuffled to a clerk who mumbled his name.

"No arrest of anybody named Holloway," he said.

"Phelps and Corregan were the arresting officers."

After more paper shuffling, he said, "Only three shoplifting arrests. None by these guys. Maybe they turned it in this morning. I'll check it out. Can I have your name?"

I gave my name and phone number. I went in to see Kate and told her about my call to Midtown North.

"Why waste the time?"

"Don't you think it's peculiar that Patrone was killed and there's no arrest record of the shoplifting? He felt pretty strongly about arresting her."

"You're not thinking we've got murder over a little shoplifting, are you?"

"That's what I was thinking."

"I told you when I hired you that a lot of paranoia goes with the job. Coincidences happen."

I didn't like it, but I decided to forget about it. It wasn't easy to do, because one of the tabloids had a front page photo of Patrone lying dead in front of his safe with blood all over the place. The article said he was killed around six, just after the store closed.

I touched bases with Midtown North the next morning and learned that Corregan and Phelps had finally reported the shoplifting. I told Kate.

"Told you," she said.

I was working the new divorce surveillance when Phelps, the younger of the arresting officers, stopped me in front of a bar on Sixth Avenue near the park.

"I want you to know that me and my partner had nothing

to do with Mr. Patrone's death," he said.

"OK." Apparently, they made the association too.

"Ms. Holloway bought us off, all of us. Patrone too. They told me you work for the Klass Agency, and I could trust you with that."

It was an unusual admission, but I guess being suspected of murder was worse. "Who's they?"

He hesitated. "Corregan."

I was self-righteous about a lot of things in those days, including cops taking bribes, but the young cop got to me with the innocence of his plea. If he had been tough about it, I might have been tough back, but it wasn't worth the trouble.

"Want do you want me to do?" I said.

"Just be quiet about it, I guess."

"It might be a good idea for you and your partner to talk to Homicide."

"But –"

"You could get dragged in a lot worse if you don't."

He thought about it. "Maybe you're right. I'll talk to Corregan." The senior partner always had the last word.

I saw my new subject leaving *Murphy's, Near the Park,* and I asked Phelps to excuse me.

"This is important," he said.

"So is this. You won't get any trouble out of me, but think about what I said."

I wasn't crazy about dropping the whole shoplifting business, but it was either that or go to war with the NYPD, which would probably embarrass Kate and cost me the job with the agency.

My new subject, wearing tweed, was walking down Sixth Avenue with a painted redhead. He wore that shitty grin and he had a bounce in his step that happens with a lot of guys when they know they're going to get laid. I followed them into the New Grand National across from the New York Hilton. One of them must have been registered, because they went straight to the elevator and to the fifteenth floor.

I waited in the hallway outside their room for almost an hour. They didn't come out, and that was plenty to go to court with, especially with the other observations I had made in the last two days. I reported to Kate from a pay phone in the lobby. I also told her about my conversation with the young cop.

"Hmmm."

"What do you mean, 'Hmmm?' That doesn't sound good."

"It's OK," she said.

"You have to do better than that."

"Come to my office in the morning," she said.

I told the secretary that Kate wanted to see me, and she said that two detectives were in with her.

I wrote the divorce report in longhand, and had just given it to the typist when Kate called me inside. She introduced me to Detectives Haven and Marsh. Both were tall. Haven was near retirement age, but he was better looking than Marsh, who tried to make up for drab with a Fu Manchu mustache.

"They'd like to talk to you privately. Use one of the interview rooms," Kate said.

I led the way to the room, but Haven took a seat at the empty desk as if he owned the place. He gestured for Marsh and me to sit in the client chairs.

"So you were you working *Silk and Lace* on Monday? Did you make any kind of arrest?" Haven said.

From the next chair, Marsh eyeballed me as if he thought he could read something in my facial expressions. I didn't know what Kate had told them, but I chose not to lie.

"I held somebody for a couple of uniformed guys, Corregan and Phelps."

"Yeah, that was it. It was a late report. They say you detained a black female at approximated 2:30 p.m."

Not talking was one thing, but telling a lie was something else. "Not a black female. A white female, blonde."

"Told you," Marsh said.

"The report says that the woman in question was one Jane Holloway, East 136th, the Bronx. The patrolmen say Patrone had second thoughts, and they never booked her."

"I wasn't there when they let her go."

"But she wasn't black?"

"She was dark with a dark wig. She was a blonde underneath."

"What did you do, look under her skirt?" Marsh snorted.

Now was the time to tell them that I recognized her as Jenny Holloway, but stupidity still had me, and I didn't mention it.

"Do you have a key to *Silk and Lace?*"

"Why should I?"

"You shouldn't."

"Did you see anything unusual when you were there?"

"Like?"

"Somebody who didn't belong? Anything."

"There were a couple of other people working, but I don't know 'em. I was the only one who didn't belong."

"That ought to be enough," Haven said. "You got any questions," he asked Marsh.

"You think the uniforms pulled some kind of shit?" Marsh said, and he stroked down his mustache with his finger and thumb.

I shrugged. "Why?"

"No reason."

After the detectives left, I went to my desk to work on my expenses, but I kept thinking about Jenny Holloway and the two cops. They would have finished their business with Patrone long before the six-o'clock closing. The whole thing gnawed at me, and I finally went to Kate and told her about it.

"When they didn't make a harder follow-up on the discrepancy about the shoplifter, I smelled a cover-up," I said.

"The street cops were covering up shoplifting, not murder. The NYPD does *not* cover up murder," she said.

Her mountain of experience was real, but I didn't know how far she would go to protect her agency from getting into a conflict with the police. I gave her an oral report on the divorce case, and she went into the critique.

"You went up on the elevator with them?"

"It was the only way I could find out where they were going."

"But –"

"I know. If I didn't find anything, I would've been useless for the rest of the case – but you could have turned it over to somebody else. That's the advantage we have over a one-man shop. You told me that when you hired me."

"You broke the rules."

"And I closed the case. Someplace in your manual, it says 'be resourceful.'"

"Don't be smug. We're not out of the woods on this Patrone thing." She was as concerned about it as I was. She just wasn't saying it.

She didn't have any new case to give me, but I hung around the office the rest of the day. In the middle of the afternoon, I received another call.

"Devoe, this is Officer Corregan. I hope you are going to back us up on our story."

"I think you might all have a problem," I said, and I told him about my meeting with the two detectives.

"This is just too screwed up!"

"It sure is. You shouldn't have said she was black. Do you think Ms. Holloway has something to do with the murder?"

Slight pause. "Nah, she left before we did."

"So you're gonna keep covering?"

"We didn't know the faggot was going to get himself choked and pureed."

"What do you mean 'choked?'"

"He was choked with a silk scarf, then he was bludgeoned with something in the office, that fancy lamp I think."

"Miss Holloway wore a babushka. Could she have –"

"Hers was green. The one that did it was red."

"Why did you lie about who you arrested?"

A slight pause. "We didn't arrest anybody. We just made a report . . . I don't have to talk to you about this."

"Phelps says she bribed all three of you to keep her name out of the papers. Now that he's dead, Homicide is likely to want to find out about her. You can't keep it quiet. How much did she give you?"

He paused for a few seconds. "She gave Patrone a thousand

bucks. Me and Phelps she gave five-hundred each."

"What do you do if Ms. Holloway decides to talk to Homicide?"

"They got no way to connect it with her."

"And what about the other employees in the store."

"Patrone told us how cool you were getting her into his office. They never even saw her. Look, Devoe, do you want some money out of this?"

"Don't insult me. How did she pay you?"

"Cash."

"How'd you get it?"

"I walked her to the bank and back. What is this, a third degree?"

"The best thing you and your partner can do is tell Homicide what happened, and –"

"No thanks. The more people who get in on this thing, the more chance I get to lose my pension."

"And the more chances somebody has of taking on a murder rap. You're in this too deep to keep lying."

"We gotta get together on this thing."

"*We* don't gotta do nothing. You and Phelps get together. I'm out of that part of it."

"You didn't tell 'em it was Jenny Holloway?"

"No."

"So you lied, too. Look, nobody hears about this, you got it?"

"I got it," I said, but I was steamed.

I was being dragged in so far that I might have to think about kissing my P.I. career goodbye, and it was probably too late to get back my old job on Wall Street. I told Kate that I hadn't told the plain-clothes guys about Jenny Holloway.

"Shit!" she said. It was the first time I had heard her utter that one.

"You didn't either?"

"We'd better come up with something quick," she said. "If there's one bunch of cops we can't piss off, it's Midtown North." Our office was not in that particular precinct, but a lot of our work was.

"We don't do murder investigations unless we're working for an accused or we're otherwise contracted to do so," I said, virtually quoting from the agency manual.

"Or we have to cover our asses," Kate said. She was quoting an addendum she had never put in print.

I understood her point. Telling the truth might be the only way out, but I had an idea. "I should talk to Ms. Holloway."

I picked up Kate's phone and reached Jenny Holloway's answering service.

"Tell her it's a matter of lingerie," I said, and I gave the agency phone number, along with my extension.

"Don't get the agency mixed up in it," Kate said after I hung up.

"Aren't *we* already mixed up in it?"

"You're good, Devoe, but you're a lot of trouble, and you take a lot of chances."

"I might take another one," I said, and I told her what I was going to do.

"If you screw up –"

"Like I said, I'm taking a chance."

By the time I reached my desk, Ms. Holloway was already calling me back, and that answered the first of my questions.

"What's so urgent?" she said.

"I just want to straighten some things out."

"What kind of things?"

"Stories, yours and mine – and the police."

There was a pause. "Uh . . . come to my place at seven."

Holding me off until seven gave me another answer.

Jenny Holloway's sexy, "come in" was a lot different from her, "Who the hell are you" of a few days ago.

She was dressed in a flowing pink gown with darker colors showing through at interesting places. After she closed the door behind us, she led me to a living room with Persian rugs and upholstered chairs with spindly legs. She gestured me to the sofa.

"You do know that Patrone was murdered," I said.

"Patrone?"

"Don't play stupid, Ms. Holloway. If you didn't know what this was about, you wouldn't have let me come here."

"I suppose you're right."

When I sat, she sat close beside me. She wasn't heavy, but the sofa didn't look like it would support even my 180 pounds.

"Cigarette?" she said.

"I don't smoke."

I could smell the burnt-hay aroma of marijuana in her hair and gown, but she chose not to offer me any of her grass. Instead, she asked if I would like something to drink.

"No, thanks."

"What *would* you like to have?" she said, going back to the sexy tone and leaning toward me.

"I want to know who killed Patrone."

"I had nothing to do with it."

"Maybe not, but you bribed him and the two arresting officers, and that *will* come out."

"No."

"I'm afraid so. If Homicide clears up the murder, there's a good chance they'll learn that you were the shoplifter."

"I don't care about the murder. How much do you want to keep quiet about my arrest?"

"This is not a shakedown, Ms. Holloway."

She rose and started down the hall, passing two open doors on her way to another bedroom, and I followed her.

"What did Patrone do with your money?" I said.

"What do you mean?" She stopped before she reached the bedroom and turned toward me.

"The young officer told me about the bribes," I said.

"That dumb bastard was supposed to keep it quite."

"Murder loosens a lot of tongues."

She was sullen, then sexy. "What would it take to *tighten* your tongue?"

"How much did you get from Patrone's safe?"

"Mr. Devoe . . ."

She stepped toward me, put her arms under mine, and laced her fingers behind my back. She pressed forward and arched away. I was showing a certain interest that she couldn't miss in that position.

"I have a career," she said. "And you know what will happen if the public, you know, if they learn about my shoplifting problem."

She moved her breasts against my chest to see if I was carrying, which I was, but not in a shoulder holster.

"Can't you tell them you were wrong about the identity?" she said.

"How much was in Patrone's safe?"

"When he opened it, I didn't see inside."

"Why did he open it in front of you?"

"To put my money in . . . Mr. Devoe, please." She looked at me for a moment and tried to bring her lips to mine. I would love to have been free to join in her exploration, but there was too much at stake.

I arched away. "How much did you and Corregan get?"

"Ohhhhh," she said, and she moved her whole body against me.

"That's enough," Corregan said from behind me.

I knew she had chosen seven o'clock to make sure that he arrived before I did. I had expected him to try to jump me when I went into the bedroom at the end of the hall, but he surprised me by coming from a different room. He pointed a .38 at me.

"You spoil everything," she said.

"Get away from him, and put some clothes on," he told her. "Keep your hands over your head," he said to me.

Jenny hesitated and smiled, but I saw the fear that said she would like to be out of this as much as I would. She didn't trust Corregan, but she had to play his game. She went into the bedroom at the end of the hall.

"You're not going to kill me here, and if you think I'm going to walk through the lobby like a good little hostage, you've another think coming."

"There are other alternatives," he said.

He was right. He could kill us both.

"Who choked him? You or her?"

"I ain't talking to you."

"How much did you get from the safe?"

"*Shut* up."

If I told him that Kate knew where I was, he would think it was a ploy, but it was just as well that I didn't, because he was figuring me for far dumber than he was.

With the revolver in one hand, he patted my chest. When he couldn't find a shoulder holster, he told me to turn around. As I did, I came down with my right elbows on his neck, and hit nerves that caused his knees to buckle. He dropped the pistol without firing it.

I came up with my left fist and hit him in the side of the head. I hit with my right under his chin. He spit out a piece of his tongue along with a spray of blood. I came down with my fists knotted and hit him at the back of his neck. He fell forward, and I stepped out of the way and let him hit the floor. By that time, Jenny Holloway had picked up the gun and was pointing it at me.

She was barefoot in flare jeans and no top, and her fingers were shaking.

"Give me that," I said.

"No."

"What are you going to do if you accidentally kill me? Dye your hair? Wait tables? Maybe you can find a whore house where they take –"

"I didn't know Corregan was going to rob Patrone and kill him. Then he blackmailed me about it. I just wanted to get out of the . . ."

I would have let her talk, but she just trailed off, figuring that I wouldn't believe her anyway.

"How about Phelps, the other officer?"

"He just took the bribe. Corregan and I came back at closing after he checked. He knocked on the door, and Patrone was happy to let him in, but he was surprised when I came in too."

I reached out for the gun.

"I, he, I can't lose that show," she said.

It was too late now, and she knew it. Whether she served time was problematic.

"I didn't know he was going to –"

If I were a cop and she wasn't holding the gun, I would have read her rights long before now. She kept talking, bouncing between truth and lie and even she didn't know what was which.

Corregan was up on all fours now.

"If you don't give me the gun. He's going to be your boss

forever," I said.

"No," she said.

I slapped the gun to the floor, and picked it up. Corregan was looking up at me, still dazed.

"He didn't tell me he was going to rob the safe."

"Then why did you go back?"

"He said he would make sure that Patrone didn't tell. I told him that he never told before and there was no reason –"

"But you went back anyway."

"He convinced me."

"Huh?" Corregan said.

I stepped away from both of them toward the telephone that hung on the wall in the kitchen. I dialed, but before I was connected, someone banged at the door.

"Whatever's going on in there, it's over," Haven shouted.

I went to the door and unlocked it. I handed him the gun as soon as he stepped inside. Marsh was with him.

"He tried to kill us," Corregan said from all fours in the hallway.

"No," Jenny said.

"Put something on," Haven said.

She covered her breasts and hurried back to the bedroom.

"He jumped me," Corregan said.

"Yeah, I know," Haven said. I was sure Kate told him what I was doing.

"I didn't have anything to do with the . . . with anything," he said.

"You have a right to remain silent . . . ," Haven began.

The more I learned about the murder, the more I believed that Jenny Holloway had little to do with it. She was surprised when Corregan carried out his plan, and when she saw what he did to Patrone, she was afraid of him.

The DA's office never charged her, and she and Phelps testified against Corregan. The case ended in a plea bargain two days into the trial. By that time, Jenny Holloway was dumped from the syndicated game show where she lied for a living.

"I heard she's going to be on a new ABC soap," I said, as I sat with Kate at one of the polished mahogany tables at *The Top of the Sixes.* It was just after Corregan's trial, but we were celebrating a more lucrative victory on another case.

"You think she was innocently dragged into the whole thing, don't you?" Kate said.

"Sort of."

"Have you seen her since then?"

"Of course not."

"You're going to learn about women one of these days."

"I hope."

"But you may be more trouble than you're worth."

She might be right about that, but I was getting the hang of the job.

The Tower House

James S. Dorr

Anton eased his steel gray Thunderbird past the big house with its single, stone tower, a shortcut he took from work. But this time was different. He'd often imagined the house a castle, the people in it a king and queen with – he'd spotted them once through its diamond-paned window – two princess daughters. Its normally manicured lawn, though withered now in the heat of a long July, a palace courtyard. But this time he'd learned that its owner was evil.

Rich people had whims, in their own ways like kings who once had ordered their knights out on quests, but, in this modern age, whims that, instead, destroyed people like Anton. That ordered "reductions in force" without notice – that caused him to be fired. So, as he pulled over for one last look at this house he had loved, this rich king's castle that brought back memories of stories of heroes he'd read in high school, he saw a stone and, on his own whim, hefted it.

William Tarninger's wife had just turned when the stone crashed through their living room window.

"Martha, are you all right?" Tarninger shouted. Seeing her nod, he peered out the window and saw the younger man disappearing into a gray, white-topped convertible.

Martha was trembling. "I-I was just looking out at the lawn, thinking how dry it was, and then . . . then it almost *hit* me.

I didn't really see who threw it . . ."

"I did, Martha." He put his arm around her shoulders. "Not his face, but I saw enough as he was running away." He knew the car from the lot at the factory where he worked too, but in a safe vice-president's job.

And he had connections.

The T-bird was Anton's one source of real pride. When he'd left the Marines, and all he could find stateside was a near-minimum wage factory job, he'd used what he'd saved of his overseas pay to buy it, beat up, from a used car lot. He'd then put whatever else he could scrape up into restoring it, having it painted metallic gray – the color of Medieval knights' armor – until it stood, shiny and clean, in the street outside his apartment now, his trusty battle steed. Except that its top was torn.

He didn't think of the tower house yet, not until he'd unlocked the car's door. There in the front seat, thrust in through its slashed top, he saw the stone he had found the day before.

He put the stone in the glove compartment and turned on the engine, relieved to find no other damage. He drove to the city's public library, checking the reference room's street directory, finding out the name of the man who owned the house. From there he went to census data, then to a directory of prominent citizens, building a dossier:

Tarninger, William, manufacturing executive, Korean War veteran, two-term state senator, voted against state job training bill; wife, Martha, amateur painter, active in club work; one daughter, Carol, in an exclusive college for women; another, Daphne – he liked the name Daphne, a name for a princess, reminding him of his own girlfriend's name, Diane – poetry published in small magazines, just finishing high school.

He made up his mind. The daughters would be tainted, but the queen, Martha, was not of the king's blood. She might be okay. He would write a letter offering her a chance to redeem her family's honor . . .

"Have you read this?" Martha screamed two days later, holding the letter out to her husband. Tarninger glanced through the handwritten script as Martha continued. "I think it's from that young man you said threw the stone through our window. Something about his car being damaged, and now it's *my* duty to pay for the repairs. As if I'd have anything to do . . ."

Tarninger shook his head, thrusting the letter into his pocket. Whoever this man was, he seemed to be clever. He'd figured out what he was supposed to – that the slashed car top had been repayment for the window – but somehow he'd also found out Martha's name. And, worse, he'd entirely missed the point, that the stone's return had been a warning to leave Tarninger and his family and house alone.

But two could play that game.

"Probably some nutcase," he finally said. "I'll make a few calls. Make sure he doesn't annoy us again."

Anton came back from job hunting to find two letters in his mailbox. The first was from his girlfriend Diane. It said that she could no longer see him. That she still loved him, but she understood he was in some kind of trouble. That two men had threatened her in an alley and roughed her up and told her to write him and warn him to leave town.

He lunged to the phone and dialed Diane's number. "Diane?" he shouted.

"This is Tomi, Diane's . . . uh . . . ex-roommate." The voice on the other end sounded frightened. "Who is this calling?"

"Look, do you know where she is?"

"She moved out yesterday. She . . . wait a minute. Is this Anton?"

"You're damn right it's Anton. I . . ."

He heard the click as Tomi hung up, then slammed his own phone down. Leave town, he thought. They'd already chased his girlfriend from him. He went to the refrigerator, cracked open a beer, then remembered the second letter and opened it. This one, an eviction notice, was from his landlord.

He finished his beer and had two more while he tried to think. If the king had gotten to his landlord too, there was nothing he *could* do but move. But not out of the city. He packed his suitcases, went down to his car and, relieved to find there was no *new* damage, he drove it to a body shop a friend of his worked at.

He too had friends. Not friends who would do something criminal for him. Not exactly. But friends who could get a new top for his car, and could have it repainted. A dull, flat black, like the armor knights errant wore. And other friends who made deliveries to houses even in rich people's neighborhoods. Who could put him up for a few days while they found out people's comings and goings.

"William, come here!" Martha shouted. "Carol – no Carol! You stay upstairs."

Tarninger came into the living room to find his wife cradling their younger daughter, just now returned from a poetry reading. He glanced at his watch – it was nearly midnight. He started to speak, but then saw Daphne's face.

He took a deep breath. "H-honey," he finally asked, "are you okay?"

"William – someone attacked our daughter," Martha said for her. She turned back to her sobbing daughter. "Daphne, it'll be all right. You can tell Poppa."

"Poppa, I . . . I was in the parking lot," Daphne stammered. "I'd just left the reading, when someone grabbed me. He forced me in his car – it was too dark to see his face. He didn't say anything, just drove around until he stopped, then pushed me out and . . . I still didn't get a chance to see his face . . . then drove some more until we got here and he pushed me out again . . ."

"Did he rape you, honey?"

"William!" Martha said.

Daphne was crying too hard to continue.

"Honey, remember this," Tarninger said, "that whatever happened we still love you. I'm going to make a couple of phone calls. First the police, then . . ."

"P-poppa, no!" Daphne stammered.

"She's right, William," Martha said. "They'll just ask a lot of questions. And if Daphne didn't even see who it was . . ."

"Okay, then there won't be any police. But I am going to call Dr. Boland. I'll arrange to have you stay a couple of days in the hospital – just in case – and then, when you feel better . . ."

"Y-yes, Poppa?"

"Then you'll join us in the mountains. Martha, I'm going to have to stay here a few days more to make some arrangements. I've got an idea who did this to Daphne – I'm going to make sure he never does *anything* like it again. But, in the meantime, I want you and Carol to pack tomorrow and go to our cabin, to start our vacation earlier than we'd planned. I'll have someone pick up Daphne's car and I'll drive it up to join you later, so, for tomorrow, you can use the Mercedes. You understand, Martha?"

The word was already out on the streets, that there was a man with a price on his head. But this was a man who drove a shiny gray car with a white top, not an all-black one. A clean-shaven man, not one who had grown a stubble of beard or, as soon as he'd heard of the contract, had gone to a drugstore and, later that night, dyed his hair. Nevertheless, he stayed inside until, the next afternoon, a friend called him.

The call was about two women who'd just been seen loading their suitcases into the back of a silver-blue Mercedes sedan.

At first he might have let this news go, but now he knew the queen was evil too. The letter he'd written had been to her alone, but then there had been the threat to Diane, and his eviction. And now the threat to his *own* life as well. It didn't matter – the battle was larger now. She had joined into it.

And it was to the death.

And so he got in his own car and drove, not to the tower house, but to an intersection he knew the women would pass on their way to the Interstate. When he had spotted them he took his time. He followed them all the way to their turnoff, and up the winding road into the hills.

He waited until the road was deserted – the sun long since down by now – the big Mercedes moving fast around a curve, when he gunned his engine. He started to pass, then braked and swerved into the larger car's fender. He nudged it just enough for the queen to lose control, just for a moment, to feel her right front wheel churning gravel as, hitting a soft spot, the car lurched and spun, then crashed through the guardrail and over the cliff beyond.

Tarninger received the phone call at five o'clock in the morning. It had taken that much time for the highway patrol to reach and identify the victims.

He put down the phone – picked it up again to make his own calls. Then put it down again. Daphne had been hurt – raped – bad enough that she'd still need psychiatric help when she left the hospital. Now Martha and Carol dead.

And he would be next.

He had that feeling. He'd had it before – back in Korea. A couple of phone calls could bring men to guard him, but, no, it was a personal fight now.

The last time he'd felt *that,* he'd gotten a medal.

But now – more phone calls. His lawyer, to make sure that Daphne would be okay. A friend who was a building contractor. The evening newspaper's ad department.

Anton saw the ad that afternoon when he glanced through the help wanted section: "Needed, a man to talk to about a torn car top. Apply in person."

He put on his old combat fatigues – a knight's modern armor – and called a gun-collector acquaintance.

He got in his car and drove to the castle.

He pulled into the driveway, leaving his car beneath the tower – no parking out on the street for him *this* time. He strode to the house, his boots crackling over the mulch-covered lawn, his shadow lengthened by the setting sun almost eclipsing the diamond-paned window.

"Tarninger!" He issued his challenge.

A window opened.

"Up here, Anton. In my wife's studio – upstairs, to the left."

He leveled his newly-obtained AK-47 – what passed for a lance these days – and fired a burst at the lock on the front door. He crouched and ran, shouldering through, then rolling to the side, firing another burst up the stairs – the king might have henchmen! Finally satisfied they were alone, he charged up the stairs himself, slapping a fresh clip into the rifle, not caring about the noise. Knowing the thick hedges outside would muffle it, that and the hedges the neighbors' homes had too, their windows shut tight, their air-conditioners turned on high to combat the evening's heat.

"This way, Anton! To left, down the hallway."

He followed the voice, more reckless now. Stalked into the darkened room it came from.

A sudden light flared and he saw a face, lit by the flame of a wooden match. A gaunt face, not fat as he had expected. A face with sad eyes.

"Would you care for a cigarette, Anton? We can still talk."

Anton shook his head. "If it was only about my car – but you took my job. You had your goons rough up Diane. You got me kicked out of my apartment – "

The older man grimaced. "What about Daphne? Or my wife and my other daughter? Not to mention I didn't have anything personally to do with your job. I think you have more to answer for than I do, Anton."

Tarninger lit his own cigarette, took one puff, and, just as Anton raised his rifle, *he dropped the match.*

Anton fired in that moment, as a pool of linseed oil burst into flame on the floor at his feet, then jumped back to see the fire spread to drapery-covered easels, accompanied now by sudden bright flashes. He knew what those flashes meant – from his own service. The igniting of fuses.

He ran to the stairs, not caring now whether the king was dead yet or not. Almost stumbling, outside and to the lawn – the lawn covered over with dry, straw mulch.

Just as a sudden crack of dynamite split the tower that his car was parked next to.

Caused stone to plummet.

Just as the battlement-hedges exploded, surrounding the house and yard in a ring of flame.

And, as he stood waiting with no place to go – imagining himself, finally, victorious, in the midst of the ruins of this fallen castle – the flames spread inward.

Happiness, or the Cash Equivalent

T. P. Keating

The sudden blast of winter sunshine must have dazzled the guy on the lemon-yellow bicycle, as he shot straight through the red light. He realized his mistake immediately, coming to a swift halt. Fortunately, no people or vehicles crossed his path, so he back-peddled to make good his minor misdemeanor (a rare occurrence for a cyclist). Then he leant his wiry frame on the handlebars, waiting for amber and green. But some days all you see is red.

A woman raced past me from the sidewalk and planted herself dead center in front of the cyclist, both her hands gripping the handlebars, her face thrust towards his for an eyeball to eyeball scenario. She was young and slim, with curly chestnut hair and attitude to burn. I stopped at the traffic island in the middle of the road to watch, half from professional habit as a private investigator, half from sheer curiosity.

"Hello, mister land-speed record, the rules apply to you too, you know?"

"Sorry, the sun blinded me."

"You call that watery stuff sunshine? It's been overcast for days." The traffic moved as the lights changed, but she held her ground. A black sedan honked behind the bicycle.

He shouted to be heard. "Look, I said I'm sorry for what happened. We all just want to get on with our lives, yeah?"

Several cars in the blocked lane joined in the honking.

She stepped aside and let him go, turning to watch him as he sped off. When the traffic came to a halt once more, she reached the opposite sidewalk and went left. I put it down to another example of temporary urban madness and focused on the working day ahead. My office is only three blocks down from my apartment, so my commute never alters. I found myself walking behind her for a few yards. Then she ducked into a tobacconist's while I carried on my way.

At the next intersection, I stepped into the road. Jerk! A cyclist ran straight into my side. Not that man and machine were going at any speed, and my bulk softened the blow. It was more annoyance than hurt.

"Hey, moron, where did you learn to ride, the demolition derby?" I barked out the charming words before I could think. I guess that's what they mean by road rage. No one is immune to the big city. He took my salvo without batting an eyelid.

"Sorry, I got distracted."

"It's you again."

"Excuse me?"

"You ran through a signal on red not five minutes ago."

The woman raced up to the bike once more, still fuming. She did the handlebar grab, eyeball to eyeball thing again.

"Hey, if it isn't Speedy Gonzalez. Well, *arriba-arriba* this." She made to throw a punch at him. Remembering that I'm supposed to be an upright citizen, I grabbed her wrist and restrained her.

"Lady, if you punch that cycle helmet, the only one who'll get hurt is you."

The cyclist carried out his escape maneuver in one fast-flowing motion. Using a convenient gap between cars, he span round 180 degrees, mounted the sidewalk and peddled off furiously, back the way he came. I let her go and we stood there like idiots while vehicle after vehicle roared by. When they stopped, we continued on our separate ways, her to the right on this occasion, me to the left.

"Hey mister, hey," a woman shouted from behind me. I turned to find the irate pedestrian. She'd become a semi-permanent fixture during these last 10 minutes.

"I'm not always so forthright," she said, forthrightly.

"Sure, okay."

"Like, how hard can it be to stop at red?"

"It's a sad sign of the times. Stab someone once, and you're praised for not stabbing them more often, or with a longer knife."

"Er, right," she added, with a look of uncertainty. Which I found a bit rich, really, considering that she'd started the conversation. That's when I caught a glimpse of him from the corner of my eye. A lemon-yellow blur that hurtled towards us on the sidewalk, like some foot-propelled bullet, tipped with a giant scowl.

"What the –" I began. Before we could move, he'd thrown two small objects at us. Orange and blue. I took the blue one on the side of the head, while the orange one hit her full square on the forehead. The water-filled balloons exploded on impact. He'd raced around the corner and disappeared.

"You're wet," she observed.

"Only on the outside," I replied, dryly. She didn't like my sense of humor. Well, I didn't like the direction my day had taken since she showed up.

"Mister, I . . ."

"Lady, enjoy the rest of your life." I turned on my heel and strode off at a brisk pace, determined to fill the remainder of the day with familiar P.I. routine. Ah, routine. So relaxing, so understandable, so, well, routine. How I regretted holding her hand back. Virtue is its own punishment.

If he'd gained satisfaction from his childish prank, then the ignorance he'd first been accused of was well deserved. Still, he did try to make good his original mistake. Mind you, running into me like that could hardly be called a mistake, even if my opinions were colored by personal involvement. But, how else are we to formulate personal opinions? With these distracting thoughts, I reached the lobby. I took the stairs in twos, unlocked my office door and, perhaps for the first time ever, positively beamed at the sight of several days' worth of paperwork that would keep me occupied, off the street and away from intersections. I changed into a spare jacket that I kept behind the door, and dabbed at the final drops of water on my shirt and tie. Then I blew some of the dust off my desk and rooted around for a pen.

Yeah, like it could continue for long. Towards mid-afternoon, my world intersected with hers once again. She wore large Jackie O. shades, but it couldn't be anybody else. I would've complained about her following me to work, though as I kept tabs on people professionally, I let it pass. She took the seat across the desk from mine, the sunshine through the slats of the venetian blind forming horizontal bands on her green wool pantsuit.

"Don't tell me, it's our Tour de France reject, isn't it?" She gave me a funny look. Make that, yet another funny look.

"He was a courier, apparently. A car knocked him down this morning and didn't stop."

"A case of poetic justice?"

"I don't read much poetry, but if you're as reckless as him on these streets of ours, how long are you gonna survive?" Point taken.

"Have the police interviewed you?"

"Not yet."

"And you are?"

"Samantha James. Miss."

"Do they call you Sam or Sammie?"

"No."

"Fair enough. When did you two split-up?" If I'd leant over and kissed those kissable glossy ruby lips, she couldn't have been more surprised. Or maybe not. "Sammie, you two had ex-lovers written all over you. Passionate and crazy, so crazy that it makes a kind of crazy sense. Don't get paranoid, it's my job, remember? That's why you came to me."

"Listen, when they start looking at his background, my name is bound to get mentioned. It's been kinda tough since we broke up, and I don't want to relive all that pain again. That's all. Find the driver of the car and give Nick some closure. That's Nick Blake."

It sounded plausible. But a small alarm bell always goes off when it sounds plausible. "So, how long ago did you break up?"

"About six weeks."

"Here's my list of fees." I slid the foolscap sheet towards her. "It's all printed clearly, no surprises. The retainer is quite competitive. Cash preferred. Checks to be made payable to

Malcolm Muir. M.U.I.R."

"That's okay, I know how to spell Malcolm." So, she possessed a sense of humor after all. We'd get along nicely, and nicely is all I need with a client. Alarm bell or not, when a gorgeous, tearful dame with an open checkbook needs me, who am I to turn down a case? She anticipated my next question.

"A friend who works for the police department said the car was a white Honda, perhaps with a sticker on the rear window. At least that narrows it down." Sure, like a grain of sand is easier to find on one beach, rather than ten.

"It narrows it down fine," I replied.

The beach turned out to be the entrance to the lot of Berry's Coffeehouse, a one-story, glass-fronted building. I strolled in and spoke to the few staff on duty. They confirmed the description of the car without adding any new details. No customers saw the collision. The street opposite the entrance contained a closed and partly demolished gas station, surrounded by a wire fence. Perhaps a few passers-by provided other witnesses, but I'd never find them.

With the tide out, I decided to make the best of it. Perhaps a jelly donut and a large coffee could help explain the matter. I took a plastic seat by the window and gazed idly at the busy street. A second coffee and donut might kick the brain into gear. I was willing to risk it for the sake of the investigation. One of the staff came over and handed me a small, brown envelope.

"Who's this from?"

"The guy driving that pickup out of the lot."

"Recognize him?"

"Nope."

Inside, on a sheet of paper, letters cut from several publications spelt a word, "amfetamines." Honestly, they don't teach them nothing at school nowadays. I made my way to Berry's payphone.

"I've heard all about the amphetamines, Sammie."

"Then you understand why I left him. I told him they'd do him no good in the end. Are you saying it's drug-related?"

"No, but I am saying that I need all the facts in order to investigate properly. Anything else you'd like to tell me?"

"You're doing a swell job." She hung up. I faced two possibilities. If the accident was genuine, case closed. If intentional, the driver may well need the services of an anonymous repair shop. My contact in the trade wasn't above the odd bit of moonlighting.

The phone didn't ring twice before getting picked up. I've seen slower pick ups in clip joints. As we weren't great types for small talk, we immediately got down to business.

"My auto shop buddies tell me that a white Honda with a rear window sticker turned up today."

"Needed work?" I asked.

"Major."

"Major, as in?"

"As in, it's now a piece of unrecognizable scrap metal." That ruled out the genuine accident theory. Someone hated Nick Blake enough to rub him out, no expense spared. Then spill the beans regarding his amphetamine addiction. Someone hated him real good.

"Was there anything actually wrong with it?"

"Yeah, the sticker." Paint-shop Bob paused.

"Would some greenbacks jog a faulty memory?"

"It's coming back to me. Yeah, a buddy of mine saw that it read 'Shortland's Zoo says Save the Whales'."

"I'm not paying you for that."

"You don't want me to start working for a rival, do you?"

"Your check's in the post." I hung up. Maybe I'd been too hasty, maybe there was a city zoo connection at the bottom of Nick's death. So Sammie would be funding my trip to the zoo. I've looked for information in a lot worse places. Coffee and donuts, you always do me proud. And I couldn't wait to see the penguins once more.

Shortland's Zoo has been here forever. It's not hard to imagine that it predates every city in the mid-west. Perhaps it even hides a few dinosaurs in a dark corner. My enquiries started at the main office. Sammie accompanied me. As she was paying, I could hardly say no.

Belinda Shortland runs the show now, according to the shiny brass nameplate on a Victorian-looking house at the heart of the zoo, surrounded by an acre or twelve of well-kept lawn. She was a slim, Victorian-looking lady in her mid-50s, with a sensible pale-yellow suit and short, gray-blonde hair. She couldn't spare more than a few minutes, which proved long enough to tell me that she didn't remember Nick Blake personally, although he did work in the aquarium complex.

"What did he do?" I asked.

"Couldn't say. Sorry, it's a big zoo," she said, with a shrug.

"Yeah, that's our city all right."

"Good luck with your investigation." She busied herself with a desk diary and I took the hint.

We made our way to the aquarium complex, a series of connected, concrete structures. Inside, the signs took us in front of a gift shop to the administrative offices. A sign hung on the locked door read Gone to feed the dolphins.

"I guess the employees double up on several duties," Sammie observed.

"To pinch a few cents from the running costs, no doubt."

We reached a sizeable indoor pool via a dimly lit arcade devoted to the jellyfish of the world. I selected places at the back of a bank of seats, with the show already in full, well-attended swing. Long, sleek, gray dolphins swam with great power, launching themselves majestically out of the water, through hoops, and showering the first rows when they splashed back down.

"Can I put a third jelly donut on expenses?" I asked. Before she could reply, another brown envelope turned up.

"Hey dude, a man told me to give you this." With which the kid whizzed back outside. Another selection of cut and glued letters formed a kind of sentence, "amfetamines meat outside shark display now." The writer had strained his lone brain cell today.

"Sammie, you'd best stay here. Tell me how the rest of the show goes." I made a swift exit.

The doors to the shark display were closed, while the large anteroom had the same faint lighting I'd encountered before. Then giant TV screens flickered into life. The walls of the anteroom were covered in them. An image of a swimming shark spread itself over most of a wall, before circling me. Very disconcerting. A man joined me, dressed all in black, with a black fedora that hid his face.

"Thanks for showing, Mister Muir."

"What do you know about the late Nick Blake?"

"That he was no amphetamine junkie. As far as I'm aware, he never touched the stuff."

"What's the zoo angle?"

"Did you enjoy the dolphin display?"

"Yeah, very educational. What of it?"

"The show takes a lot out of the dolphins, but they always put on a good display."

I made the connection. The dolphins received the amphetamines to maintain their performance rate. To maintain their ability to generate income, to put it bluntly. This wasn't a zoo, this was a circus. A killer whale replaced the shark.

"Nick worked with the dolphins?"

"No, he worked with a bunch of rats. They hired him as a courier. One day he found out what he was transporting. Perhaps he got nosy or a package broke. Whatever. He didn't like what he found."

"So he threatened to go to the authorities?"

"You've got the picture."

The TV screens flickered out, footsteps retreated and a door closed nearby. A pity, I didn't manage to recommend night school to him. So, I'd have to play rat catcher all by myself – business as usual, in fact. I retraced my steps to the administrative offices.

The locked door didn't hinder me for long. Beyond it lay a narrow corridor with two doors on each side. I didn't bother with picking any more locks, out of consideration for Belinda Shortland and the gun pointed decidedly at me. Her reaction to my entrance proved astonishingly swift. She held her gun hand less than steady, and her eyes never stopped moving.

"When did you get addicted to amphetamines?" I asked, softly.

"I'm not addicted, I only use them for . . . hey, none of your business, snoop. Put your hands on your head." She backed into a door, which opened behind her, giving me room to pass. "Now keep walking, nice and slow." I stepped into a larger space, which the light from the corridor barely illuminated. Water lapped gently beyond view, and the bare floor felt wet.

"What now, Belinda? I swim with the sharks?"

"You'll be dead before you hit the water, snoop." Enough with the snoop already. "Keep walking." I took baby steps. "Walk, I told you." She fired the gun.

Somewhere not too far in front of me, a sudden frenzy of motion disturbed the water. A crash came from behind. I turned to find two figures engaged in a bitter struggle on the floor.

"Malcolm!"

"Sammie, you're full of surprises."

"Malcolm quick, can you . . . arrgh, that's my bra strap, you bitch." Two silhouettes full of venom, they traded punches with only a grunted accompaniment. A gun came sliding across the wet tiles to my shoes.

They separated, scrambling to their feet, then the slug-fest continued. I needed greater visibility. Cautiously, I took a path around the combatants to the corridor. The wall on the left held a panel of switches, some in the up position, some down. I flicked one down. The corridor fell into darkness. Great.

"Muir you fool," one of the ladies shouted, but she probably expressed an opinion they both held. I'd kept my finger on the switch, so I flipped it back up, then flipped up several more.

Loud jazz filled the aquarium. A trumpet launched on a soaring solo over the pounding waves of drums. A large sign above the pool announced "Sharks" in flashing red neon. By the intermittent glow I saw her plummet into the water. The body sank immediately beneath the churning surface.

"You okay, Sammie?" I held out my hand and hauled her back to her feet.

"I will be," she said with a tight smile. "I'm sorry I had to knock her out, but it got pretty vicious back there."

"Yeah, I know the feeling, it was you or her."

"For a gumshoe, you're plenty easy to follow."

More traditional indoor lighting replaced the neon sign, while the jazz stopped in mid-flight. Grateful to have my attention drawn from the reddening pool, we turned to face the corridor.

"My letter-gluing friend, I presume?" I asked of the fedora-wearing informant. He looked barely twenty.

"Travis Shortland, nephew of Belinda and soon-to-be rightful owner of the zoo. I owe you two big time."

"Just assure me that it'll be run without amphetamines," I said.

"Mister, you've got it," he promised.

Takeout

Stephen D. Rogers

"Gino's Pizza. Pick up or delivery?"

"Delivery."

"Go ahead."

"A large pizza with double pepperoni and anchovy."

"Large double pepperoni with anchovy. Anything else?"

"You got poppers?"

"Medium and large."

"Are they hot?"

"People have lived."

"I'll take a large."

"Anything else?"

"That's it. 48 Coburn Street, second floor apartment. Tell the driver to knock three times."

"Three times. That will be twenty minutes."

Nicky checked the note next to the telephone and dialed the number written there. "This is Nicky from Gino's Pizza. Some guy just ordered a double pepperoni with anchovies and a large popper."

"You got an address you got fifty bucks."

"48 Coburn Street. Apartment on the second floor."

"I'll swing by with your money later."

"I'm off at ten."

"Don't worry, you'll get the fifty." Thompson disconnected, grinned at the ease with which he'd found Marino.

You can change your name, alter your face, fake your shoe size but just try to stop hankering for your favorite food.

Only once had Thompson caught someone because the guy simply had to call the love of his life. Unique takeout orders were a whole 'nother story.

Thompson checked his gun as he walked out to his car.

Marino wasn't supposed to be dangerous but that too could change. Being on the run made some people only nervous, others down-right paranoid.

The one time Thompson had taken a bullet it was fired by an accountant who wouldn't hurt a fly. He could cook the books but he couldn't bring himself to eat meat. After hiding for seventeen days in a motel room he sported a tremor that would have put a junkie to shame but he still had the ability to call for an order of Five-Flavored Tofu.

And fire a gun when Thompson came through the door.

Leaving the past where it belonged, Thompson checked the mirror and pulled out into traffic. The key to success was focusing on the job at hand.

Marino.

Coburn Street was about fifteen minutes away in a neighborhood of large houses that had been cut up into tiny tenant-at-will apartments. Ten years from now people with too much optimism would buy the properties and renovate to turn a profit. Then the cycle would begin all over again.

Everything was patterns, endlessly repeated. Understanding that was what allowed Thompson to find people when they wanted to remain hid.

Marino was no different than any of the others. He might have been a small-time hood who tried to think big but he still couldn't escape being himself.

All it took was a simple telephone call to every pizza place within fifty miles. Marino hadn't even left town.

Thompson would relay the message, pay off the pizza guy, and print the final bill for his client. Maybe he'd even get a good night's sleep for a change.

Turning left onto Coburn, Thompson slowed to look for house numbers. There ought to be a law that numbers had to be visible from the street. And if there was a law it ought to be enforced.

There was three seventeen.

Thompson accelerated again.

Some of the houses were already looking fixed up. Maybe it would only be five years before this street became a hot address.

Three kids were bouncing a ball off cement stairs, stepping out of his way to let him pass.

Thompson caught another number in the two hundreds.

His client wanted Marino to meet him on public, neutral ground. While Thompson couldn't be certain he was only facilitating conversation instead of setting up a hit, the case would be closed by the time anything happened and Thompson would be working something else.

A gray cat ran in front of his car.

One twenty-seven.

Thompson stopped, waited for a van to finish backing out of the driveway. The vehicle turned towards him, the high beams blasting his night vision before he had a chance to look away.

That was helpful.

Thompson pulled to the side of the road and closed his eyes. He counted to thirty before continuing down Coburn.

He passed eighty-seven.

Two houses down someone was sitting on a porch swing. When was the last time Thompson saw that?

A young girl was standing under a streetlight. Waiting for a friend? Looking for a friend?

Sixty-three.

Tomorrow was trash pickup.

Also recycling.

Fifty-two.

Thompson slowed.

There was forty-eight with lights on the second floor.

Thompson parked and rechecked his gun.

He could hear several televisions from the street, two people arguing from somewhere on the left. Even from this far away he could hear the pock, pock of the ball bouncing off the cement stairs.

After confirming the house number, Thompson started up to the second floor, resting his hand in the pocket that contained the gun. Gino's Pizza. Double pepperoni and anchovy. Stick a foot in the open door so he can say his piece.

A door slammed across the street. A telephone rang. Someone shouted at a dog.

Thompson knocked twice. "Gino's Pizza."

Marino shot him through the door, Thompson flying back and landing halfway down the stairs, tumbling down the rest.

He couldn't get his hand out of his pocket and the other couldn't stop him from falling, the pain from spreading.

He was dumped out onto the sidewalk. Dazed. His leg hurt.

His hand was covered in blood. His shirt.

Nicky was standing behind the counter, shooting the shit as Gino spun a pizza dough in the air, when he suddenly remembered the double pepperoni and anchovy. "Damn."

"What?" Gino sent up a cloud of flour.

"That P.I. who wanted us to watch for the special order. I forgot to tell him the guy said knock three times."

Gino shrugged. "Screw him if he can't take a joke."

"He still owes me fifty bucks."

"How many times I got to tell you to write down the orders?"

"Ahh, blow it out your ear."

Fender Bender

Simon Wood

Racing back to his car, Todd cursed the ATM. Why was there always a line when he was in a hurry? His job packing boxes wasn't much, but he didn't want to lose it by being late again. He hopped back into his car and crunched it into reverse. The Honda Accord was way overdue for an overhaul, although an overhaul wouldn't do much for its ancient transmission. It was toast. Half the time, he didn't know what gear he was selecting. The Accord stuttered in the parking stall.

"Get in there, damn it."

Gears snarled as Todd struggled to find a forward gear. He jumped off the clutch and the car leapt backwards, slamming into a Porsche Boxster's headlight.

"Shit," he muttered.

His antics had drawn quite a crowd and they'd all witnessed his screw-up. Nowhere to run, he thought. He found first gear without effort this time and eased the Accord forward to assess the extent of the damage.

Everyone had an opinion and had no problem telling him where he'd gone wrong and how much it was going to cost him. He crouched in front of the Porsche and picked at the broken headlight and buckled bumper. There was a couple hundred dollars of damage to the average car, but on the German exotic, he was looking at thousands. His car, the piece of shit that it was, didn't exhibit any signs of damage – just like Todd, who didn't exhibit any signs of insurance.

"Does anyone know who the owner is?" Todd asked.

No one did.

"You'll have to wait," someone suggested.

"I can't. I'm late for work."

"I don't think you have much choice," someone else said.

"I can't. I've been late twice this week already." Todd delved inside his car for a scrap of paper and a pen. "I'll leave a note."

He wrote: "People think I'm leaving you my contact and insurance details. I'm not. Sorry."

Todd folded up his note, wrote sorry on the outside and stuck it under the windshield wiper. He shrugged, hopped inside the Accord and raced off.

He felt guilty and sorry for shafting the Porsche driver, but at the same time, he was buzzing with the thrill of his lawlessness and his speedometer showed it. He was accelerating past forty-five on Telegraph. He took a deep breath and eased off on the gas.

In the scheme of things, what he'd done wasn't so bad. It was an accident and it was more likely the Porsche driver's insurance could afford the repairs than he could. Anyway, with a car like that, he thought, you're asking for trouble. Todd pulled into his employer's parking lot safe in the knowledge that the matter was over.

Todd liked to take Sunday mornings easy. He lounged in bed until ten then took a walk to the newsstand to pick up the Sunday paper. He wandered back through the apartment complex, pulling out the color supplement and flicking through the magazine, ignoring the front-page splash about some big drug bust. He took a different route back to his apartment and passed close to his assigned parking space. He slowed as he approached his car. At first, he'd thought his windows had steamed up overnight, but the weather had been too warm for that. As he closed, he realized he'd been way off. Every one of the Accord's windows had been smashed. All four tires had been slashed. He ran a hand over the scarred paintwork. A crowbar was buried up to its hilt in the front windshield, and a note was sticking out from under a wiper. He pulled it out and read it. "Guess who?" it said.

Todd didn't need to guess. He knew who had done the damage. It was the Porsche owner. Todd hadn't forgotten about the fender bender, but it had been days since it happened and he thought it was over, a stunt that would dissolve in his memory over time. Well, he just found out his stunt was insoluble.

He'd screwed it up this time. Someone must have taken down his license plate before he'd driven away. He was going to pay big for this one. He tugged out the crowbar and tossed it on the backseat through a glassless window.

Returning to his apartment, a thought dogged him. Someone may have taken down his license plate and reported him to the police or Porsche driver, but how did the Porsche driver know where he lived? He opened the door to his apartment.

"Mr. Todd Collins, I presume," the small man said, getting up from Todd's couch.

Two linebacker types, one black, the other Hispanic, flanked the small man. The small man seemed genial, but the linebackers looked ready to tear Todd's head off. He could have bolted, but judging by the bulges under the three men's jackets, he didn't expect to get far. He guessed he'd just met the owner of the Porsche.

"I'm Todd Collins." Todd stepped inside the apartment and closed the door.

"Do you know who I am?" the small man asked.

Todd went to say, "the Porsche owner," but he decided against it. He thought it best not to antagonize the situation any more than he had already. He shook his head, finding that his vocal chords had failed him.

"Good. That makes things simpler. It's probably not a good idea that you do. It's only important that I know who you are. Understand?"

Todd nodded.

"I bet you're wishing you'd left your insurance details now, aren't you?" the small man said.

"I can make up for it. I can pay."

The small man held up a hand and shook his head. "It's far too late for that." He looked Todd up and down. "Besides,

I doubt you could afford to pay. The damage is incidental. However, the consequences of your misdemeanor have been severe. Put the newspaper down."

Todd, confused at first, hesitated before doing as instructed. He placed the Sunday newspaper on the chipped coffee table. The small man separated the newspaper from the supplements and opened it out. He tapped the front page with the back of his hand.

"See what you've done."

Todd glanced at the headline.

Drug dealer busted during routine traffic stop

"The car you hit belongs to an employee of mine. Driving home the other night, he was pulled over for a busted headlight. The cops discovered two kilos of coke in his possession. He's in a lot of trouble and I'm minus an employee. Do you see now? Do you see what you've done and why it has led us to your door?"

"I'm sorry."

"That's not important."

"I didn't know."

"I wouldn't expect you to know. But I've lost a valuable employee who had a job to do. Now he can't do it. This is where you come in." The small man stabbed a finger in Todd's direction.

Todd's stomach twitched. He didn't like what was coming. He knew it was retribution for what he'd done, but it wasn't the kind he wanted. Points on his license and a fine he could accept. But the small man's kind of retribution filled Todd with dread.

"Me?" Todd stammered.

"Yes. You'll have to fill in."

The linebackers wrinkled their noses. They knew Todd wasn't the right man for the job and he agreed with them.

"What do you want me to do?"

The small man beamed. "That's the attitude. These two said I was making a mistake."

The linebackers frowned.

The small man dug in his pocket and threw a set of keys to Todd. Todd caught them and examined them.

"Those fit a black Jag. You'll find it outside Denko's

restaurant in the city. Bring it to me in Oakland."

"When?"

"Oh, I like you. I debated just beating the crap out of you, but I wanted to give you a chance to make up for your error and you've done that. You've assessed the situation and decided to stand by your mistake. I admire that." The small man stood and dropped a note on Todd's newspaper. "Bring the Jag to me tonight. Addresses are on the paper. See you at midnight."

The black linebacker brushed Todd aside to open the door. It was a petty gesture, but Todd wasn't going to tell him. Todd grabbed the small man's arm on his way out. The small man stared at Todd, his look piercing. Todd knew enough not touch him, but he didn't care. He knew what was being asked of him was illegal. He just needed to know how illegal.

"Will I find drugs in that car?" Todd demanded.

The linebackers stiffened. The small man nodded at his arm. Todd released his grasp.

"Unfortunately, you don't have a choice, Todd," the small man said, his tone barbed. "Be at the Oakland address at midnight."

Todd resorted to public transportation to get him into San Francisco, seeing as the linebackers had finished off the Accord. He was looking at a few thousand to replace the tires and windshield. It was cheaper to get another car.

A combination of BART, MUNI and good old-fashioned walking brought him out on the corner of Bush and Powell. Mid-block on Bush, Denko's was classy and unique for the city. It had its own parking lot. Strictly, it wasn't a parking lot. To the right of the restaurant was a dead end alley, which had been cordoned off to make a parking lot. Two valets protected it. They looked as if they were relations of the small man's linebackers. Obviously, the small man was making Todd work hard to make up for his screw up. It wasn't going to be easy, but it was doable.

He breezed on by the restaurant, counting his steps, then turned right at the next block onto Powell. He turned right at the next cross street and counted his steps again. When he counted eighty-seven, he stopped in front of a narrow apartment block, which looked squeezed by its neighbors. The door was locked, but there was a buzzer entry system. Todd pressed the first one his finger fell on.

"Yes," a woman answered.

"Pizza delivery," Todd said.

"We didn't order any pizza," she barked.

"Sorry, is this 7A?"

"No, 8A, moron."

"Sorry. Can you buzz me in?"

She growled and the door clicked.

Todd let himself in and bounded up the first flight of stairs. The good news, as he had hoped, was the landing window opened out onto the restaurant's alley parking lot. The bad news was that there were no fire escapes. They were all on the front of the building. He flicked the safety latches and slid the window open. Surprisingly, it opened with ease.

One of the valets trotted up the alley to collect a Range Rover. Todd waited until the SUV and owner were reunited, then he climbed onto the ledge and jumped out. He connected hard with the ground. Electricity crackled through his legs, intensifying in his groin. He bit back a scream and crumpled onto his knees. The valets didn't notice him. They were too busy hustling for tips. Todd crawled behind the nearest car to survey the lot.

Todd had a new problem. There were two black Jags in the parking lot, one an XK8, the other an S-type. The small man had told him to pick up a black Jag, but he hadn't told him the model or license number. He fumbled in his pocket for the keys. He aimed the remote in the direction of both cars and pressed the unlock button. The S-type chirped and blinked its lights. The valets whipped around at the noise. Todd burst out of the shadows, charging for the Jag. The valets did likewise. Todd was lucky on two counts. The valets were big, but not fast, and he was closer.

He reached the car first, dived in front of the wheel and gunned the engine, all before the valets were halfway to him. He cranked the steering and hit the gas. The Jag leapt forward, smearing its fender across the back of a Lincoln Navigator, setting off its alarm. The Jag bounced off another car before he gained control.

One of the valets raced back to the gates while the other blocked the alley with his body. He made himself wide by crouching and splaying out his arms. If they were playing chicken, Todd knew he had the upper hand and floored the gas.

"Time to jump, buddy," Todd said grinning.

Todd's grin slipped when he realized the second before he hit the guy that the guy wasn't going anywhere. He smashed into the windshield and disappeared over the roof.

The remaining valet had closed the gates, but hadn't locked them and Todd blasted them open. They slammed back against the side of the restaurant, busting its neon sign. Todd jumped on the brakes to prevent the Jag from slamming into the apartment block opposite. Traffic slithered to a screaming halt and he floored the gas pedal, fishtailing down the street and jumping the first red light he hit.

His heart out-revved the S-type. Neat adrenaline raced through his veins and sweat poured off him. Heading towards the Bay Bridge, his pipe wrench grip on the steering wheel softened and his foot eased off the gas.

He laughed. His panic and fear changed into exhilaration and excitement. His crime-fueled buzz was hard to deny. He liked being a criminal. It beat stacking boxes.

The drop off point was in Oakland's warehouse district, near the rejuvenated Jack London Square, except the address wasn't in the fancier end of the neighborhood. Todd pulled up in front of a whitewashed building that was in desperate need of a fresh coat. The building had an address, but no sign giving any clues as to its business.

Todd got out of the Jag and banged on the roll up door. Before he was finished banging, the door retracted. He hopped back into the S-type and drove the car in.

The warehouse's interior was in marginally better condition than the exterior, but was well lit. The place was barren, except for a scattered collection of Snap-On tool chests and half a dozen car lifts. Cars Todd couldn't afford occupied the lifts. The small man stood in the middle of the warehouse floor with the familiar linebackers and a few new friends. Todd parked and got out.

"Christ! What the hell have you been up to?" The small man examined the busted headlight and scarred paintwork. "Do you do this to all the cars you drive, or just mine?"

The roll up door closed with a bang. The noise echoed off the walls.

"It wasn't easy getting the car out. You didn't say anything about stealing it."

"I didn't say anything about smashing it up either. Or were you just trying to impress me?"

"Sorry." Todd didn't know what else to say.

The small man waved the issue aside. "Don't worry, I just wanted the car back. The condition is unimportant."

"Are we square? Can I go?" Todd sounded tired, more tired than he felt.

"Not yet." The small man patted Todd on the shoulder. "You're close. There's just one more thing before accounts are squared away. Reuben, give him the keys."

The Hispanic linebacker tossed a set of keys to Todd and he caught them.

"Those fit that Lexus over there. I want you to drive it to Dallas."

"Texas?"

"The one and only. Don't look so worried. This job is a lot easier than the last one. All you have to do is drop it off at Ruskin's. It's a dealership. Then you're done and our business is concluded."

"That's a good two day drive. I can't do that. I have a job."

The small man's irritation evaporated his grin. He yanked out a gun and jammed it in Todd's face. "You drive or you die. Your choice. You've cost me a lot of money and I think I've been damn charitable giving you this chance to redeem yourself. So what's it to be?" He snapped the safety off the pistol.

"Drive," Todd managed.

The preamble was over. A minute later, he was on the road, Texas bound. The euphoria he felt stealing the Jag seeped away with the boring drive ahead of him. The small man had really screwed him this time. He'd given him a schedule that meant no time to pack any clothes or leave a message. He hit the road as he was dressed. He couldn't blame the small man too much. If he'd done the right thing in the first place, he wouldn't be on I-580 now.

"You're a dumb, dumb man, Todd," he said to himself and turned the radio up.

At the Arizona state line, he slept in the car. Deep into New Mexico, as evening descended, his funk got to him. His stale breath cloyed at his nose and his BO was ripe. He'd washed up as best he could in a gas station restroom, but his clothes were rancid. He pulled off at the next town and raided the first Wal-Mart for a change of undershorts and a couple of T-shirts. He changed into his fresh clothes in a restroom, dumping the dirty ones in the trash. He crossed the Texas state line in good spirits and fresh smelling, although his stink seemed to have impregnated the Lexus' interior.

"Damn it," he groaned.

He hadn't seen them, not that he'd been keeping an eye out. He'd been playing it safe, keeping to the speed limit and using his turn signals. He was low level, not registering on anyone's radar. But the red and blue light bathing the Lexus' interior ended that pretense. He eased the sedan off I-40 and onto the shoulder.

The state troopers wandered up behind him, but only one came up to Todd. The other lagged at the rear of the Lexus, trying to look uninterested, examining the car's rear with some well-practiced flashlight work. Todd powered down the window.

"License and registration, please, sir." Traffic was light at that time of night and the trooper was easy to hear.

Todd delved in the glove box for the documentation. His mouth went dry. A nickel-plated .357 rested on top of registration documents. He whipped the document out and slammed the glove box shut before the trooper could see anything.

The trooper took the documents and Todd's driver's license. He gave them careful consideration.

"Is this your vehicle?"

"No, I'm just delivering it."

"Where to?"

"Ruskin's in Dallas. It's a dealership."

"And where's it coming from?"

Todd didn't have an answer. He hadn't thought to check what the registration documentation said. Sweat appeared on his forehead and under his arms. "Another dealership," he ventured.

"Then where are your dealership tags?"

"I don't know. It's my first job. I didn't know I needed them."

The trooper didn't look impressed. "Well, you do."

"Oh." Todd tried to sound as innocent as he could.

The trooper handed the documents back. Todd leaned across for the glove box when a thought struck him. They hadn't told him why they'd pulled him over. A dry click echoed in his ear as he popped the glove box and the .357 fell out.

"Don't move a muscle, son," the trooper said and pressed his gun into the back of Todd's head. Gun drawn, the trooper's partner opened the passenger door and snatched up the fallen .357. "Nice and easy now, climb out of the vehicle."

Todd did as he was told and, without being asked, interlaced his fingers behind his head. The trooper escorted him to the front of the Lexus and cuffed him, while the trooper's partner searched the car. A couple of passing vehicles slowed to get a better look at the theatrics.

"Why are you carrying a concealed weapon?"

"I didn't know I was."

"Do you have a license for the weapon?"

"Lyle," the trooper's partner called. "You'd better take a look at this."

Trooper Lyle scowled at Todd. Todd shrugged. The trooper snatched Todd's bicep and marched him over to the passenger side of the car. Lyle's partner had the door panel in his hands. Taped to the inside were clear packets filled with a white powder. No one needed to explain what it was.

"The panel was loose and fell off when I touched it."

"Taking it to a dealership, were you?" Lyle said with disgust.

"I don't think this is all of it," Lyle's partner said. "This backseat is padded, but I wouldn't want to sit on it." He banged the seat with his fist. His hand left no indentation.

"You've got some explaining to do," Lyle said.

A cell phone rang. The troopers looked at each other and shook their heads.

"Have you got a cell phone, buddy?" Lyle's partner asked.

Todd shook his head.

"It's coming from there." Lyle pointed at the trunk.

Lyle tugged Todd back from the car. Lyle's partner chased around to the rear of the Lexus and popped the trunk. "You'd better take a look at this," he said.

Lyle glared at Todd. A hot sweat broke out over him as Lyle dragged him to the trunk.

Shrink-wrapped in plastic was the contorted shape of a man. The suffocating plastic sucked into his open, screaming mouth and a cell phone blinked, sticking out of his shirt pocket. Todd recognized the dead man from his picture in the newspaper. He was the Porsche owner the cops had picked up.

Todd sighed. He didn't have to ask who would be on the other end of the phone. The small man was at the root of this. He'd set him up. Stealing the Jag must have been something to buy him time while he took care of the Porsche driver. The cops would know the Porsche driver was linked to the small man and the small man couldn't let a loose end like that exist without cutting it off. He needed someone to do the trimming, so why not let Todd be his scissors?

"Son," Lyle said without a hint of pleasure, "you are royally screwed."

Dreams Unborn

Michael Bracken

1974

In Baker – a small town on the northern California coast that barely registered as a blister on Highway 1, where only two stoplights impeded traffic on its way north from San Francisco and where the Coast Ranges prevented most radio and television signals from bringing in the latest fashions, a town where generations of families lived, worked, and died and where only now did teenagers dream of leaving – the evening sun hung low in the sky, nearly hidden by storm clouds.

"We've reserved the ballroom at the Oceanview Hotel and the Rockhounds have agreed to play," Susie Van Pelt said. She had long reddish-brown hair that hung from the ruler-straight center part, gold wire-frame glasses, and a splash of freckles across the bridge of her pert nose. As senior class president, she chaired the graduation party committee.

Around the dining room table in her parents' home sat the other committee members – Caryl Mason, Linda Sullivan, Paula Hudson, Patrick Bates, and Susie's steady boyfriend, Douglas Birdsall – all duly elected by their classmates to organize the biggest blowout of the year. The high school graduation party had been a town tradition as far back as anyone could remember; even the first Baker High School graduating class of six young women had celebrated with a reputedly sedate tea party.

Patrick glanced at his watch before Susie could continue. "I have to leave by seven," he said. "I'm meeting Jewelle downtown."

"We should be done by then," Susie said as she pulled open a bag of corn chips and offered them around the table. Caryl Mason, a short, slightly overweight blonde, took the first handful of chips then passed the bag on.

Wind-blown leaves scratched nervously along the sliding glass door behind Patrick. A branch tapped an irregular rhythm against an outside wall. All afternoon San Francisco-based weather reporters had been predicting a storm, though no one in the room had heard the predictions. With graduation day almost upon them, weather reports had little meaning.

"Who wants to head the decorating committee?" Susie asked. She had a spiral-bound notebook open before her. Elected class president because of her efficiency, she'd already preplanned most of the party. "We need somebody with lots of friends to help out."

Paula Hudson volunteered Patrick's name.

"Give me a break," he said. He pushed his shoulder-length black hair away from his face. "I couldn't decorate a bonfire."

Under the table, Douglas pushed aside Susie's skirt and placed his hand on her inner thigh. She reached under the table and pushed Douglas' hand away, then glared at him. Douglas' curly brown hair wasn't nearly as long as Patrick's and he wore little round John Lennon glasses.

"I'll do it," Linda Sullivan said. She'd come to the meeting from cheerleading practice and still wore her pleated purple skirt and white tank top. "The Pep Squad will help."

Susie wrote Linda's name in her notebook and continued down her list of objectives for the evening. Two hours, two dozen sodas, and three bags of chips later, they had outlined the entire graduation night party, from starting time to catering service to admission price.

When they were sure they'd thought of everything, the meeting ended and the committee members began to leave. Linda and Paula headed home; Caryl hurried to her evening job at the bowling alley.

Patrick stood in the doorway of Susie's house and said to Susie and Douglas, "Don't expect much. I don't know where I'll be ten years from now."

"It doesn't matter," Susie said. A cool breeze slithered through the open door and sent a chill up her exposed legs, tickling her inner thighs. "You just need to know where the rest of us are."

"That won't be easy." Patrick had accepted chairmanship of the ten-year-reunion committee.

"You'll keep in touch with enough people, you shouldn't have any problem finding all of us," Douglas said. He had his hand on the door, inching it closed.

"Most of us will still be around," Susie said. "Can you imagine a future for some of these guys that doesn't include the mill or the boats?"

Patrick stepped onto the porch. Storm clouds filled the evening sky, blocking out the last of the sun's rays.

"Jewelle's expecting you," Douglas reminded Patrick as he pushed the door another inch closed.

Patrick finally took the hint, turned, and stepped off the porch. Long strands of black hair whipped across his face as he walked down the tree-covered path through shadows twisted by the wind.

Douglas closed the door, then pulled Susie into his arms, crushing her against his chest. He said, "I thought Pat would never leave," and then he kissed her. Their glasses clicked together.

Susie pulled away. "Help me clean up before my parents get home."

"It can wait," Douglas said. "They aren't due back until tomorrow." He coaxed Susie toward the couch, encouraging her to sit with him.

"How do you think it went?" she asked.

His hand slipped under her sweater, across her abdomen, and over her bra. "Fine," he mumbled.

"Really?" She settled back against Douglas. "You think the graduation night party will turn out okay?"

"It'll be fine," Douglas murmured into her neck as he kissed his way up to her ear lobe. One hand found the clasp of her bra and worried at it.

"I can't let anything go wrong," she said. "This is going to be bigger than Homecoming or the Senior Prom. It'll be the last time we're all together until our ten-year reunion."

Thoughts of the party slowly disappeared. Susie's mouth found Douglas's and she returned his kiss. She shifted position, allowing Douglas to unclasp her bra and push it aside.

She lay back on the couch, pulling Douglas on top of her and feeling the bulge in his pants press against her leg.

He pushed up her sweater and her bra and took her breasts in his hands. He squeezed and she jerked in pain.

"Not so hard," she whispered.

He covered her mouth with his as one hand slid up her thigh, pushing her skirt to her waist.

"Why don't we go to the bedroom?" Douglas whispered into her ear. Then he pushed himself off the couch, struggled out of his jeans and his underwear, and stood naked before her.

Susie had never before seen his erection. She stared.

Douglas pulled at her wrist, urging her up. "The bedroom," he said gently. "It'll be easier."

"No!" Susie said. "We can't." Suddenly modest, she pulled her skirt over her lap and pulled her sweater over her breasts.

"But – but –" Douglas sputtered.

"I don't want to get pregnant," Susie said. "I can't take a chance. I'm going to UCLA in the fall."

"I thought you were on the pill," Douglas said.

"I . . . I chickened out," she explained. "I couldn't ask Sally Filmer's father for the pill. Sally's mother plays bridge with my mother. God, I would just die if my mother found out."

"Susie," Douglas pleaded. "I . . . oh, damn it, I gotta go to the bathroom."

He hurried across the living room and into the bathroom, locking the door behind him as he switched on the light. He'd never gotten this far before and now he couldn't stop. He reached down.

Susie knocked on the bathroom door. "Are you okay, Doug?" she asked. "I'm sorry. I really am. I wanted to but I just couldn't."

When he didn't answer, she said, "I brought your clothes. I'll leave them by the door. I – I'll be in the kitchen cleaning up."

Rain spattered against the bathroom window.

Baker expanded at glacial speed, gaining new residents through a birth rate that barely exceeded the mortality rate. Few families needed new homes, choosing instead to live with relatives until a house passed down through the generations, or gathering together uncles and cousins to build additions when families expanded. Three years earlier, Bill Harrison had stared up the barrel of a .38 Special when his contracting business failed following the financial collapse of an inadequately-planned housing development had forced him into near-bankruptcy. Only his wife's soothing reassurance had allowed him to continue on until he accepted a position as the town's building inspector following George Anderson's unexpected retirement.

Outside Bill's house, the wind whistled along the loose vinyl siding, caught a shutter that hadn't been properly fastened, and slapped it against the house. A shingle from a neighbor's house skittered across the roof.

"You hungry?" Bill asked as he opened a loaf of white bread and pulled out a single slice of Wonder. His daughter sat on the far side of the white Formica and chrome kitchen table. He was so glad she had taken after her mother, had her mother's shapely figure and not the cube shape of generations of Harrisons.

Jewelle didn't look up. "I already ate."

"What'd you have? Anything good?"

"Soup," Jewelle responded. "Tomato soup."

Bill buttered his slice of bread, took a bite, and chewed slowly. When Jewelle didn't add anything to her description of dinner, he said, "I saw your mom this afternoon."

"And?"

"She's still the same."

Jewelle finally looked up from her history text and stared over the top of the ceramic chicken her mother had proudly placed in the center of the table when Jewelle brought it home from sixth grade art class. Her mother had done things like that and her father had never protested against all the poorly-drawn pictures decorating the refrigerator, nor against the ceramic ashtrays and beaded necklaces and macramé plant hangers she'd made and her mother had immediately put to use.

When his daughter didn't respond, Bill said, "I thought you'd like to know. You haven't asked about her."

Jewelle closed her book. She brushed back a long lock of dark hair. "It's been a year already," she said quietly. "Mom's always the same."

"You used to see her every day," Bill continued. He still visited the hospital each afternoon to sit with his wife, even though he could do nothing for her. Her losing battle with cancer had kept the already-drained savings account empty and had sucked dry the last of his emotional reserve. "I know she'd like to see you more often."

"She doesn't see me now," Jewelle said. "She doesn't know I'm there. She doesn't even know you're there."

Bill took a deep breath. They had had this discussion before. "Maybe not," he said quietly.

"I know she doesn't," Jewelle said. "There's nothing I can do for her. I've tried. God knows I've tried. I wish she'd just die and get it over with."

"Jewelle!"

The shutter slapped the house again.

Jewelle stared at her father. "Well, I do. I can't stand not knowing – not knowing when she's going to die – not knowing when you're going to start living again."

Bill watched his daughter gather her books into her arms, press them tight against her ample bosom, and storm from the kitchen. A moment later she reappeared, a sweater in one hand, her purse in the other.

"I'm going out."

Bill ran his thick fingers through his closely-cropped salt-and-pepper hair. He wanted to ask Jewelle where she planned on going, with whom she planned to go, and when she'd be home, but he didn't. He knew anything he said would only provoke an argument. He watched her step outside and pull the door closed behind her, then tears filled his eyes and he tried to blink them away.

The clouds finally opened and a steady drizzle fell against the house.

Rain beat a staccato rhythm against the plate glass windows of the Sprouse-Ritz. Inside, Patrick Bates stood before a rack of sunglasses, tugging at the zipper of his faded denim jacket – the jacket with the red peace symbol embroidered on the back. The zipper had stuck again and he'd grown warm waiting for Jewelle Harrison to join him at the store.

He tried on sunglasses, staring at himself in the tiny mirror with each different pair he slipped on.

"You look like a dork," Jewelle said as she stepped beside him.

Patrick shrugged. He'd just been killing time until her arrival.

"How'd the meeting go?" Jewelle had walked four blocks in the rain and she brushed a long, wet lock of hair away from her round face.

Patrick wrapped one arm around her shoulder and pulled Jewelle close, feeling her warmth against him. "Everything's been worked out," he said. "I don't have to do much."

"Tom Sawyer," she said. "You always get out of the hard jobs, don't you?"

He replaced the last pair of sunglasses he'd tried on.

"You ready?" He pulled her toward the door.

"Sure," Jewelle responded wearily.

Patrick stopped and stared deep into her eyes. "You okay?"

"My father climbed on me about my mother again."

Before Patrick could respond, lightning seared the evening sky and thunder rattled the store windows. The store lights dimmed as the storm slammed against the town with its full force.

Patrick grabbed Jewelle's elbow and hurried her out of the store and across the parking lot to his car. She settled in while he ran around and slid into the driver's seat. He'd been dry inside the store, but the short run to the car had soaked Patrick's jacket and his hair.

Water dripped from his sleeve as Patrick slid his key into

the ignition and brought the car to life. He snapped on the headlights. A dozen small-town faces pressed against the plate glass window of the store stared out at them as Patrick swung the car around and splashed through the deepening puddles around the already overflowing storm sewer grates.

He pointed the car north and crawled through the rain to the other end of town, behind the bowling alley, and up Catholic Hill. As he crested the hill, Patrick turned off his headlights so they wouldn't shine on Mrs. Gundellini's house, then coasted down the other side to the back of the cemetery. They were invisible to the road out front, hidden from the sight of anyone more than a hundred feet away.

As the car coasted to the far end of the cemetery, hidden beneath the canopy of trees, Patrick cut the engine. Rain pelted the car, the sound of each drop echoing faintly inside the car.

"It wasn't always like this," Jewelle said. "My mother was a beautiful woman."

"I never really knew my mother," Patrick said.

"She was always so happy, so – so – so alive, damn it." Jewelle turned away from Patrick and stared out the side window. She bit her lower lip to keep from crying.

Patrick placed a hand on Jewelle's shoulder and felt her silent sobs. Trying to reassure her, he said, "It's okay."

"There's not a damn thing I can do for her now," Jewelle said a moment later. "I tried to visit. I really did. I went almost every day. I would tell her about school and about us and –"

Patrick barely heard her voice, barely understood the words.

"My father doesn't understand," Jewelle said suddenly. She turned to face Patrick. His face lay hidden in the shadow, his expression lost in the darkness. "Nothing I can do will ever bring her back the way I knew her."

"I can't bring my mother back, either," Patrick said quietly, as much to himself as to her. "I tried."

"She's going to die and I know it and my father knows it and there's nothing I can do." Jewelle collapsed against Patrick's shoulder and cried.

Patrick slowly stroked her hair, feeling the damp strands as they laced through his fingers. Each night before bed he'd prayed to God for his mother's return, he'd promised everything he knew to promise, and he'd lit candles for her at the church. At four he hadn't understood why God had taken his mother away; hadn't understood why his father blamed those around him for her death; why his own existence and his resemblance to his mother caused his father so much pain. By six he'd learned to live with his father's pain, had come to accept his own grieving, and had realized that God wasn't answering his prayers. He would never again lose someone he loved; he'd made a blood oath when he was nine, when he thought his babysitter, Mrs. Carvelli, was going to die because he didn't know what hemorrhoids were and thought them fatal.

Nearly twenty minutes passed before either of them spoke.

"We're going to see the world together, aren't we?" Jewelle asked.

"Everything," Patrick promised. "After graduation."

"We'll leave behind all the bad memories," Jewelle said. "Like you promised."

Patrick sat silent, still holding Jewelle against his chest in the confines of the car.

"San Francisco," she said. "I've never seen San Francisco and it's so close."

"We'll see San Francisco first," Patrick promised. "College will be the ticket out of here. College first, then we'll see the world."

"I sent more applications off yesterday," Jewelle said. "I still don't have any responses. I waited too long. Now they won't take me." She thought a moment, then quietly said, "Maybe they don't want me. Maybe I'll never get out of this town."

Patrick stroked her hair.

"Tell me about the party. Tell me about tonight's meeting. Tell me about something nice," Jewelle said.

Patrick described the party plans, how the hotel would be decorated and which band would play, how Susie Van Pelt had commanded the meeting and about Douglas Birdsall.

"Doug was so hot he couldn't wait for us to leave," Patrick said. "He almost pushed me out the door."

"He won't die a virgin," Jewelle said. "If Susie doesn't put out soon, he won't wait for her."

They both laughed.

"So what about graduation night?" Jewelle asked.

"It'll be the biggest damn party of our lives," Patrick said. "We'll probably use all the money in the Senior class treasury."

"But we won't need it any more," Jewelle said, "because we'll all leave this damned town as soon as we graduate. No more school."

"It'll be a celebration of the end of life as we know it," Patrick suggested. "We could double with Siro and Lisa."

"You think?"

Patrick kissed her forehead and they watched the rain trickle down the windshield of his car.

A patchwork quilt of dark shadow and bright sunlight lay over Catholic Hill. Four preteen boys playing tag with puberty weaved their way through the headstones and the trees. Their tennis shoes slipped on the slick grass, still muddy from the previous night's storm. The only sound in the cemetery came from their voices.

"I don't like it here," Mike Morelli said. Sweat gathered on the back of his neck and made it itch. "It's creepy."

"Chicken." His three friends taunted him. "It's just a bunch of dead people. They're never coming back."

Morelli trailed behind them through the headstones, seeing the names, the dates, the epitaphs. He hadn't been on Catholic Hill since his grandfather's burial years earlier when his grandmother sat beside him on the trip from the church to the cemetery, hugging him tight with one frail arm, and whispering Italian prayers in his ear; when a once-strapping bull of a man long-since collapsed into himself and walking only with the aid of a stout cane had stood with his grandmother, his parents, and him, and said, "Nobody escapes from this town. Not even Antonio. Not even dead." The old people surrounding him had frightened Morelli; their death masks of wrinkled skin, the smell of garlic and Old Spice and fish, and the sound of their labored breathing and wheezing as the priest said his final words before the dirt rained in hollow thuds upon the casket.

He shook away the memories and asked, "What are we going to do?"

They shushed him.

"Steve's brother is bringing a girl up here after practice. I heard him say so."

"I bet he touches her tits."

"Her tits? I bet he gets all her clothes off." A voice caught halfway between child and adult cracked out the words.

"Did you hear where they'd be?"

Morelli stepped on a branch forced to the ground by the storm. It snapped under his weight.

"Around the back. You can't see it from the road."

Morelli followed without comment. The others had often hidden in the trees at the back of the cemetery, trying to catch glimpses of teenaged couples making out. This was the first time they'd convinced Morelli to join them.

"Hey you kids!" An old woman stood on the other side of a split-rail fence yelling at them.

"Christ, it's Mrs. Gundellini."

"What are you doing in there? You don't belong in the cemetery!" she yelled. Her voice had the irritating sound of overtaxed machinery.

They ran, but Morelli slipped and fell face-first into the grass. His shoulder grazed a marble headstone and pain shot down his arm.

"I'll call the cops, that's what I'll do. I see you Mike Morelli. I'll call your father." She waved her fist at them, a fist as wrinkled as a prune and as tough as leather.

"She saw your face, stupid," one of the others told Morelli when they'd run over the crest of the hill and out of Mrs. Gundellini's sight.

"You think she'll really call my father?" Morelli asked. They'd stopped running and leaned against headstones catching their breath. The patchwork quilt of shadows had darkened. On the far side of Catholic Hill the trees grew closer together and blocked out more of the sun. Morelli felt like he was walking through an ever-darkening tunnel. He shivered.

The others seemed unaffected.

"And the cops, too."

"She's a mean old biddy. Screams at everybody."

"I heard she used to teach school."

"A century ago, maybe."

"A Catholic school."

"Which one, Our Lady of Perpetual Hell?"

They all laughed.

"What about Steve's brother?"

"I don't want Sergeant Garvelli to catch me back here. I'm going home."

The others agreed. Morelli didn't care if Sergeant Garvelli caught him in the cemetery and he didn't care if his father knew he'd been there, but he felt glad one of the others had suggested they leave. The next time he visited Catholic Hill – or any other cemetery – would be too soon.

As they followed a path through the woods and back into town, one said, "I saw my sister's tits once. It's no big deal."

"Your sister's six years old, jerk."

Morelli followed the others in silence, listening to their preteen patter, the friendly and not-so-friendly insults, the moronic jokes and puns, until he finally tired of them. He told the other boys he had to get home, then he cut through the Friberg yard, down the alley for two blocks, then halfway through town and into his own back yard.

He stopped and stared at his mother's flower garden, knowing the babysitter would be inside with his little sister, wondering if Lisa dreamed of leaving Baker as often as he did, wondering if she would leave with him when he left.

After carefully picking a half-dozen of the prettiest flowers, he carried them inside. Lisa Anderson sat at the kitchen table, spooning baby food into his little sister's mouth. Her white blouse, unbuttoned far enough that Morelli imagined he could see more than he really could, was stained where his sister had spit up something green.

"I picked these for you." Morelli held out the bouquet of flowers.

"They're nice," Lisa said as she accepted them.

Morelli blushed when her fingers brushed against his.

Then his little sister gurgled and strained peas dribbled

down her chin. Lisa turned from him, laid the flowers on the table, and carefully wiped the green spittle off of his sister's chin.

"Would you go out with me?" Morelli asked. He'd had a crush on Lisa since she'd first started baby-sitting his little sister a year earlier, but he'd never told her of it. Instead, he'd watched her, studied the curve of her thigh and the swell of her breast, noticed how her blouse fell open when she bent to pick up his sister, and sat so he could stare up the length of her firm legs when she wore a skirt. She was so different from the other women in his life – not like his mother with her bulging thighs, expansive buttocks, and overflowing brassiere; not like his sister with her tiny, undeveloped features; and not like the girls in his class who tried so hard to look grown up but who, in blue jeans and sweat shirts, looked little different from the boys.

"Maybe when you're older," Lisa said.

Morelli stared at his feet.

Lisa finished spooning peas into the baby's mouth, then wiped away the last of the mess. Morelli watched as she threw the empty jar away and washed the spoon, moving easily around the kitchen as if it were her own.

Finally, she said, "You'd better get ready. Your father will be home soon and Siro will be here to pick me up."

"Do you love him?" Morelli asked.

Lisa stopped, a dishtowel wrapped around one hand. "Who?"

"Siro. Do you love him?" He'd often seen them together, walking hand-in-hand, laughing at one another's jokes, sharing root beer at the A&W. He'd seen them together and he'd imagined himself walking in Siro's shoes, holding Lisa's hand.

Lisa looked at Morelli closely, for the first time recognizing what had been evident all along.

"I think so," she said carefully.

"Then you don't love me." Morelli crossed his arms and pouted.

"I like you, Mike." She reached across the table and tousled his hair. "We're friends, right?"

The baby laughed at her brother. "Da-da-da-da."

"Sure," he said.

"Always be friends, right?"

"Sure."

"Nothing will ever come between us. We'll always be friends."

The baby burbled again.

"You'll marry Siro and you'll have a bunch of kids and I'll never see you again."

"I don't think so," Lisa told him.

Morelli's father pushed open the front door and called his greetings. The baby saw him as he entered the kitchen and she held her arms up.

"Mrs. Morelli received a phone call before she left for the hospital," Lisa said as she handed Mr. Morelli a folded scrap of paper. "She told me to give this to you and to tell you one of the nurses on the third shift called in sick and she might have to pull a double tonight."

While Mr. Morelli unfolded the paper, Lisa gathered together her school books, her purse, and her jacket.

"Get ready, champ," he said to Mike. "We have to go down to the music shop."

Siro Pasetti knocked on the screen and Lisa stepped onto the porch beside him. Morelli watched as Siro took her hand and they headed down the walk to his car.

"Your music teacher said such good things at the last parent-teacher conference that your mother special-ordered an electric bass for you," Mr. Morelli said.

"The graduation party is only a few weeks away," Jewelle said as she cleared dinner dishes from the table. They'd had meat loaf for the third night in a row and they'd finally eaten the last of it. "I haven't a thing to wear."

Bill Harrison opened his wallet and shook it over the table. Out dropped a crumpled dollar bill and a pair of business cards.

"You don't have to be so dramatic," Jewelle said.

"There's nothing I can do," her father said. "Friday's payday but the car's been acting up again. It won't last much longer. Without the car –"

"I know," Jewelle said as she filled one side of the double sink with soapy water. "No car, no job." She'd heard it before, more times than she could remember. Ever since her mother had gone into the hospital, her father hadn't had any extra money. "But this is important."

"I know it is," Bill said. He remembered his graduation party nineteen years earlier, the year he'd begun dating her mother. It had been just as important to him then as it was to her now. "But your mother comes first."

Jewelle rinsed a plate in the sink. "Patrick asked me to be his date. I should have something nice to wear, shouldn't I?"

Bill grimaced.

"Maybe I can make something," Jewelle said. "If you'll just buy the material."

"We'll see," her father said. "Maybe I can squeeze a little out of the next paycheck. Maybe the car won't cost so much to fix. Maybe –"

"I know, I know," Jewelle said. "We'll see."

"Right. We'll see."

"Will you be going out tonight?" Bill asked. He handed his daughter the dirty silverware.

She shook her head. "I don't think so. Patrick hasn't called. I'll probably call Lisa, though."

Bill finished clearing the table, wiped it clean, and headed toward the living room.

"Dad?"

He stopped, one foot already touching the living room carpet.

"About the dress," she said. "I understand. I'll make do."

Patrick Bates sat alone in the dark, a crumpled letter in his hand. Cherry incense burned in a special holder on top of his dresser. Led Zeppelin screamed through his earphones. He'd read the letter a dozen times and the outcome never changed.

His father pounded on the bedroom door. "What are you doing in there, Patrick?" He pounded again. "I smell something funny." He pushed the door open and flipped on the light.

Startled, Patrick jerked his head around and saw his father standing in the doorway. He pulled the earphones off and asked, "What do you want?"

"Nobody normal sits in the dark." His father scratched at the expanse of belly exposed between the waistband of his work pants and the bottom of his dirty T-shirt. "You smoking dope or something?"

"Nobody normal has you for a father," Patrick said. He pushed himself to his feet and jammed the letter into his pocket. He couldn't deal with his father right then.

"What's that supposed to mean?" Patrick's father demanded. Then he belched. The smell of stale beer and cigarettes nearly overpowered the incense.

Patrick removed the needle from the Led Zeppelin album and switched the stereo off. The stick of incense had almost finished burning and he let it alone.

"It means I don't want to put up with you anymore," Patrick said. His entire life he had depended on his father for clothes, food, and the roof over his head and his father never failed to remind him of that fact. "It means I'm moving out of here as soon as I can."

"You think you're a man already, huh? Then get yourself a job and pay some bills, you little shit."

Patrick stood close enough to smell his father's sweat, the acrid odor of a man who worked long, hard hours in the lumber mill. The faint smell of redwood clung to his father's clothes.

"Soon enough," Patrick said. "And it won't be at the mill, either." Patrick grabbed his denim jacket from the top of his bunk bed and pushed past his father.

"It's lumber or fish," his father called after him as Patrick opened the front door and stepped outside. "You ain't got any other choices."

"Not if I stay here," Patrick mumbled as he climbed into his car a moment later. He ground the engine to life, dropped the car into gear, and sped away from the dilapidated mobile home they shared a mile north of town.

A few minutes later Patrick pulled into the bowling alley's

parking lot, cut the engine, and climbed out. At the public phone inside, he dropped a dime in the slot and dialed Jewelle's number. After a dozen rings, he hung up, waited for his dime to clatter out, then phoned Siro Pasetti.

When Patrick pulled to the curb and honked his car's horn, Siro and his six-year-old brother John rushed from the Pasetti house. Siro pulled open the passenger door and shoved his little brother into the back seat.

"My parents are going out tonight," Siro explained. "They asked me to watch him."

Patrick shrugged. Siro's little brother had tagged along before and never gotten in the way.

"You ready to rock-and-roll?" Patrick asked. He shoved an 8-track tape into the player mounted under the dashboard. The music of Bachman-Turner Overdrive blared from the stereo speakers mounted on the rear window ledge.

John lay in the back seat of Patrick's car, his jacket pulled tight around his thin frame, his hands pressed against his ears. Patrick always played the music too loud and his head hurt.

Siro lived on a dead-end street and Patrick spun his battered yellow Grand Prix in a tight circle before heading into town.

"U. C. Berkeley turned me down," Patrick said. He pulled the crumpled rejection letter from his pocket, then tossed it from his open window. Except for the junior college in Santa Rosa, he'd yet to be accepted at any of the colleges to which he'd applied.

Siro strained to hear.

"Then my father came home and started in on me. I got out of there as soon as I could." Patrick honked the horn at a pair of teenaged girls standing on a corner. "Then I tried to call Jewelle and she wasn't home."

One of the girls waved at the car and Siro waved back.

"God, I need a drink," Patrick shouted over the music. "It's been one hell of a day."

They had already passed the heart of town and were about to turn around at the bowling alley.

"Stop at Santelli's," Siro shouted back. "I'll go in."

A few minutes later Patrick pulled to the curb and popped the tape out of the tape player. He and John sat in silence while Siro hurried across the street.

Siro quickly returned. "The old man's nearly blind," Siro said as he dropped into the seat with the six pack in his hand. "He didn't even ask for I.D."

John leaned over the seat and watched as Siro popped open two beers and handed one to Patrick.

"I didn't forget you, squirt," Siro said. He pulled a can of Pepsi and a Hershey bar from his jacket pocket. He handed them over the seat to his brother.

Patrick dropped the Grand Prix into gear and headed south to Chapman's field where they sat on the car's hood drinking beer. John sat between them.

"Listen to the ocean," Siro said. "It's got a voice of its own."

John listened to the roar of the surf, the waves crashing against the rocky cliff below Chapman's field, the random cry of a gull somewhere overhead.

"The ocean doesn't talk," Patrick said. He'd already drank most of the beer.

"Pasettis have been fishermen since Jesus walked on the water," Siro said. "We know."

Patrick belched. "If the ocean talks," he asked, "then what's it saying?"

"It's saying you've had too much to drink."

"Bullshit talks and bullshit walks." Patrick pushed himself off the car and walked to the edge of the field where it dropped away into the ocean below. "I'll tell you what it's saying," he yelled back. "It's saying we ain't ever gonna get out of this town, that's what it's saying."

Siro shrugged. "I never wanted to leave," he said. "There's no place else to go."

"There's everyplace else to go," Patrick yelled. "You ever wanted to see what was on the other side of the ocean? You ever talked to it, asked it what's over there?"

"Doesn't matter," Siro said. "I'll never see it."

"That's right. And you know why? Because you're too stupid. When you graduate high school you'll work on daddy's boat, won't you? No college, nothing. You'll smell like fish all the damned time and if I ever come back to visit I'll find you in one of those dago bars in the harbor trying to drink the smell away."

Siro patted his little brother's shoulder. "It's getting cold, John. You'd better get in the car."

"Is Pat okay?"

"I'll take care of him. You just get in the car."

"Why did he call you a dago?"

"He didn't. He's just upset," Siro explained.

As John slipped off the hood and walked around the car, Siro called for Patrick to return.

"In a minute." Patrick waved Siro away, then unzipped his pants and urinated over the edge of the cliff, writing his name in the wind.

*F*aded elegance permeated the Oceanview Hotel. Once a haven for lumber barons and wealthy vacationers up from San Francisco, the Oceanview now catered to weary travelers crawling along the Pacific Coast Highway in their overloaded station wagons and battered microbuses, and, more often than not, they opted for the newer, more modern Surfside Motel just north of town.

Ed Johnson remembered those days near the end of the hotel's glory years when he'd been a bellhop, earning far more in tips than he had in salary. Now, after years of hard work, he owned the hotel and he couldn't afford bellhops.

He stood in the entrance, impatiently tapping his foot as Bill Harrison, Baker's building inspector, walked up the street toward him.

Johnson glanced at his watch when Bill pulled the door open. "You're late."

"I'm sorry," Bill said. Half-moons of sweat stained his armpits. He wearily straightened his wide polyester tie and shifted his clipboard from one hand to the other. "My car broke down south of town. I had to walk." He would call the DeGrasso brothers later to tow his car into their shop. He hoped they would wait until payday to get their money; they'd waited before.

"Let's get on with this," Johnson insisted. A corpulent man grown fat from inactivity and too much greasy food, he wore a reasonably new three-piece suit well tailored to his girth. His thinning hair had been trimmed neatly above his ears and he ran one pudgy hand along the side of his head. "I don't have all day."

"Neither do I," Bill said under his breath. He planned to return to the hospital soon and he anticipated a long walk back the way he'd come.

Johnson followed the inspector along the threadbare carpet. "Where should we start?"

"At the top," Harrison said. "We'll work our way down."

For the first hour the two men toured the upper floors of the hotel as Harrison pointed out a variety of small infractions. On the fifth floor he discovered a fire extinguisher long over-due for a refill, on the third floor he found an improperly marked exit, and throughout the offices on the main floor he discovered overloaded electrical outlets and a knot of extension cords around and under the desks. As Harrison pointed out each infraction, Johnson nodded and said, "I'll see that it's taken care of."

The basement, last stop on their tour of the hotel, had become a repository for old newspapers, improperly sealed cans of paint and paint thinner, old mattresses and unusable furniture. Harrison carefully picked his way across the basement in search of the fuse box.

"This is a mess," Harrison said. He stepped around a leaning tower of newspapers. "An absolute mess. You have any problem with mice down here?"

"We did last summer," Johnson told him. "So we got a cat. We haven't had any problems since."

Harrison noted the mess on his clipboard. "Where's that fuse box?"

Johnson pushed aside a broken cedar chest and squeezed his bulk past it. "Back here."

"Damned inconvenient place for it, isn't it?"

Johnson shrugged as Harrison opened the fuse box. A third of the fuses had been replaced with nails cut short and more than a dozen wires leading from the box had been improperly spliced.

"Looks like a bunch of amateurs had a field day down here," Harrison said. "I can't let this go. You'll have to rewire or I'll have to close down the hotel. You've got a hell of a fire trap down here."

"I can't afford to rewire," Johnson said. He didn't admit these things easily. "I can barely keep this place open as it is."

"That's not my problem," Harrison said. He hadn't yet written anything on his clipboard.

The two men stood silently appraising each other in the dim light of the basement. Finally, Johnson reached into his back pocket and pulled out his wallet.

"Look, maybe you can get that car of yours fixed," the hotel owner said as he pressed a crumpled pair of fifties into Harrison's hand. "And I'll see what I can do about getting this place cleaned up."

After a long moment spent weighing his options, Harrison's hand closed around the money and it disappeared into his pocket. He peeled off the top sheet and handed it to the hotel owner. "I'll be back in thirty days to check on the fire extinguisher, the exit, and the extension cords."

"I'll take care of everything," Johnson assured the inspector.

"You already have," Harrison said.

Jewelle stood at one of the clothing racks in Seabolt's Dress Shop, gently fingering the sleeve of a powder blue chiffon dress. She stared forlornly at the $59 price tag and thought of the eight dollars in her piggy bank at home. Her back to the door, she heard the tiny brass bell tinkle as someone entered the shop.

A moment later, her father quietly walked up behind her. She'd left him in the hardware store next door picking out washers for the leaky bathroom faucet.

"Is that the one you want?" he asked.

Jewelle turned. "But you said –"

"I know," he interrupted. "Don't make me explain what happened, but I've got the money now." Her father lifted the dress from the rack and handed it to her. "Try it on."

Jewelle took it into the dressing room, pulled the flower-patterned curtain closed, and quickly changed clothes. When she stepped out of the dressing room, her father whistled appreciatively. "You'll be the most beautiful girl there."

Mrs. Seabolt, a corpulent woman fairly bursting out of her own dress, bustled up behind Jewelle and fussed over her.

"I'll bet you're looking for something to wear to the graduation party aren't you? You won't believe how many girls I've had in the shop these past few days. I guess maybe there still are a few places where a girl still wants to look like a girl. Bell-bottoms, schmell-bottoms, we'll have you fixed up in a jiffy, we will."

Jewelle didn't quite know what to say and stood quietly as Mrs. Seabolt prattled on.

"I'll have to take this in," Mrs. Seabolt said as she shoved a pin into place, "and let this out."

She spun Jewelle around and continued fussing. A chalk mark here, a pin there, a dozen questions about the adjustments she was making. "How does this feel?" and "What about this?" and "Too tight, too loose?"

Jewelle nodded or shook her head as appropriate, all the while continuing to stare at her father when she wasn't answering one of Mrs. Seabolt's questions.

"You sure it's the one you want?" he asked when Mrs. Seabolt had finished fussing.

"Absolutely."

He turned to the corpulent store owner. "How long to make the alterations?"

"If you can just wait a few minutes, I can take this in back and have the changes made in no time at all. You should see the alterations I've had to make to some of the dresses, but these are nothing, just take me a few minutes is all. Just a few minutes and I'll have it all wrapped up and ready to go."

Within half an hour, Mrs. Seabolt had made all of the adjustments to Jewelle's new dress on her antique Singer sewing machine and had the dress packed and ready.

"What about shoes?" Bill asked his daughter as he accepted the change from the two fifties he'd handed Mrs. Seabolt. "Don't you need new shoes?"

Jewelle thought of the scuffed white pumps shoved to the

back of her closet. "I can polish the ones I wore to Aunt Fergie's anniversary."

"That was three years ago. Do they still fit?"

She shook her head; she'd gained a shoe size since then. "But I can squeeze into them. It's just for one night."

"Nonsense," Bill said as he led his daughter down the street to the shoe store. "We'll get what you need."

The afternoon sun steadily grilled Lisa Anderson and Siro Pasetti as they walked around Monteleone's Used Car Lot. They threaded their way through the cars on the front of the lot, the newer models that had been freshly washed and waxed.

"I think I have a new boyfriend," Lisa said.

"Yeah, who?" Siro asked as he kicked at the tire of a Rambler.

"The Morelli's son, Mike."

"Nice kid."

"He keeps bringing me flowers and things, asking if you and me are serious."

"We're serious." Siro looked at her across the hood of a Chrysler.

"He wants to marry me."

Siro started laughing. "He's a little young, isn't he?"

They stopped in front of a year-old Monte Carlo and Siro studied it carefully.

"This looks pretty good," Siro said as he wiped sweat from the back of his neck. He had changed the subject and they both realized it.

"What can I do for you kids?" Monteleone asked as he huffed his way from the tiny office at the back of the lot. He wore an ill-fitting blue suit, the knot of his rep tie loosened and the collar of his white shirt unbuttoned. "You aimin' to buy, or you just killing the afternoon browsing through the selection here?"

"How much are you asking for this?" Siro indicated the Monte Carlo.

"Well, son, I'm gonna bet that little beauty is out of your

ball park, but I'll tell you what I'm asking," Monteleone said. "Before I go to all that trouble, though, let me ask you again, are you just lookin' or do you plan to buy?"

"To buy," Lisa answered. In the front pocket of her tight-fitting jeans was all the money she'd earned working at the A&W the previous year.

"Well, glad to see the little lady has an answer for me." Monteleone dug through his shirt pocket and pulled out a crumpled sheet of paper. "The Monte Carlo's a damn nice car," he said. "Power steering, power brakes, almost no miles on her to speak of."

He found the price on his sheet and read it to them. Lisa blanched. It was nearly four times what she had to spend.

"You got anything less expensive?" Siro asked.

"Well, I don't run no junk yard here son. What kind of money are we talkin'?"

Lisa started to say, "I've got about sev –"

Siro nudged her. "Let's say she's got enough to bargain with."

Monteleone laughed as he ran a thick hand through his thinning black hair. "Ain't you one of Pasetti's boys? I'd know a Pasetti if I was deaf and blind. Your father still driving that Nova I sold him last year? Your old man drove a hard bargain for that car. I almost lost my shirt. Now, about how much you got to spend?"

"It depends on what we see," Siro said.

"Jesus, son, I ain't gonna waste my time showing you the real beauties if you only came to buy a dog." Monteleone pulled a handkerchief from his pocket and moped at his brow. A two-day heat wave had followed the last storm and he was ill-prepared to deal with it. Sweat ran down the back of his neck, soaking the stiff collar of his crisp white shirt.

When Siro didn't respond, Monteleone said, "Let me show you what's on the back lot. I've got a few older models – workhorses, not show cars – back there."

Lisa and Siro followed Monteleone as he threaded his way through the lot.

"There's five or six cars back here all under a thousand. I've had the DeGrasso brothers look at all of 'em and they say all the cars are in good mechanical shape. Guaranteed."

"There's somebody out front," Siro said. "If we see something, we'll let you know."

Monteleone glanced toward the front of the lot. A well-dressed young couple with a toddler in tow had opened the Monte Carlo's doors and the husband had slid behind the wheel.

"You do that," Monteleone said as he hurried off.

"See anything you like?" Siro asked when he and Lisa were alone.

"Not back here," she answered.

They stood before a battered blue Volkswagen Beetle. The left front fender had collapsed in the same accident that had left a long yellow gouge halfway down the driver's side. They walked past the Volkswagen and examined the other cars.

"Maybe I should wait," Lisa said, disappointed. Her father had finally given her permission to buy her own car and had agreed to meet her at Monteleone's after work that day.

They examined an old Dodge with rotted upholstery and Siro patted the fins on a battleship-gray Cadillac. On the other side of a VW Microbus, they found a brown Chevrolet station wagon.

"It's clean," Siro said. He pulled the door open and looked at the odometer. "And not too many miles on it, either."

Lisa frowned. She hadn't set out to buy a practical family car. She'd wanted something a little flashier to drive to college in the fall.

Monteleone rejoined them. "You like this one, do you?"

"No, I –" Lisa started.

"A good choice. Clean as a whistle, good on gas, and only eight hundred dollars."

"But that's –"

"Negotiable, right?" Siro interrupted Lisa.

"Son, everything in this world in negotiable, even deals with the devil." Monteleone laughed at his own joke.

"Can I think about it?" Lisa asked.

"Take as long as you want sweetheart," Monteleone said. "But unless you put a deposit on that car, I can't guarantee it'll still be on my lot tomorrow."

"I know that," Lisa said, "but my father's supposed to meet me here in an hour. I can't do anything till he arrives."

"I understand. There ain't a teenager alive can buy a car offa my lot without his parents' permission." Monteleone patted at his forehead with a sweat-stained handkerchief. "Why don't the two of you walk on over to the A&W and think about it. I'll still be here when you get back."

Jewelle Harrison sat in the passenger seat of Lisa Anderson's new station wagon, fiddling with the radio dial. Static distorted the reception of every station she tuned in.

"Where'd you hear that?" Lisa asked as she pulled from the student parking lot at the high school. Hers was only one in a long line of slowly moving vehicles. Within half an hour, after the last of the school buses had departed and most of the family cars had been disgorged from the lot, some of the senior boys would spin donuts in the gravel-covered student parking lot, or drag race down the newly-paved street before the high school. The daily rituals of the senior boys and the old cars they'd hopped up during shop classes and long summer afternoons had always stayed outside Lisa's experience. Now that she owned her own car she needed adolescent displays of abnormal testosterone levels about as much as she needed to lose a few million brain cells.

"Caryl Mason," Jewelle answered. She gave up on the radio and switched it off.

"She's nuts," Lisa said. She concentrated on the driver ahead of her, a pimply-faced junior with a brand-new diver's license, the family car, and a complete inability to distinguish between the brake and the accelerator.

The two girls were silent as Lisa drove toward the center of town. The junior ahead of her turned left three blocks away from the school, bucking and jerking his family's car up one of the side streets.

Finally, Jewelle said, "Caryl believes it."

Lisa shrugged. "So? We're all going to die someday."

The sun beat heavily against the car and a warm breeze blew through the open windows. Along the western horizon, dark clouds gathered and rapidly moved toward shore.

"She spent yesterday afternoon looking through the city

records," Jewelle said. "She says if you're born here, you die here."

"Jesus, you're morbid. Next week we graduate and then we can all leave this town forever."

"She says nobody leaves Baker forever."

"That's depressing. Who'd ever want to come back?"

Jewelle shrugged. "Patrick and I are going to see the world," she said. "We're going to go to San Francisco, then we're going to see the world."

"The whole world?"

"Every inch. I plan to spend the rest of my life with him."

"He ask you to marry him?"

"Not yet, but he will," Jewelle said. "What about you and Siro?"

Lisa shrugged.

"That's not an answer," Jewelle said. "Are you going to marry Siro?"

"I'm going off to college and he doesn't want to leave Baker."

"So go to college and then come back. He'll wait for you."

"Four years is a long time."

A dark cloud passed over, momentarily casting the town in shadow. A second cloud followed a few minutes later as Lisa pulled her station wagon to a halt in front of Jewelle's house. They were inside before the first rain drops fell.

Jewelle stood at the front window and stared out at the street. "I hate this town," she said. "If it isn't raining, it's threatening to."

Then she joined Lisa at the kitchen table and opened her California history text. They still had final exams in two classes and Mr. Carrington's history test was certain to be the toughest of the two.

The rain stopped as quickly as it started. Patrick Bates turned from the window in Miss Murdock's room and watched the other members of the graduation party committee pull a half dozen student desks into a circle.

Susie Van Pelt had her notebook open on the desk before

her and she cleared her throat. "You intend to join us, Pat?"

He crossed the room and slid easily into the one empty desk.

"Graduation is next Friday," she said. "The ceremony will be held in the early afternoon and the party will be that evening. If the valedictorian and Father Calvo keep their speeches short, we should have three hours free before the party."

Susie glanced up from her notes, then continued. "If we decorate the hotel in the morning, we'll have the time after graduation to get dressed for the party."

Patrick didn't pay attention as Susie outlined plans for graduation day. Instead, his gaze shifted around the room, first taking in the travel posters behind Miss Murdock's huge oak desk, then the "Faces and Places" display where lengths of blue yarn connected photos of people to locations on a map, then to the globe in the corner of the room. Each acted as a reminder of his promise to leave Baker following graduation.

"Are you with us, Pat?" Susie asked.

He shook his head. "I'm sorry. I can't concentrate."

"Well, we're done," Susie said. She closed her notebook. "All the details have been finalized. Your work doesn't start until 1984. Will you be with us then?"

Patrick forced himself to smile. "I've never been late for anything," he said.

"Let's hope not." Susie pushed herself to her feet. Her agitation increased the closer graduation day became, just as Patrick's resolve to leave town strengthened with each passing day.

He remained sitting as Douglas, Linda, and Paula followed Susie from the room. Soon only he and Caryl remained.

"I've thought a lot about what you said," Patrick said. A few late raindrops spattered against the window. He watched as the bubbles of water strayed down the glass.

For nearly four minutes the only sounds in the room were the hum of the fluorescent lights, the drizzling of water as it fell from the gutter outside the window, and their breathing.

Finally, Patrick said, "I've been thinking a lot lately. Do you remember Joey Gunn? He went to school with us until fourth grade."

Caryl nodded.

"His father worked for the lumber company – a vice president or something – and they moved here just before Joey was born. They left when we were in the fourth grade. Three years later they came back to visit. Joey fell out of a tree up on Catholic Hill and split his head open."

Patrick shook his head as the memory came back. He and Siro had been up in the tree with Joey. They'd been roughhousing, urging each other to climb higher, daring and double-daring each other to perform some act even more stupid than any the other boys had already done. On a quadruple dare, Joey climbed out on a weak limb, released his grip on the tree, and rode the limb like a sky-high surf board. Then the branch snapped under his weight, sending him hurtling to the ground.

"He was born here," Patrick said. "And he died here."

The Oceanview Hotel cat, an unnamed black stray salvaged from the pound, slipped quietly along one of the basement shelves, squeezing between the brick foundation wall and a hodge-podge of empty cans, jars of rusted nails, broken door knobs, and miscellaneous hardware. As the cat passed behind a precariously-perched tin can, he pushed it off the shelf. The empty can clattered to a desk below, sending the startled cat screeching across the basement.

In his flight, the cat crashed into an already cracked wall mirror, tipping it into an unstable shelving unit filled with paint, paint thinner, and a two-quart jar of leaded gasoline a former handyman had set aside for the lawnmower. The shelving unit collapsed, spilling its contents onto the stacks of newspaper below the fuse box. Thinner sprayed across one stack of paper, gasoline pooled around the foot of another mountain of newsprint, and shards of broken glass littered the floor everywhere.

The cat darted out through the broken basement window, down the alley past the Hi-Ho Inn, and across the intersection of Sequoia and Main. Mrs. Gundellini slammed on the brakes of her aging Chevrolet Bel Aire when she saw the cat streak across the street before her.

She was the last person to ever see the hotel's cat.

Mike Morelli carried a microphone stand from William Rossotti's battered VW Beetle into the Oceanview Hotel. He'd offered to help the Rockhounds with their equipment when he'd seen them unloading their cars.

Morelli carried the mic stand across the ballroom floor, weaving around the seniors who were decorating the room for the party that evening. Behind him, Rossotti carried his bass guitar.

"What're you guys going to play?" Morelli asked. "Beatles? Stones?"

"Mott the Hoople," Rossotti answered. "Deep Purple. Black Sabbath. Alice Cooper. Some top 40 stuff."

Morelli nodded.

Gary Hurley squatted in the center of the stage, assembling his drum set. Ronald Orsi sat on the edge of the stage tuning his Fender Stratocaster. Robert Viera, the other guitarist, hadn't yet arrived.

"What about you?" Rossotti asked. He knew Morelli had been taking lessons from his old music teacher. "What do you play?"

"Jazz," Morelli said. "Jazz and blues. You know how Malone is."

"Yeah," Rossotti said as he unpacked his bass. "I know."

Orsi finished tuning his guitar, switched off his amp, and nodded to the others. "See you tonight. I've got to get the car back or my old man will kill me."

Hurley tapped his drum sticks on his hi-hat, did a quick roll across his tom-toms, and then stopped. He adjusted his stool, tightened one of the tom-toms, and moved the hi-hat a few inches to the left. Then he launched into two minutes of "In-a-gadda-da-vida."

When he stopped, one of the girls on the other end of the ballroom clapped. Hurley stood and bowed deeply. Then he threw kisses across the ballroom toward his girlfriend.

"Show-off," Rossotti said.

Hurley smiled. "If Robert ever shows up, tell him I'm pissed. He should have been here half an hour ago."

"He'll show. Don't worry." Rossotti plugged in his bass and handed it to Morelli. "You want to learn to play some good music?"

Morelli nodded and Rossotti spent the next half-hour teaching him to play the bass lines from "Iron Man" and "Smoke on the Water." As they finished, Robert Viera rushed in, out of breath. Rossotti didn't bother to give him Hurley's message – Viera always arrived late.

Ed Johnson and his assistant manager slowly circumnavigated the ballroom of the Oceanview Hotel, preparing for the arrival of the graduating seniors. In only a few hours the place would be overrun with teenagers listening to loud music and smoking marijuana and practicing free love all over his furniture.

The Oceanview Hotel had been host to the last twelve graduation parties and each year Johnson vowed not to do it again. Excluding churches and the high school gym, only two other places in town had rooms large enough to host the party and neither of them had placed a competitive bid in seven years.

"Put a new light bulb in back there." Johnson pointed down a narrow hallway near the stage. "I don't want them kids necking in the dark."

"What about the back doors?" his assistant asked as they examined the chain wrapped around the push bars. "Think we should unlock these?"

"And have a bunch of hooligans sneaking booze and drugs in here? Forget it. We're going to have enough trouble controlling them at the front door."

The assistant manager shrugged. He didn't get paid to make decisions. "Anything else?" he asked.

"Yeah. Make sure to put our other guests on the upper floors, as far from this noise as possible."

"We don't have any other guests."

Johnson looked at his assistant. "Nobody?"

"The Surfside is nearly full," the assistant said. "We may get some of their overflow."

Johnson snorted. Nothing had been going his way lately.

Lisa Anderson, valedictorian, stood at the podium and faced an ocean of purple, every seat filled with a graduating senior swathed in the school colors. Behind the sea of seniors, in the bleachers along the far side of the gymnasium, sat their brothers and sisters, parents and grandparents. Off-stage to her left sat what remained of the high school band – sophomores and juniors about to move up a grade.

A neatly typed, five-page speech lay on the podium before her. Principal Dexter and Father Calvo had already spoken, had promised the graduating class that they could change the world, that they could become the senators and congressmen and doctors and lawyers and leaders of the next generation; that they could make the decisions that changed the world; that they could become anything they chose to be. Dexter and Calvo had filled the gymnasium with empty promises, the promises given to every graduating class everywhere every year.

"Today is the last day of the rest of your life," Lisa began, the wrong words spilling from her mouth as she started to read.

The seniors laughed.

Her eyes nervously searched for Siro somewhere in the sea of purple. When she found him, she realized he wasn't laughing. She took a deep breath and glanced down at the speech. It had been approved by the principal, two English teachers, and the head of the PTA. Nothing in it could possibly offend any of the gathered parents. All her life Lisa had sought the approval of parents and teachers. She had struggled for twelve years to climb to the top of her class, to achieve a grade-point average rarely seen at Baker High School, to become the daughter every parent in town hoped for and, as she looked out at her bored classmates and the tired parents who had already sat through two hours of speeches, Lisa made a decision.

"My speech isn't my speech," she said. "I wrote some of the words but the thoughts aren't mine." She held the speech up and carefully shredded it. Tiny bits of paper floated to the floor at her feet.

Principal Dexter rose from his seat at one end of the stage.

"I only have one thing to say – the same thing I'm sure is on the mind of every one of my classmates." She took a deep breath as the principal crossed the stage toward her.

Patrick Bates sat in the front row. He slipped from his seat and caught Dexter's pant leg.

"Let her finish," he said to the startled principal.

"Today is like serving the last day of an eighteen-year prison sentence," Lisa said. "We've been stuck in this damned town since the day we were born. Tonight we're going to party, 'cause tomorrow we won't be here." She took a quick breath. "We're leaving and we won't come back!"

The audience sat in stunned silence for a moment. Then Siro Pasetti stood and began applauding. One-by-one Patrick Bates and Jewelle Harrison and Caryl Mason joined him. Before long, the rest of the senior class stood, their applause thundering through the gym.

Principal Dexter took the microphone as Lisa walked from the stage. A radical junior who the music teacher later kicked out of the high school band stood and played Alice Cooper's "School's Out." Lisa stripped off her cap and gown and left them laying on the gymnasium floor as she walked up the aisle, past the girl's locker room, and out the door. Nearly half the class joined her, leaving their diplomas behind.

Siro caught up to Lisa in the student parking lot as she unlocked the door of her station wagon.

"I'm leaving tomorrow morning," she said. "Everything is packed. I just have to load it into the car."

"I won't be leaving," Siro said.

"I know."

"I promised my father I'd help him with the boat."

"What could I do here? The best I could hope for is to get

married and have kids," Lisa said. "What kind of life is that?"

"It's a good life. My parents are happy. So are yours."

"My parents aren't happy, they've accepted defeat. They're stuck in a rut, just like this entire town. Nobody ever leaves."

"You don't understand."

"Don't understand? What don't I understand?"

"Pat and me, how we made a pact. A blood oath. One of us would get out of here and stay away forever. But it won't be me. I'm not leaving."

"I have to get home," Lisa said. She pulled her car door open.

"The adults have hidden it from us," Siro said. "Or maybe they don't understand it, either. You can't really leave. Not forever."

Lisa dropped into the driver's seat, jammed her key into the ignition, and brought the station wagon to life. She stuck her head out the window and said, "I'll pick you up at six."

Siro nodded as Lisa backed out of her parking spot and he watched as she drove away. He'd never talked about it with anyone before, refusing to believe what he knew to be true. And now, when he'd tried to discuss it with one of the few people he trusted, she had refused to listen to him.

"Hey, Siro! Dad's looking for you," yelled his little brother as he hurried across the parking lot.

Siro turned toward John and wondered if he should explain everything to his younger brother. He decided it could wait.

"Tell Dad I'll talk to him at home," Siro responded.

"How you going to get home? Walk?"

"I'll hitch a ride with Pat."

John stared up at his older brother. Siro was already lost in thought again so he tugged on Siro's sleeve. "When you stood up and clapped, so did I."

Siro looked down at him.

"Afterward Dad told Mom he's sorry he asked you to work on the boat with him. But you should have heard some of the other parents. Boy, were they pissed when you guys walked out. Mr. Ugrin said you kids owe everything you've got to this town and you should be grateful and Mr. Hinkson said if Lisa was his daughter he'd slap the shit out of her when she got home. Would Lisa's father do anything like that?"

Siro shook his head. "No, Squirt, he wouldn't. He's a lot like our dad."

"Tell Lisa I stood up," John said. "Okay?"

"She'd like that." Siro patted John's head. "I'll tell her."

Three hours later, Ed Johnson stood at the Oceanview Hotel entrance and stared out across the tiny parking lot as the first of the graduates arrived. The boys wore pastel-colored tuxedos with bell-bottom pants they'd rented from Tops 'n' Tails, the girls wore floor-length prom dresses with full skirts. Animated, they filed past him as if he didn't exist, talking only to their friends and to Susie Van Pelt as she registered them at the entrance to the ballroom.

As the crowd of young adults grew larger, the parking lot overflowed and soon cars were parked up and down the street and around the block. The Oceanview Hotel parking lot had never been prepared to deal with crowds, having originally been an expanse of lawn later paved over when automobile travel became common.

Inside the ballroom, the Rockhounds tuned their instruments and checked their microphones before slipping outside for smokes and quick pulls from a bottle of Thunderbird the drummer had purchased at Santelli's earlier that day.

After most of the senior class had arrived, Johnson toured the inside of the ballroom, then resumed his seat behind the front desk. He'd heard about the graduation ceremony that afternoon and had tried to stop the party. Susie Van Pelt had threatened legal action against him when he'd called to discuss the problem with her father.

"Susie's eighteen," her father had said. "And you've got a contract with her. It's not my problem."

Then he'd turned the phone over to Susie, who reminded Johnson that her uncle, a county judge, could issue an injunction against him before the party began. "And you wouldn't want legal problems, would you?"

"I don't want *any* problems," Johnson had told her. "Keep that in mind because if there're any problems at all, it's your name on the contract and I'll see to it that you're held liable."

When Van Pelt had arrived, she and Johnson had managed to remain civil toward one another, but Johnson found it difficult. He didn't like matching wits with an eighteen-year-old girl.

When the Rockhounds finally began playing, he regretted the passing of the big band era and he pressed the palms of his hands flat against his ears to muffle the scream of the electric guitars.

Outside, a single cloud passed across the moon.

Patrick and Siro had taken Jewelle and Lisa to dinner before the party and they arrived together in Patrick's Grand Prix. They could hear the pounding music of the Rockhounds halfway down the block when Patrick squeezed his car between Paula Hudson's Nova and Douglas Birdsall's Volkswagen.

"They've already started," Jewelle said as Patrick helped her from the car.

The two couples walked the half block to the Oceanview Hotel, then inside past the abandoned registration table. They were the last to arrive.

"What's with Lisa?" Patrick whispered into Jewelle's ear when the two couples were temporarily separated near the punch bowl. "She's hardly said a thing all night."

"She's leaving in the morning," Jewelle told him. "Siro's not."

Patrick stared across the table at his best friend.

"Not like us," Jewelle said. "When we leave here, we'll be together."

Patrick squeezed her hand as Siro stepped around the table, Lisa following behind him.

"There's four together over there." Siro motioned toward the far wall with his free hand, indicating four empty seats.

"You got plans for tomorrow?" Patrick asked Siro.

"Sleep in," Siro said. "Monday I start full-time on my Dad's boat. No more rest for the wicked, he says."

"You see Susie Van Pelt anywhere?" Jewelle asked.

Patrick shook his head.

Lisa pointed to one of the other girls. "You see that dress? I wouldn't be caught dead in a dress like that."

"She waited too long," Jewelle said. "The best dresses must have already been taken."

As their girlfriends became engrossed in conversation, Patrick leaned over and whispered into Siro's ear. "I've got a bottle."

"Look," Douglas Birdsall whispered into Susie Van Pelt's ear later that night as he flashed a key before her eyes. "I got a key to one of the rooms upstairs. We could go up there now. Nobody would notice if we were gone for a little while."

Susie looked at the key in Douglas' hand. "Doug, no, I told you –"

"Don't worry. I've got a rubber." He patted his jacket pocket.

She hesitated.

Douglas took her hand and urged her toward the staircase. "Nobody'll notice," he repeated.

Susie glanced around the ballroom, realizing that she had already done everything she could and that the party had taken on a life of its own. Certain that no one was paying attention to them, she followed Douglas out the door and up the back staircase. Her floor-length skirt rustled as she climbed three flights of stairs.

Douglas slid the hijacked key into the lock on room 403, twisted until it unlocked, then pushed open the door and led Susie inside. He closed the door behind her, then gathered her in his arms, crushing her pink corsage between then.

Their lips met and then their tongues entwined. Before long, they lay together on the bed, their clothes folded neatly on a chair by the door.

Douglas nervously tore open the square foil packet he'd retrieved from his jacket pocket and the condom fell free, landing on Susie's stomach. They both stared at it a moment before Douglas reached out to pick it up.

Susie touched his wrist to stop him. She said, "Let me."

The telephone rang at the hotel's front desk. Ed Johnson barely heard it above the sound of the hard rock music spewing from the ballroom. The hotel's assistant manager picked the phone up on the third ring, listened a moment, then handed the receiver to Johnson. "It's your wife."

Johnson covered one ear and listened without comment, then slammed the phone down.

"Damn it," he said. "I have to leave. My wife's locked herself out again. I'll be back as soon as I can."

The assistant manager knew better than to question his boss.

"You make sure these kids don't do something stupid," Johnson said. "If they screw up anything, I'll have your ass for it."

The assistant manager nodded and watched as Johnson grabbed his jacket and pulled it on. With one last glance toward the ballroom, Johnson stepped from the hotel and walked around to his year-old Chrysler New Yorker. The drive home to Leon and back wouldn't take long, but if he knew his wife half as well as he thought he did, he knew she'd have him corralled at the house for at least twenty minutes. One of these days he would remember to leave a key with one of the neighbors.

After sliding into the driver's seat, he loosened his collar and rolled down the window. As Johnson started his car, he heard the first few notes of The Doors' "Light My Fire" filter through the chained rear exit of the ballroom, though he didn't recognize the song. As he backed his car into the alley and drove away, sparks from the fuse box in the basement of the hotel ignited a tower of newspaper soaked with paint thinner.

Fire consumed the tower of paper, then expanded to include a mattress, a box spring, and a headboard. The flames sucked fresh air in through the broken basement window often used by the hotel cat as a doorway, and the flames continued to grow, quickly consuming everything in the basement. The smoke had to go somewhere and it rose up through the ventilation system into the empty rooms and the darkened ballroom where no one could see it. Caryl Mason, sitting next to a vent with Eric Ceriani, began coughing. When she couldn't stop, Eric suggested they step outside.

Patrick Bates sat on the hood of his Grand Prix and passed the open bottle of Jack Daniel's to Siro. They could hear the pounding music of the Rockhounds as one song segued into the next and Siro tapped his foot against the pavement in time to the driving beat.

"What do you think?" Patrick asked as Siro brought the bottle to his lips and tilted it back. "Going out with a bang, eh?"

After Siro swallowed, he nodded, then wiped his lips with the back of his right hand. "Lisa's leaving tomorrow."

Patrick didn't respond. He knew how Siro felt about Lisa, but he also understood why Lisa had to leave, and why sometime in late August he and Jewelle would also be leaving.

"I told her to keep the ring. There's nobody else I'd ever give it to," Siro continued after taking another swallow from the bottle. "She's the only girl I've ever cared about."

"We'd better go back before they come looking for us," Patrick said. They'd slipped outside while Lisa and Jewelle were in the restroom.

Just then, the Oceanview Hotel exploded in a ball of flame. Startled, Siro dropped the bottle of Jack Daniel's. It splintered as it struck the pavement at his feet, soaking his pants legs with bourbon.

Patrick slid off the hood of his car and they rushed toward the hotel as the first screams became audible. A wall of acrid smoke met them at the front door and before they could fight their way through it, the hotel's assistant manager stumbled out of the hotel.

Once inside, they found Lisa standing next to the restrooms in the lobby, seemingly dumbfounded.

Patrick grabbed her shoulders and demanded, "Where's Jewelle?"

"She went back in already."

Siro pulled Lisa from Patrick's grasp and pushed her toward the door, urging her to get as far away as possible.

"But –" she started to protest. Siro shoved hard, propelling her out the door to the parking lot.

Together, Patrick and Siro fought their way through the smoke, searching for the source of the screaming, and found Caryl and Eric trapped under a collapsed section of wall in the hallway just outside the ballroom. Eric had already died, but they didn't know that as they lifted sections of wall off the two of them.

"Where's Jewelle?" Patrick shouted at Caryl. "Did you see Jewelle?"

Caryl didn't hear him as she realized Eric wasn't crawling from under the rubble. She collapsed again and took Eric's head in her lap.

"Get out!" Siro shouted at her. "It's too late. Get out!"

He tried to pull Caryl to her feet, but he couldn't lift her.

Patrick shouted for Jewelle, but his voice was only one among the chorus and he heard no response. He pushed forward through the smoke, stepping over collapsed sections of the wall, trying to find a way into the ballroom. He bent low and held his hand cupped over his face, trying not to inhale the smoke that stung his eyes.

Then Siro began screaming, and Patrick turned back. Siro's pants had erupted in flame and he collapsed to the floor beside Caryl as he slapped unsuccessfully at his legs. Patrick screamed Jewelle's name once more.

Patrick grabbed Siro under the arms and dragged him toward the door. By then the entire ballroom had become engulfed in flames and Patrick could not see through the thick blanket of smoke.

The stage and half the ballroom floor collapsed into the basement. An interior wall crumbled, spilling burning debris across the remainder of the room. Those not already dead soon would be and no amount of screaming would prevent it.

Patrick continued yelling for Jewelle as he backed into the lobby, but the flames licking at the walls around him continued driving him backward.

Siro's entire body burned like a napalm victim, the flames climbing over his chest and arms, igniting his hair. Patrick didn't realize his own tuxedo had caught fire until he'd fallen backward out the front door of the hotel still dragging his best friend. By then Siro had stopped screaming.

Patrick rolled across the pavement, trying to snuff himself out as his cheap tuxedo melted against his skin and a volunteer fireman smothered the flames with a blanket.

Mike Morelli stumbled from his bedroom, rubbing his eyes as he crossed the living room toward his father. He had fallen asleep while practicing the songs he'd learned that afternoon on his new bass guitar. "What was that noise?"

Still in her crib, his baby sister began screaming.

His father pushed himself out of the recliner and turned off the television. "I don't know," he said after he retrieved the baby. "Why don't we find out?"

Morelli followed his father onto the front porch. From three blocks away, they could see the blaze of the Oceanview Hotel as it bathed the center of town in flickering shadows. Sirens screamed through the night, calling the town's volunteer fire department into action.

Morelli's little sister buried her face in his father's shoulder, and he felt his father's arm snake around his shoulder and pull him close. They stared at the blaze and listened to the wail of sirens as the fire engines, both police cars, and the town's only ambulance arrived at the hotel.

Morelli's father said, "Your mom will be busy tonight."

The fire burned long into the night and before the sun broke over the Coastal Range the next morning, everyone in town knew what had happened. Hardly a person in town didn't have a relative caught in the fire, even if only a third or fourth cousin, and they gathered in the Oceanview Hotel's parking lot and the hospital's waiting room, demanding answers from exhausted firefighters or quietly praying for miracles that wouldn't happen.

Doctors released Lisa Anderson from the hospital shortly after her admission. She'd been rushed to the emergency room as a precaution, but the doctors on call had found no reason to admit her. She returned home, packed her belongings into her station wagon, and drove east over the Coastal Ranges as the morning sun finally peeked over the horizon.

She still wore Siro Pasetti's class ring.

Sunday afternoon Bill Harrison sat in a chair next to his comatose wife and told her about their daughter.

"Jewelle graduated high school Friday," he said. "You would have been so proud of her. She was the prettiest girl there. I took pictures of her at graduation, and I took pictures of her in the new dress we bought for the graduation party." His throat caught as he remembered the source of the money. "She was so beautiful . . . so beautiful."

He'd spent all day Saturday combing through the embers of the hotel with the fire chief and the police chief, ostensibly searching for the cause of the fire. He'd been a member of the fire investigation team ever since his appointment as the town's building inspector, but he hadn't had to investigate the site to know how the fire began – that had been only too obvious to him when he'd arrived. Instead, he'd searched for his daughter's remains, never finding anything he could recognize.

"You would have been so proud," he continued. "So proud."

His hand slipped into his jacket pocket and he retrieved the .38 Special he had contemplated using three years earlier.

He leaned over his wife and kissed her gently on the lips. "We're going to be with her now, dear," Bill said as he shut down his wife's life-support equipment.

Then he slipped the .38 in his mouth, hooked the sight behind his two front teeth, and squeezed the trigger.

His body continued to convulse as Mike Morelli's mom, the nurse on duty, ran into the room.

Patrick Bates lay in a hospital bed in San Francisco. After his melted tuxedo had been peeled away and his vital signs had been stabilized at the small hospital in Baker, he had been rushed south on a Coast Guard cutter. He stared up at the whorls of white paint on the ceiling of his hospital room on those rare occasions when he drifted into consciousness. As chairman of the reunion committee, it would be his responsibility to call the three survivors together on their ten-year anniversary.

In Baker – a small town on the northern California coast where families shared unimaginable loss and where generations of families lived, worked, and died – only Mike Morelli made plans to leave.

Contributors

Neil Schofield, born in Yorkshire, England, studied law before entering the theatre. After twelve years as technician and lighting designer, he segued into "industrial theatre" where he has spent most of his working life, writing/producing corporate events, product launches and videos. In 2000, he began writing and selling crime fiction. His story, "Groundwork," placed third in the 2001 *Ellery Queen's Mystery Magazine* Readers Awards. His preferred form is the short mystery story, though he admits to working on two novels. He lives in Normandy with his partner Mimi (short for Mireille), and his dog Nestor (short for *Nestor Burma,* "the only *real* P.I. hero in French crime fiction"). He has one daughter, Kate, a London-based theatre director.

Paula J. Matter is the author of numerous short crime fiction stories and nonfiction. Her stories, interviews and articles have been published in Germany and the U.S. She is a member of Private Eye Writers of America, Sisters in Crime, Short Mystery Fiction Society, Women's National Book Association and is the Author Advocate of Pennwriters, Inc. She lives with her family in north central Pennsylvania.

Tom Sweeney has published about three dozen short stories which have appeared in such diverse magazines as *Analog, Blue Murder,* and *Woman's World,* and in the anthologies *Fedora, Fedora II, Hardbroiled,* and *Mystery Street.* His stories have been nominated for the Pushcart Prize and the Shamus Award. He is the editor of the Private Eye Writers of America newsletter, *Reflections in a Private Eye.* He and his wife live in Portsmouth, New Hampshire, where he is working on his first novel.

Ted Hertel, Jr., is a practicing attorney in Milwaukee, Wisconsin. He served as local arrangements chair of Eyecon '95 and co-chair of Bouchercon '99, the 30th World Mystery Convention, both held in Milwaukee. His previous non-fiction publications include "Queen's Gambit: The Life and Times of Ellery Queen" in *The Tragedy of Errors* (Crippen & Landru, 1999), a critical essay examining the themes in the Queen novels and stories, and a biographical article on Linda Barnes for *St. James Guide to Crime & Mystery Writers* (1996). His short story "My Bonnie Lies . . ." (*The Mammoth Book of Legal Thrillers,* Carroll & Graf, 2001) received the Mystery Writers of America's Robert L. Fish Award for best first short story by an American author. It was also nominated for both an Anthony and a Macavity Award for best short story of 2001. Additionally, Hertel reviews books for *Deadly Pleasures* and *Mystery News.* He is married to Maggie Ley.

Dorothy Rellas' suspense novel, *Hidden Motives,* was published several years ago, and she has just finished her first P.I. novel. Her short fiction and articles on writing have appeared in *Futures,* and the anthologies *A Deadly Dozen* and *Hardbroiled.* She lives with her family in Pasadena, California.

Kevin Egan is the author of a science fiction novel, *The Perseus Breed,* and short stories that have appeared in *Whispers* and the Tampa Tribune's *Fiction Quarterly.* Writing as Conor Daly, he has published three mystery novels: *Local Knowledge, Buried Lies,* and *Outside Agency.* Two of these novels, *Local Knowledge* and *Outside Agency,* received the Washington Irving Book Award from the Westchester County (N.Y.) Library Association in 1997. He lives with his family in White Plains, New York.

Chelle Martin is a member of Mystery Writers of America, Sisters in Crime, and Romance Writers of America and was elected as Vice President of Sisters in Crime Central Jersey for 2002 and 2003. She's published in short fiction and is the author of numerous articles on writing, which have appeared both in print and online. An award-winning writer, she is now working on several novels.

Gary R. Bush's short fiction appears in the anthologies *Flesh and Blood: Guilty as Sin* and *Fedora II*. He's completed his first novel, is currently finishing a novel about murder in a ballet company, and is researching a novel about murder in the recording industry. His career has been varied, from teaching history to prisoners at a Federal penitentiary, to working as a human resources director in a large corporation. Once an avid sailor, he was sidelined by an accident and now writes full time. Bush lives in Minneapolis with his wife, Stacey, and their Kerry Blue Terrier, Max.

Tim Wohlforth's short stories have appeared in *Detective Mystery Stories, Futures, HandHeldCrime, Hardluck Stories, Mysterical-e, Nefarious55, Plots with Guns,* and *Without A Clue*. His stories have also appeared in the anthologies *Bullet Points, Fedora, Hardbroiled,* and *Techno Noir*. He co-authored the non-fiction book *On The Edge: Political Cults Right and Left*, published by M.E. Sharpe. He resides with wife and two dogs in Oakland, California.

Jack Bludis is the author of more than thirty novels, six novellas, and almost three hundred short stories using various pseudonyms in various genres. His most recent work includes the novels *The Big Switch* and *The Deal Killer*, and short stories in *Hardbroiled* and *Mystery Street*. He currently lives in Baltimore, Maryland.

James S. Dorr's fiction and poetry collection, *Strange Mistresses: Tales of Wonder and Romance*, was released in November 2001 by Dark Regions Press. He is an active member of the Horror Writers Association and Science Fiction and Fantasy Writers of America, a past Anthony Award and Darrell Award finalist, winner of the Best of the Web 1998 award, and his work has been listed in *The Year's Best Fantasy and Horror* nine of the past eleven years. His short fiction has appeared in

Aboriginal SF, Alfred Hitchcock's Mystery Magazine, Enigmatic Tales, Faeries, Fantastic Stories, Future Orbits, Gothic.Net, New Mystery, Terminal Fright, Tomorrow, The Strand, and such anthologies as *The Best Of Cemetery Dance, Bloodtype, Children Of Cthulhu, The Darker Side: Generations Of Horror, Darkside: Horror For The Next Millennium, Dark Tyrants, Gothic Ghosts, Strange Attraction,* and *Whispers and Shadows.* Dorr currently resides in Bloomington, Indiana, in the company of a large tabby-on-tortoise shell cat, with a dubious past, named Carmilla.

An avid reader and writer from an early age, when granted access to the adult library as a child, he considered it a rare honor indeed. **T. P. Keating**'s recent hard-boiled short stories have appeared in *Plots with Guns* and *HandHeldCrime.* Presently working on a darkly humorous noir novel, Keating is married and lives in London.

Stephen D. Rogers' mysteries have appeared in *About.com Mysteries, Alternate Realities, Bullet Points, Crimestalker Casebook, Detective Mystery Stories, Ellery Queen's Mystery Magazine, Futures Mysterious Anthology Magazine, HandHeldCrime, Hardboiled, Hardbroiled, Hardluck Stories, Judas, Malone's White Fedora, Murder Hole, Murderous Intent, The Mystery Review, Mystery Time, MysteryNet, Orchard Press Mysteries, Plots with Guns, Rex Stout Journal, Thrilling Detective,* and *Woman's World.* He writes the mystery column at *Writing-World.com.* He lives with his family just this side of Cape Cod.

Simon Wood has garnered more than seventy short story credits in less than three years. His work has appeared in American, Australian, British, and German magazines and anthologies. In July, 2002, Barclay Books released his first novel, the suspense-thriller, *Accidents Waiting To Happen.* Barclay Books has contracted his second novel, *We All Fall Down,* and Medium Rare Books has contracted his short story collection *Dragged into Darkness.* He is at work on his third novel *No Show.* A native of England, Wood currently resides in Richmond, California.

Small Crimes editor **Michael Bracken** is the author of *All*

White Girls, Bad Girls, Canvas Bleeding, Deadly Campaign, Even Roses Bleed, In the Town of Dreams Unborn and Memories Dying, Just in Time for Love, Psi Cops, Tequila Sunrise, and nearly 800 shorter works. He previously edited *Fedora: Private Eyes and Tough Guys, Fedora II: More Private Eyes and Tough Guys,* and *Hardbroiled.* Bracken has received numerous awards for advertising copywriting and his short story, "Cuts Like a Knife," was nominated for a Derringer Award. Born in Canton, Ohio, Bracken has traveled extensively throughout the U.S., and currently resides with his family in Waco, Texas.

Printed in the United States
23509LVS00002B/209

9 781592 245956